CRAZY FOR YOU

DOMHNALL O'DONOGHUE

MERCIER PRESS

MERCIER PRESS

Cork

www.mercierpress.ie

© Domhnall O'Donoghue, 2020

ISBN: 978 1 78117 779 2

A CIP record for this title is available from the British Library.

Printed and bound in the EU.

PROLOGUE

Clooney stormed the hotel corridor, scantily dressed in a white singlet and matching boxer briefs. He gripped a phone in place of the loaded gun that had scorched his hands moments earlier. If the stakes hadn't been so high, the vainglorious thirty-seven-year-old might have paused his rescue mission and stolen a glance at his impressive, tanned physique in one of the gilded mirrors lining the walls on either side. He might even have chanced a selfie to excite Instagram – the moody lighting in the property was particularly flattering. 'The more flesh the better!' his millions of followers would often comment on his hourly posts. He'd always been happy to accommodate – just not now.

Clooney's late grandmother was to blame for his love of expensive undergarments – how many times had she said, 'Everyone should own good quality pants unless you want to be embarrassed in the morgue'? And the morgue was precisely where he feared he would soon end up.

What the near-naked actor lacked in actual body armour, he made up for in steely determination. Such was the intensity of the situation, he wasn't even aware of the bestial grunts escaping his mouth. Thankfully, the exclusive ski resort was teeming with eccentric millionaires, all dab hands at behaving oddly; otherwise, Clooney would surely have received inquisitive glances – even been tackled to the ground by those fearful of terrorist attacks.

Ironic, given that the building's only terrorist had fled moments earlier.

For now, nothing was going to prevent him protecting the

woman he'd loved ever since he was in britches: the only person who had genuinely motivated him. Inspired him. Fascinated him. Never in his wildest dream had he imagined he would one day be responsible for averting her assassination; the world's most famous person.

Yet here he was.

Breathless, Clooney reached the elevator and slammed the call button with as much energy as he could rally. As he waited, a disorientated lady waving a Bloody Mary slurred, 'Nice bulge,' before staggering past him, unconcerned that her potent vodka and tomato juice concoction was sullying the plush ivory carpet. On an average day, Clooney couldn't resist a compliment. Today, with his laser-like focus on saving a life, her praise went over his pretty head. Frustrated that the elevator doors remained shut, he hit the button for a second then a third and fourth time.

'Jesus Christ, would you open!'

A waiter, delivering breakfast to one of the bedrooms nearby, offered Clooney an apologetic shrug.

'It is often busy in the morning,' he said by way of explanation. 'If you are in a rush –'

'I *am* in a fuckin' rush –'

'Then you could always take the stairs. We're only on the second floor.'

Without so much as a thank you, Clooney cleared the corner and sprinted down the stairwell, five steps at a time. He could hear the waiter shout after him – 'Would it be possible to get an autograph?' – a request that would have normally gladdened the heart of this world-famous 'trailblazer', as *The New York Times* had recently referred to him.

Again, not today.

How could you be so stupid, Clooney?

He felt his forehead moisten, briefly reminding him of those horrid periods earlier in his life when he'd battled social anxiety; his body publicly and embarrassingly unravelling at the first hint of awkwardness: sweating, blushing, stuttering.

Remember all those invitations you turned down? Locking yourself in your flat, too self-conscious and panicked to even greet the postman? Well, you should have stayed put, you absolute cad, and then all of this drama could have been avoided!

He finally reached the foyer. Guests sashayed across the marble floors en route to the restaurant to sample the local Alpine cuisine. How Clooney envied them: their most challenging decision that morning was choosing between a bowl of muesli and a sliver of *schinkenspeck*. Not that he could have entertained a morsel of food; in the past few moments, his stomach had become quite spirited, and he wanted to avoid discolouring his white underwear if possible.

As he hopped over a leather suitcase, cast aside by a new arrival too tired or too rich to position it out of harm's way, he spotted her through the glass doors. Not the woman whose life he was trying to save but the woman – if you could even call her that – who was the cause of all these histrionics.

Vonnie. His nemesis.

Despite resembling the Michelin Man in her over-sized ski gear, her menacing presence was clearly evident. She briefly locked eyes with him and winked coquettishly before disappearing in the direction of the slopes. Clooney had always known that the fame and adulation he'd craved since childhood would come at a price. It seemed that this wench – the supposed love of his life – was hell-bent on making him pay.

Pay the ultimate price.

PART
ONE

ONE

Seventeen Months Earlier

'Let me take those dirty bin bags off ye, my love. The only place a woman of your beauty should be surrounded by such filth is in the bedroom!'

Clooney always felt a need to help others, and the evening of Isla's fancy-dress party – a gathering that would change his life forever – was no exception. Kitted out like his childhood idol Madonna, he'd arrived at his best buddy's house an hour early. As soon as he and his conical bra had crossed the threshold, the actor had begun playing a supporting role to the hostess, assisting with last-minute, tedious chores.

Cutting lemons.

Filling ice trays.

Plumping cushions.

Nothing that would burn any calories, granted, but help that had been appreciated by his jittery pal who could, in turn, focus on other aspects of her to-do list, like cooking food or preparing cocktails. Or simply releasing her frustration that the clock was against her by slamming presses and drawers – as she was currently doing.

'Jesus, hold them from the bloody bottom, will ye?' Isla, dressed as Catwoman, growled in her thick Navan accent after spotting Clooney dragging the two black bags across the spacious, ultra-modern kitchen floor and out to the bins in the back garden. 'The last thing I want is leftover dinners scattered across me lovely Moroccan tiles.'

While Clooney was a good foot taller than Isla, this evening the hostess' stressed state meant she dominated the room. He suspected her feline costume, which perfectly showcased her athletic physique, was also encouraging her to release her inner claws. On an average day, his pretty, blonde buddy was the personification of calm, cool and collected. This wasn't one of those days. So Clooney didn't dare tell Catwoman to cool her jets, fearful she might take the knife she was wielding to the Jean-Paul Gaultier-inspired costume that had cost him the best part of a week's wage. In addition to the golden corset and matching pointy bra, his ensemble consisted of fishnet stockings, a pair of ankle boots and a curly blonde wig. Determined to impress guests later that evening, he wanted his tribute to the Queen of Pop to remain free from attack. Instead, he suppressed a laugh, entertained by Isla's out-of-character hysteria, and animatedly lifted the bags a good metre above the tiled surface.

'Thanks, babes!' she eventually yelled out from behind him, clearly having taken a couple of breaths (and knowing that everyone's threshold for abuse had limits). 'What would I do without ye?'

Emerging onto the patio, Clooney basked in the knowledge that he was being of assistance. Nothing made him happier than receiving praise. Growing up gay in Navan in the 1980s and 1990s had meant being ridiculed and ostracised, particularly by the male contingent. As well as developing a sharp tongue to protect himself from hairy moments, Clooney had discovered that the most effective way to diffuse another's unmerited contempt for him was to be supportive, helpful and of value.

To that end, he'd facilitated cheating amongst his less academic classmates.

He'd lionised their modest talents to the high heavens.

He'd set them up on dates with his many female friends.

As a result of these efforts, when others discussed him, Clooney's sexuality – along with the inevitable judgement – was relegated to the bottom of the list, superseded by more favourable descriptions such as warm, kind and 'fucking sound'. In comparison with many of his gay contemporaries growing up at the same time, Clooney had survived his youth relatively unscarred. But the do-gooder instinct had never left him.

Of course, it hadn't been his oratorical artistry alone that had protected him in his youth; he'd also had Isla, whose side he'd barely left since meeting her in playschool at the tender age of three. Despite her snotty nose and obsession with building houses from toy bricks, the boy had been smitten by her, and they'd been a two-person army ever since.

'Don't think I haven't noticed that you've said *nada* about my costume,' Clooney teased, back from the garden – although he immediately regretted interrupting her, seeing how consumed she was with brushing egg-wash over a tray of *vol-au-vents*.

'Deadly, yeah.'

'Thanks.' He decided not to push it and simply washed his hands instead. Hopefully, the guests due to arrive shortly would be more forthcoming with their appreciation. 'So how many people are you expecting?'

'What? Em, about fifteen. Although, at this stage, I'd be delighted if nobody turned up because I'm worried I won't have enough food – particularly if yer man from two doors down comes. That savage would ate the dirt from under your fingernails. Please, God – let me have enough!'

Isla was being hyperbolic. Tonight's mistress of ceremonies had spent the afternoon in three different supermarkets, and judging by the way the fridge door, and the two presses beside it, kept popping open, Clooney wouldn't have been surprised if Marks & Spencer had shut up shop due to empty shelves.

'Before I forget, as a reward for all your help this evening, m'dear, here's some good news for ye: Vonnie is coming,' Isla revealed dramatically as she began preparing a large jug of Sangria. 'You'll get to meet her at long last!'

'You're kidding me! Please don't be kidding me. Are you kidding me? You know I'll start crying if I find out you're lying to me!'

'I'll give you good reason to start crying if you don't sweep under the table – there's so much dust under there, ye could almost stuff a cushion with the shite!'

What was there was about the size of a stamp, but Clooney decided to do as he was told.

'I'm not kidding ye, by the way,' she added, pouring a bottle of red wine into the jug. 'She'll be here with bells on. Figuratively and literally, knowing her love of crazy costumes.'

'I thought you were allergic to her?'

'I am. I most certainly am. But she overheard us talkin' about the party in the staffroom and she asked if she was invited. I couldn't say no – much as I wanted to!'

'Do you know what I wouldn't say no to? A glass of bubbles! Meeting Vonnie at long last deserves some celebration. What do you say?'

'Yes, please, Louise!'

'Maybe that will help ye to …'

'Help me to what?'

Relax.

Calm down.

Chill the fuck out.

'Get into the party mood, my love!'

'Good save.'

Clooney had been hearing about Isla's new workmate for the past few months, although 'workmate' might have been overly generous when describing the gal's position. Since the beginning of the year, Vonnie, a self-described 'visionary artist', had been volunteering in the local primary school where Isla worked, teaching arts and crafts to the Junior Infants. The principal had felt sorry for her and had cautiously agreed to welcome her into the school for a one-off workshop but, months later, she was still there – showing up every Wednesday and Friday morning, despite having been told politely that her services were no longer required. Clooney had always thought Vonnie sounded only fabulous and applauded this I'm-not-taking-no-for-an-answer attitude. Frustratingly, since he spent the majority of his year in Connemara, filming the Irish-language soap opera *Brú na hAbhainn*, the pair hadn't yet met.

'I can't wait for us to be introduced, Isla!' he said, his annoyingly chirpy voice indicating his excitement. 'I knew there was a reason I came tonight.'

'Eh, what about my Sangria and all my lovely nibbles?'

'Those too.'

'You're not allowed touch them until everyone else has gotten some, alright? Well, maybe the odd one or two. Ye don't mind, do ye? Although, by the looks of things, ye seemed to have lost your appetite recently – there's not a pick on you these days, ye lucky bastard!'

Isla's kind words were almost drowned out by the racket she was making, carrying trays and slamming the oven door.

'Stop! But don't! Do you think I've lost weight? Do I look well, babes?'

'That's all the flattery you'll be getting from me tonight, d'ya hear?'

Clooney made his way to the fridge to retrieve some Cava. 'I wonder what she'll be wearing,' he mused as he popped open the bottle. 'It better be fuckin' outrageous, or I'll be left devo.'

'Three guesses.'

'Okay, em … Cleopatra?'

'No, Marie Antoinette.'

'Oi! I'd two guesses left!'

'Sorry, I haven't time for stupid games; I have to finish my make-up. I'll be back down in a minute. What time is it, m'dear?'

'A quarter to eight.'

'That gives us about fifteen minutes before the madness starts! I'm getting into the mood now! Thanks for all your help – you're a keeper, that's for sure.'

Alone, Clooney sat down at the table and looked at the bubbles rise in his flute. He was adamant he wasn't going to get intoxicated tonight. When in the company of his best friend, he tended to lose the run of himself – polishing off six or seven bottles of wine between them was a regular occurrence. It was never a pretty sight – certainly not the next morning. But he was due to fly to Jamaica on a press trip with a group of fellow travel journalists – a fruitful sideline he'd carved out for himself – the following week, and that was all the motivation he needed to be measured with his intake. In preparation, he'd been working hard in the gym to shift his ever-threatening moobs and trim his waistline so he could be in somewhat presentable shape for hitting the Caribbean beaches. And so hangovers, along with carbs, were a no-no. It was encouraging that Isla had noticed his efforts.

He would have this one tipple and nothing more, he decided.

Clooney would soon realise that worrying about his alcohol consumption was pointless. His night was going to be spent, glass-free, chatting to a certain French queen.

Unlike everyone else, Clooney would delight in listening to Vonnie's quirky anecdotes.

TWO

'If you're fortunate enough to be the chosen one, there are a few house rules I insist you respect.'

Vonnie was showing Sally, a prospective tenant, around her dark and damp terraced house – a familiar experience for the petite forty-three-year-old. Since taking on a lease some ten years earlier, she'd shared the two-bedroom premises with no fewer than forty housemates, some of whom had only tolerated her insufferable dictatorship for a matter of days.

'You're not permitted to cook chickens in the oven, it's far too costly,' Vonnie instructed, toying with the hefty skin tag positioned between her lower lip and chin. 'If you have a hankering for a roast, I'd suggest you purchase one, ready-made, from Tesco. I'm sure you'll agree it's far more economical.'

Now in the pokey living room, Vonnie directed Sally to take a seat, which the immaculately groomed young lady did somewhat unwillingly: the sofa was deathly black – a far cry from the cream shade its manufacturer had initially afforded it. In addition to its questionable colour, it emanated a waft of cat wee, and Sally suspected that the wet-looking patch perilously close to her was not part of the initial design.

'Seeing as we're discussing house rules,' Vonnie continued, remaining vertical, thereby affording her the all-important power in the relationship, 'be sure to bring a nice, warm coat – I'm unwilling to turn the heat on unless there's a blizzard outside. And even then … I trust you're of the same thinking?'

Vonnie caught Sally examining some of her creations on the

walls. Her furry nostrils flared with pride.

'I see you're admiring my work. As an adult, I'm an artist, did I mention that?' she boasted.

'Three times. Do you mind me asking, why do you say "as an adult, I'm an artist"?'

'I don't understand your question.'

'Sorry.'

'You should be.'

'Indeed. What I meant was, why don't you simply say that you're an artist rather than prefixing it with "as an adult"?'

The situation left Vonnie torn: on the one hand, she appreciated the interest being shown by this woman, but on the other, she was irritated by her tone. She detected a measure of patronisation.

'Everyone's an artist as a child, aren't they?' Vonnie eventually replied, keeping her temper in check. 'How many hours did you spend colouring pictures in school? To be an artist as an adult means it's your profession. Your vocation. Your calling.'

Sally continued to be confused.

'You wouldn't understand. So few do. Oh, and no more than three showers per week,' Vonnie added, steering the conversation back on track. 'If you want more, I suggest joining a gym. By the looks of things, you could benefit greatly from a membership. No offence, obviously.'

Sally decided not to challenge Vonnie on her ridiculous demands or tartness. Even though the rental market in Ireland was worse than ever, within minutes of entering this cesspit she'd deduced that sleeping under the stars would not only be safer, but also warmer and cleaner.

'I see.'

'And speaking of bills,' Vonnie said, removing her jam-jar glasses and rubbing her eyes, 'I suppose I should be upfront about how they are split.'

'Fifty-fifty, I'd assume.'

The grimace that quickly hijacked Vonnie's face told Sally her answer was way off the mark.

'My dear father passed away a couple of years ago ...'

'I'm sorry to hear –'

'And he always had a dream.'

Sally tried to give the impression she was sympathetic and interested, but not too much so; she reminded herself of their initial introduction an hour earlier when she'd made the mistake of revealing that her sun-kissed skin was the result of a recent holiday to Marbella. Stood in the chilly hallway, Vonnie had swiped the conversation from her, and for over forty minutes – without appearing to take a single breath – had delivered an exhausting monologue detailing the time she'd purchased a flight to the south of Spain. At the last minute, Vonnie had cancelled because her late cat, Snuggles, had astutely concluded that 'Mama was going away and raised hell!'

'Daddy's dream was to build a pond in the garden,' Vonnie explained now, as she finally took a seat, safe in the knowledge that Sally knew who ruled the roost. 'He had cut-outs from gardening magazines pinned to the walls of his garage – he knew exactly what he wanted. Then – BANG! – cancer struck.'

'I understand; both my parents died from can–'

'So as we buried him, I decided there and then I would realise his dream on his behalf and build the pond. The owner of the house has given me his full blessing. He knows it will only add to the value of the property. I've almost everything in place and am just waiting until the end of summer when the weather improves. The rain has been relentless, hasn't it? You'd hardly think it was June.'

'What a wonderful thing to do. I'm sure your father would be very prou–'

'Because of the expense, I am only able to contribute a small amount to the household bills – a token, really.'

'I see.'

Having accepted that her tiresome search for accommodation had not concluded that evening – along with the fact that her new pencil skirt was now fit only for the scrapheap thanks to Snuggles or one of his undomesticated comrades – Sally decided to indulge Vonnie. At the very least, she would come away from the encounter with an excellent story to tell the girls when they met for chicken wings the following evening.

'How do you suggest dividing the bills then?' she quizzed, trying not to stare at Vonnie's bushy moustache.

'I'll contribute about €10.'

'A week?'

'Every two months!' Vonnie corrected, outraged by this audacity. From the off, she'd battled an instinct that the young woman wasn't the right candidate for the house, and this lack of compassion only verified it.

'That seems reasonable,' Sally mocked.

Vonnie examined Sally's face. 'You probably don't have a boyfriend? If you do, he isn't welcome, I'm afraid – the space isn't big enough. That goes for friends as well.'

'I don't have a boyfriend at the moment.'

'No, I didn't think so. Your looks aren't your strength. And if you'll allow me to be candid, you're also a little bit selfish.'

'You think?' Sally replied, fighting the urge to burst out laughing.

'Don't take it to heart – you are still very young. I was like you at your age: "Me, me, me!" Hopefully, you'll grow out of it. Maybe then, men might find you more attractive. Might. You'd have to lose a few pounds as well, I'd say. Yes,' Vonnie decided, reaching over and squeezing Sally's waist, 'take my advice and join the gym, and maybe then your fortunes might change. Might.'

'I take it you have a partner.'

'No. I have my cats and my gallery, and that's more than enough for me. I did tell you that as an adult, I am an artist.'

'I don't think you did. You can tell me another time – I'm in a bit of a rush tonight, unfortunately.'

Vonnie's arched eyebrows indicated that she wasn't impressed her artistic endeavours were receiving such little respect.

'Thank you very much for your time,' Sally said as she rose to her feet.

'*My own gallery!*'

'Good for you,' the visitor praised, pulling her soggy skirt away from her legs. 'I hope it is a big success.'

'Do you know, you are the first person who hasn't asked me about my gallery. Everyone is usually fascinated.'

'I'm sure they are,' Sally quipped under her breath, making her way through the hallway and towards the front door.

Vonnie had had enough.

'Look, everyone who knows me, knows me to be honest, so here you go: I don't think you're the right person to share this house with me.'

'I'm saddened to hear that, but I understand your position.'

'You have no curiosity. You've got an opportunity to hear exciting and, possibly, life-changing stories and adventures, but you don't even care.'

'Actually, there is something that I am curious about.'

'Really?' Vonnie beamed; she knew there was no way anyone could be so indifferent to her distinguished personality and colourful life. 'Do you want to come back in?'

'No, I must go, but I've been wondering why you're wearing a Marie Antoinette costume? Is that your usual outfit of a Friday?'

'This old thing,' Vonnie casually replied, secretly delighted that her sartorial efforts were receiving the attention they deserved.

'It's what's known as a *robe à la Française*! You'd never think I got it in a car boot sale!'

While the tattered, eighteenth-century replica had cost as little as the price of admission to Versailles Palace, the dress was undoubtedly impressive. Complete with gold fringes and tassels, ribbons and ruffles, the funnel-shaped cream bust and matching billowing skirt was one of Vonnie's favourites, and she jumped at any opportunity to give it an outing.

'I'm going to a fancy-dress party, Sandra.'

'Sal–'

'Although I hardly need an excuse – I just love dressing up!'

'Well, I hope you're going to bring some cake and let them eat it!' Sally teased as she opened her car door.

'Why would I bring anything? I'm not throwing the party, my friends are. It's their job to provide their guests with food and drink – and cake.'

'I was trying to make a joke. You know, the famous quote ... Never mind.' Sally got into her red Ford Fiesta and, after turning on the engine, rolled down the window. 'Wait, just to clarify, you turn up empty-handed at a party? Don't you bring anything? Not even a packet of biscuits?'

Vonnie slammed the front door shut, having indulged this upstart's ignorance long enough. Walking towards her bedroom to apply her make-up, she wished there was a guillotine at her disposal: there were a few heads she'd love to chop off, starting with that brazen madam.

THREE

With the party in full swing, Isla and Clooney peeped through the living-room curtains, uncertain whether to laugh or call the police. Outside, Vonnie, beautifully dressed as Marie Antoinette, was arguing with an unimpressed taxi man. While they couldn't make out exactly what they were debating – haggling over the price of the fare, perhaps – the two friends realised things were getting ugly when the former French monarch chased the driver around the car and whacked him across the back of his head with her fan.

'Ouch!' Isla mocked, closing the curtains so as not to be associated with the drama taking place in front of her house. As a new resident in the estate, she didn't want to get a reputation – she'd already felt the presence of a few squinting eyes from across the road. Navan was a big town with bigger mouths. 'She better not carry on with that shite in here. I'm ragin' she convinced me to invite her! And everything has been going so well so far.'

'She's even more fabulous than I'd previously imagined, babes! I love her attitude!'

'Clooney.' Isla wasn't in the mood for joking. After all the work she'd put into the party, she was determined that this reluctantly invited guest wasn't going to hijack proceedings. Come Monday morning, she didn't want the only aspect of the night discussed in the staffroom to be Vonnie.

'Hopefully, she has all that rage out of her system now,' Clooney said, trying to reassure his hostess. 'Although I wouldn't like to have that poor driver's head in the morning. That whack looked sore.'

'Given the way you're currently drinking – or not drinking, more to the point – you'll have no head in the morning. Unlike me.' Isla topped her glass up with the last few drops from the bottle of Cava. 'You sure you don't want some more bubbles, m'dear? I don't want to be the only one who's three sheets to the wind.'

'Positive. Sure, I'll need to have my wits about me if things kick off with herself.'

'If she puts a foot out of place –'

'Relax, Catwoman – I'll keep an eye on her. And it will be my pleasure.'

Isla scanned her best friend's face. 'It's good you seem to be feeling so well in yourself these days. Unlike …'

'Unlike?'

'You know what I mean. I don't have to worry that you're going to …'

'What? Start sweating? Like I did at your brother's wedding?'

'Or that time the chef came over to enquire if we'd enjoyed our meal?'

'Or when we bumped into Nuala on Watergate Street?'

'*Water* is right – you were wetter than the Boyne River!'

Isla was referring to Clooney's battles with social anxiety, which had arrived with great fanfare a few years earlier. Randomly breaking out in a sweat was one symptom; cheeks reddening like the strawberry currently draped on the edge of Isla's glass was another. For all the highs that went hand-in-hand with being an actor, Clooney had discovered that the lows were more devastating and frequent. On the one hand, the industry asked artists to be open and vulnerable – traits that could be called upon on set or in the rehearsal room. On the other, it demanded they should also be as tough as old gumboots, able to deflect the constant rejection and indignities that were common occurrences in the world of entertainment.

A few years ago, it had all gotten too much for Clooney, and his body had had no qualms about letting him know. Making matters worse, the physical manifestation of this anxiety had left him in a permanent state of embarrassment and upset, ashamed that the body he'd once thought so robust was continually letting him down – even in the most mundane situations, such as asking how much the lamb cutlets cost at the butcher's, or giving a stranger directions to their hotel.

'Don't worry, Isla, my love – I've got it under control.'

Clooney was telling the truth. As soon as he'd realised what was happening to him, he'd sought help – making simple yet effective changes to his life. Upping his exercise regime had been top of the list, which had the added benefit of eliminating that belly so prevalent amongst men navigating their mid-thirties.

'Anyway, enough about *moi*,' Clooney said, ensuring his wig and corset were in place, 'I can hear the front door opening. Marie Antoinette has arrived. Hump the diet; I hope she's brought cake!'

FOUR

Vonnie glided into Isla's semi-detached house, triumphantly shaking off all residue of the tiresome exchange she'd just endured with that greedy taxi driver. The journey from her home to Isla's was less than a kilometre – and she would gladly have made it by foot, but her magnificent, regal costume wasn't cut out for such expeditions – and yet the skinflint had demanded €12.

'How about I give you a 10 per cent discount on the admission for my art gallery instead?' she had tried to barter. Unsuccessfully. So in the end, he'd received his full fare, along with a little surprise for later – as the driver climbed back behind the wheel, Vonnie scratched the side of the car with one of her decorative and sharp-edged hair clips.

That will teach him.

Passing the other guests, Vonnie knew no one would be able to compete with her outfit. Nobody ever could. And that was saying nothing about her chalk-white skin and plump, rosy cheeks, entirely in keeping with the style of the eighteenth-century. She knew there were many things at which she excelled – painting, cooking and the art of conversation being just three – but she took particular pride in her reputation for always being the best turned-out at fancy-dress parties. This talent, like many others, came effortlessly. For as long as she could remember, Vonnie had always adored escaping reality and dressing up. If it weren't for the fact that, all too often, she'd been at the receiving end of rocks, rubbish and whatever else those jealous thugs who walked Navan's streets could get their dirty hands on, she'd have been only delighted to showcase her treasure chest of outfits daily. The real world rarely interested Vonnie. What took place in her imagination was far more enjoyable.

'I'm a typical Piscean, the dreamer of the zodiac – my head is constantly in the clouds!' was the justification this astrology fanatic would always use.

Her bedroom was akin to the Abbey Theatre's costume department, with railings and shelves weighed down by dresses, cloaks, shoes, wigs, masks and props. Vonnie detested spending money, apart from on this, her one true passion (art aside). For costumes, she'd happily pay a king's ransom – although that never prevented her from bartering with the seller at the jumble sale or taking advantage of the kind-hearted volunteer working in the charity shop.

But that night, her Marie Antoinette ensemble wasn't receiving a shred of the attention it deserved.

'Jealousy isn't a good colour on you, Siobhán,' she hissed at an unforthcoming colleague standing outside the downstairs toilet – her name was actually Sinéad – 'and neither is pink. Maybe you should head out to the garden. The subdued lighting out there is much more forgiving.'

Unlike most Irish people, who would sooner have their eyes gouged out than be complimented, Vonnie readily embraced any kind sentiments directed at her. And if they didn't arrive, she simply tooted her own horn instead. 'It is magnificent, isn't it?' she said to a cluster of underdressed guests gathered by the kitchen sink. 'Can you properly see the detail at the back? Let me tell you a little about the history of fashion – judging by your outfits, you could benefit from my insider knowledge.'

'Maybe later.' It seemed fellow guests were happy to smile when Vonnie praised herself, but were determined not to get caught in a corner with her.

Vonnie forced a smile. 'Okay so, maybe later then.'

She didn't know her hostess well and even felt that Isla was a bit of a bitch, one who lacked appropriate enthusiasm when Vonnie discussed her life's adventures in the staffroom every Wednesday and Friday. She'd enjoyed the self-appointed role of 'artist-in-residence' for over eight months and, initially, all the teachers, Isla included, had been only delighted to interact with her – especially if that meant they got their classes taught for them. However, as the weeks had come and gone, Vonnie had begun to notice that she now passed the majority of her time in the school alone, or being told by other staff members – especially Isla – that they couldn't talk as they were 'in a rush!' But when she'd accidentally heard about Isla's end-of-term fancy-dress party, she had decided to park her reservations about the hostess and other staff members, and make an appearance. And it was a good job she had because, without Marie Antoinette's fabulous and decadent presence, the entire affair would surely have been a disaster.

As small pockets of guests chatted away to each other, Vonnie decided to overlook the fact that she was – once again – being excluded and took an unopened bottle of Prosecco from the fridge. Even though its quality wasn't worthy of ballads or poetry, it was better than going thirsty. After filling a glass, she discreetly placed the bottle behind the curtain; she could tell by the look of some of the attendees that they were the very reason people locked their cars. Was it any wonder they weren't inviting her to join in their conversations – the magnanimity for which Vonnie was famed would only highlight their shortcomings.

'What on earth is a gal as spectacular as you doing drinking on her own?'

Vonnie looked around. Standing in front of her was Madonna, complete with an Adam's apple, a hairy chest and even hairier armpits. He was unsightly, she felt, but at least he'd made an effort, and, unlike the other guests, he gave credit where it was due. Little did she know it at the time, but he was the only person at the party who basked in compliments more than she did.

'I'm just taking a moment to catch my breath,' she explained, sitting down at the kitchen table and using her fan to punctuate her point. 'Everyone has been harassing me since I arrived, bombarding me with questions about my costume.'

'Can you blame them?' Clooney teased. 'If there were awards, you'd surely saunter off with top prize!'

'I'd imagine so,' she nodded before taking a generous mouthful of her Prosecco.

'May I join you?' Clooney took a seat without waiting for her agreement.

Vonnie examined him. 'You have nice eyes. Kind eyes.'

'Have I?' Clooney beamed, delighted that he'd used eye drops to clear the windows to his soul of any bloodshot redness.

'Maybe not, actually,' Vonnie corrected. 'I have contacts in, and they are barely any use. And the lighting is terrible in here. Like the rest of the décor.'

'I see.'

'At least somebody does. I feel like one of those old blind monks living in a derelict monastery up the mountains. I can just about make out the tip of my nose.'

'And what a lovely nose it is too – if I may say so.'

It was Vonnie's turn to beam. 'You may.'

Clooney pulled his seat closer to Vonnie; the Queen of Pop had much to discuss with the Queen of France, and there was no time to waste. 'You know, Madonna has channelled Marie Antoinette on numerous occasions. Probably her best-known incarnation was for a performance of "Vogue" for the MTV Music Awards in 19–'

'Speaking of alcohol …'

'I didn't mention alco–'

'Do you think you could top me up?' She pushed a now-empty glass towards him.

'It would be an honour. I'd hate to get on the wrong side of Marie Antoinette! I think most people have brought their own bottles, which one is yours?'

Vonnie decided that the stolen Prosecco currently skulking behind the curtain should remain where it was for later on in the night, so she told her new admirer a little white lie. 'I brought so many with me and, with careless abandon, shared them out with everyone. I'm too generous for my own good! In saying that, I think a communal spirit is far more rewarding than everyone being out for themselves, don't you?'

'You've certainly changed your ways since the eighteenth century,' Clooney joked. 'I quite like this philanthropic version of you, Marie Antoinette.'

'Are you a Scorpio by any chance?'

'I most certainly am! How did you know – I haven't a clue about star signs, I'm afraid. I've always thought them to be a little silly.'

'Of course you have – Scorpios are suspicious of everything.'

'I suppose you could say that.'

'I did say that.'

'The one thing I remember about astrology is that we Scorpios apparently make the best detectives – very curious. Is that right?'

'Okay then, Sherlock Holmes – what's my sign? It's straightforward. I'm a textbook example!'

'God, I barely know –'

Before he could finish his sentence, a loud crash sounded from the sitting room.

'Isla's new table!' Clooney gasped. 'I bet she's langers! I'll be back in a minute – stay where you are!'

'Typical Scorpio, always wanting to help others.'

'Guilty as charged! Give me a minute, your Majesty.'

While unimpressed that this strange, oddly handsome Scorpio had opted to salvage a piece of tatty furniture rather than tend to her more pressing needs – *he can't control how the stars and planets made him, I suppose* – Vonnie found her mood to be light and merry. She wasn't 100 per cent sure whether it was the bubbles she'd just polished off or the praise she'd been receiving from Madonna, but whatever the case, the night was turning out to be much more pleasant than anticipated.

FIVE

'That one is annoying my happiness tonight,' Isla said.

'So what, you're trashing your gaf as a result?' Clooney took the overflowing glass of wine from her hand and returned the wooden table to its rightful position. Isla had been living in the house on the outskirts of Navan for just under a year – her first rung on the property ladder – and all the furniture was straight off the factory's conveyor belt. Clooney knew she would be depressed if anything broke.

'All I'm going to say,' his best friend slurred, the stress of the evening having resulted in the alcohol hitting her in almost record time, 'is, give her an inch …'

'She's harmless. Unlike you tonight, my love!' The two of them would have needed a calculator to work out how often they'd taken care of one another after a few tipples; tonight, it was clearly Clooney's turn. 'She's obviously a bit lonely, that's all.'

This brief wrangle was indicative of the most significant difference between them: Isla took a zero-tolerance approach to people and their nonsense, while Clooney gravitated towards society's most vulnerable. His sexuality had always made him feel like an outsider, so perhaps it wasn't surprising he'd developed a need to protect those who didn't slot neatly into the status quo. If he cried, it was rarely for himself; usually for someone innocent, persecuted. Someone like Vonnie, if the looks and sneers she'd been receiving from the other guests all evening were anything to go by.

And if he received a little praise for being altruistic and kind along the way, who was he to argue?

'You do realise she came empty-handed and had the cheek to rob a bottle of my Prosecco?'

'Maybe it was an oversight on her part?' Clooney suggested, hoping his new buddy wasn't of the penny-pinching variety.

'She then hid the rest of the bottle behind my new curtains! Finlay saw her.'

Clooney tried to hide his disappointment: meanness was a trait he loathed. He knew only too well what it was like to have an unenviable bank balance – what jobbing actor didn't? – but there was no excuse for arriving at a party empty-handed. Even a can of Fanta Orange would have been something! It was an etiquette that had been instilled in him by his parents, but sadly one not all self-respecting adults followed. In fact, tight-fistedness had compromised a couple of his friendships over the years.

'What is it you always say?' Isla persisted, ill-prepared to see her pal taken advantage of. '"If they aren't generous with their wallet, they're not generous with their spirit." Or soul. Or some shite like that.'

'I'd say very few people have given her much – if anything – over the years; maybe she just isn't accustomed to the concept –'

'Oh, lol! Listen to you, Freud! Do as you bloody well please, mate, but don't say I didn't warn ye!' She gave him a gentle kiss on the cheek, then whispered, 'Here she comes, and it seems she wants you to fawn over her da Vinci-standard artwork! Lucky you! Did you know that, *as an adult*, she's an artist?'

'"As an adult?" What does that mean?'

But Isla staggered across the room to her other guests. Clooney turned around, and, inches in front of him, stood Marie Antoinette, glass overflowing with plundered booze in one hand, sketch pad in the other.

'There you are! I thought you'd forgotten about me,' she challenged, layers of make-up able to conceal neither her displeasure nor her moustache. 'I wanted to show you some of my work. As an adult, I'm an artist – did I tell you that already? Somebody else probably did. Did they mention I own a gallery where I showcase my work?'

Behind them, a couple of revellers dressed as Kanye West and a large-bottomed Kim Kardashian stared at Vonnie before unapologetically bursting into laughter – the loud music doing little to drown out their aversion to this French royal. If that wasn't bad enough, Kim threw a sausage roll, which landed in the middle of Vonnie's wig. Clooney prayed his new acquaintance hadn't deduced that she was the source of this mockery, but a single look was all it took for him to realise that she was fully aware they were ridiculing her, and his heart sank. Granted, they had only just met, but the sudden change in her demeanour struck Clooney. The authoritative posture she had possessed earlier in the kitchen abandoned her, and the confidence that initially shone from her face had disappeared completely. Her grip of the sketch pad tightened convulsively; she was furious yet saddened; frenetic yet embarrassed.

Clooney had misgivings about Vonnie's apparently ungenerous ways, but he couldn't help feeling sorry for this woman. Clearly, she was far more fragile than she let on, and her evident enthusiasm for being someone else – in this instance, French royalty – suggested to the amateur psychologist in him that she was far from comfortable in her skin. Vonnie's social etiquette might have been deserving of criticism, but, at that moment, Clooney felt an urge to protect her. Like Ebenezer Scrooge, he saw a mental slide show of his youth, back when he was the focus of other people's sneers and sniggering. He knew first-hand how horrid, mortifying and lonely that felt, and wished he could cheer her up in some way.

'Oooh, is that some of your artwork? I'd love to take a look if you'd allow me,' he said, moving the conversation forward.

However, over-eager as he was to hearten Vonnie, his voice carried too much condescension. 'I'm sure they wouldn't look out of place in the Louvre!'

'Well, I wouldn't go that far,' she replied, suddenly wary of him too.

Clooney reached out for the pad, but Vonnie pulled it away.

'What's wrong?'

'I feel you're mocking me. Like everyone else.'

'Oh my God, I can assure you I'm doing nothing of the sort! That just came out the wrong way – the tone. I'm sorry.'

He sensed he had lost her trust, which only confirmed his suspicions that she'd been hurt badly in the past. She was well over forty, for crying out loud; why had he felt the need to speak to her as though she were still a resident in the maternity ward?

'If you want to see my work, come into my gallery tomorrow,' Vonnie instructed, her voice regaining its strength. 'It's on Watergate Street, next door to the Bank of Ireland.'

Forced into a corner, Clooney, like most Irish people, would have agreed to all sorts of requests for the sake of a peaceful life, but tonight was different somehow. He was acutely aware of how blessed he was, and it was clear to him that Marie Antoinette was not.

Wasn't this what parents had instilled in their children since time immemorial? His parents, anyway.

Love thy neighbour.

Help those less fortunate than you.

Be a decent fucking person.

'I would love that,' he said. 'Seriously.'

Vonnie managed a slight smile. 'You'll be dazzled, I'm certain of it.'

'I have no doubt.'

'By the way, have you figured it out?'

'What's that?'

'My star sign!'

'Vonnie, my love, it's not something –'

'Pisces! You got it in one! You probably picked up on some of Pisces' main traits – generous, easy-going and compassionate,' she suggested, swiping a large handful of *hors d'oeuvres* from a passing tray. A grimace followed the first mouthful. 'Disgusting. Like the rest of this party.'

'That must have been it – generous, easy-going and compassionate,' Clooney said, fighting the urge to laugh.

'You do realise that Scorpios and Pisceans are very compatible?' Vonnie added, chancing a sausage roll. 'They make great pals. Soulmates even.'

'Is that true?'

'Are we friends?'

'I hope so.'

'That would be nice.'

Vonnie looked around the party. Tilting her head back, nose in the air, she then threw the rest of her drink into her and without a goodbye, flitted towards the door. Before disappearing, however, she removed one of her hairpins and pierced Kim Kardashian's inflated arse.

'Oops! It seems someone's costume has hit a "bum note"!'

And she was gone.

As Clooney now had an important engagement the next day, he decided to follow the queen's lead, and returned to his own quarters in his family home nearby.

SIX

'I always knew that, as an adult, I'd be an artist, but I never thought I'd end up as curator of my own gallery. Sometimes, it seems you've no control over your destiny. It was as if art demanded my full attention!'

Clooney had called to Vonnie's modest gallery the morning after the party full of curiosity and expectation, but was immediately disappointed. An assembly of tatty, poorly framed creations hung on the stained white walls. Most wouldn't have looked out of place at the bottom of a skip. The materials used were quite inventive, he thought, trying to see the bright side.

Coat hangers.

Bicycle wheels.

Fishing rods.

'What a magical place you have here, Vonnie,' he lied, his actor's training standing him in good stead. 'I'm so surprised I'm only discovering this gallery for the first time today. How long has it been open?'

'It's coming up on our third anniversary. Daddy was an accountant for most of his life, and this was his office.'

'Really? You'd never think this was once full of books and ledgers! I love how spaces completely change their purpose over –'

'My daddy and I have always been admirers of art, but not just in the traditional sense; in all its forms. Art can be found everywhere – in the manufacturing plant, in the science lab or at the bottom of the River Boyne. We collected vast quantities of objects over the years, including what you see in front of you.

We discovered them in alleyways, jumble sales, even friends' attics. When Daddy passed away –'

'I'm sorry to hear –'

'I converted it into a gallery.'

'What a thoughtful tribute.'

'I would love to have it open all the time but, because of my "day job", I can only be here five days a week. That's the main reason so few people visit.'

'I'd imagine,' he nodded, stealing a glance at the guest book that sat open on a nearby desk. From what he could make out, it had just a solitary signature: *Vonnie J. Gallagher.*

'I dream that the gallery will eventually be my main source of income.'

'But I thought you worked as a volunteer at the school?' Clooney was confused.

Vonnie quickly turned the conversation. 'I'm not too fond of being a teacher, if I'm frank. I don't think it's my calling even though I'm something of a natural at it.'

'I don't doubt that.'

'In addition to this gallery, I also want to build a gazebo in memory of Daddy one day. It was just the two of us for most of my life. Mammy died when I was a teenager. Before that, she was always sick. A bit selfish if you ask me. But Daddy made up for it. Apart from me, gardening was his one true passion.'

'How did your mother die?'

'Is that the time?' she abruptly asked without looking at a watch or clock. 'Let me show you this wall, Mr I-love-asking-questions Scorpio!'

'I'm sure if you keep up the hard grafting,' Clooney said, following her to the other side of the narrow space, 'you'll soon realise all your goals.'

'No better star sign for fulfilling your dreams than a Piscean!'

'Is that so? I'm sure both your parents will be supporting you from afar.'

'Daddy will. Look at this powerful composition,' she instructed, pointing at an empty bottle of mayonnaise.

It wasn't just the gallery that had failed to meet Clooney's lofty expectations. The previous night, he'd been genuinely impressed by Vonnie's appearance and costume. Today, the contrast could not have been more pronounced. He was well aware that it was inelegant to comment on how another person looked (with his thinning hair and crooked nose, he was far from an oil painting himself – well, maybe he'd make the grade as one of the examples that currently surrounded him), but he couldn't help notice she resembled a brick: heavy, stocky and cumbersome. As for her movements, he doubted the Bolshoi Theatre would be queueing up for her balletic services anytime soon. She was also shorter than he'd first thought and, when she stood still, kept shifting her weight from foot to foot, giving the impression of a boxer preparing to enter the ring. Her eyesight was clearly of the unenviable variety if the thick jam-jar glasses were anything to go by. And the rasping voice suggested her health could do with some monitoring. The most significant disappointment, however, was that today's clothes consisted of an ugly Paisley blouse and a green, woollen skirt, both speckled with stains. Marie Antoinette would be turning in her grave.

As she continued the tour, Vonnie suddenly thrust a leaflet towards him; on it, the words 'ENTRANCE €20' were written in bold capitals.

But you invited me! was the response Clooney would have liked to have given. Instead, he reminded himself that the arts (a generous description, he conceded) needed support. He took out the required entrance fee and handed it to Vonnie. In fairness, that gazebo wasn't going to build itself.

'Now let me show you some of my own work. I think you'll be impressed.'

As Clooney followed her around the corner of the gallery, he hoped his new friend was some modern-day Picasso, and that her urge to solicit praise for her work had substance. For the second time in a matter of minutes, his expectations were sorely challenged.

'Ta-da!'

Clooney was grateful to be there on his own. If Isla or any of his other friends had been there with him, they'd surely have doubled over laughing at the sight in front of them. An assortment of lines, shapes and squiggles were painted in dull colours onto crumpled pages. While Clooney accepted that modern art was open to interpretation, the efforts in front of him were too easily understood.

They were, quite simply, out-and-out shite.

'You don't need to give me your feedback straight away,' Vonnie prompted after a painfully awkward silence, unsure of how best to decode Clooney's low-key reaction. 'I know my work is a little, um, individualistic ...'

'That would be a good way to describe it. I've certainly not seen anything like it before.'

'Society is always telling us what to do and not to do. I wanted my work to be free from rules and regulations.'

'I think you've certainly achieved that, Vonnie.'

'Would you like me to paint you? You can be my muse today!'

Clooney blushed a little, unable to hide his delight at being seen as model material. His new health regime was paying dividends!

'Me? Really?'

'Yes, you. There's no one else here – a travesty if you ask me.'

'You want to draw me like one of your French girls?' he joked.

'You want to dress up as a French girl?'

'No, it was a ... from *Titanic*? Kate Winslet ... Never mind.'

'So?'

'So?'

'Me. Paint you. I think you'd make a great model.'

'Well, I'm flattered to be considered –'

'Many artists over the centuries have found beauty in the grotesque.'

'Right.'

'I'm not taking no for an answer.'

Judging by the scribbles in front of him, sitting for Vonnie would take a matter of minutes, maybe seconds, so Clooney agreed. Even though Vonnie wasn't exactly offering admiration, he did love being looked at.

'Okay, great. Take a seat on the windowsill; there's good light there.'

'Will I leave on my coat?'

'Yes, that check shirt isn't very nice.'

'Eh no, I suppose not.'

Clooney sat on the windowsill and looked out onto the busy street below. Tired drivers were going home after Saturday shopping; parents were trying to quiet excitable children muddy from football or rugby training. Here he was, sitting for a woman with the artistic capability of a saucepan.

Isn't it only fabulous!

Just as he was about to strike a pose, unknown objects – leftover takeaway food, perhaps – slapped the outside of the window with a bang. Clooney jumped.

'What the ...?'

He turned to Vonnie. A look of panic crossed her face.

'Not again,' she mumbled, barely audible.

Hesitantly, she joined Clooney at the window. On the footpath below stood a group of teenagers. Through a thick plume of cigarette smoke, Clooney could make out facial expressions full of menace and mockery. One, the tallest with a shaven head, stuck his middle finger up at Vonnie and mouthed the words, 'crazy fuckin' bitch'. Clooney's chest tightened.

'Does this happen often? I could have a word with them if you'd like?'

'You'd do that for me?'

'Of course I would. Although they don't look the sort to be open to reasonable discussion.'

'Don't worry your pretty head – I've bigger plans for them than having an adult chinwag. Thank you for your offer, though. No one's …' She returned to her easel, touched by Clooney's gesture. 'As a thank you … My usual fee is €100. But I'll give you a friendship discount of five per cent. Only if we're friends, that is?'

Clooney forced a smile, uncomfortable at the serious tone of her question – not to mention the intense way she clutched the paintbrush. It was a wonder it didn't break in her hand.

'Friends for life,' he laughed, trying to keep the mood light.

'Friends for life,' she repeated. The words sounded nice in her mouth. 'Friends. For. Life.'

Clooney's instinct told him he'd need his wits about him for this friendship.

'By the way,' Vonnie continued, starting work on her latest masterpiece, 'there are a few dead rats in the storeroom in the corner. You might be so kind as to fetch them for me after we finish? I have a plan for those hooligans outside.'

SEVEN

'Norman, come here, and I'll put suncream on you!'

When seventeen-year-old Clooney had left Navan for the bright lights of Dublin city, he'd vowed never to return home, apart from a couple of days at Christmas. It wasn't that he'd been at war with the town, just that he'd been full of ambition and determination, convinced that to succeed as an actor, he needed to keep his focus on the future rather than dawdling in his past. Eighteen years later, he knew this was merely youthful folly, and he now spent much more time in the family home than he'd anticipated.

Production of *Brú na hAbhainn*, the soap opera in which he'd been playing entrepreneurial restaurateur Pól for five seasons, took place in Connemara between August and February. For the other half of the year, he mostly sailed the seven seas as a travel journalist, writing about his adventures in national magazines and newspapers. However, there were weeks here and there when he was without an address, and at these times, he'd developed the habit of returning to Navan to enjoy clean sheets and his mother's cooking.

It wasn't just a convenient sleeping arrangement or an opportunity to hang out with school pals like Isla. Clooney's parents were both septuagenarians and had battled various illnesses and injuries in recent years. Even though he was optimistic that they'd many years left, nobody ever knew the date or the day, as his late grandmother had often lamented, so his unusual work schedule afforded him a fantastic opportunity to spend time with the old pair while he could.

When it came to love, Clooney's parents were like teenagers: smitten. Both had lost their parents when they were just children, so they played numerous roles in each other's lives: wife, husband; mother, father; sister, brother; educator, best friend.

Simply put, either would be a mess without the other.

In fact, Norman had once insisted that, should Helen die, he wanted to follow her into the grave the following week. 'I'll give you the send-off you deserve, Mud, and then I'm coming to join you!'

Romantic as this sentiment was, Clooney often teased that it was a shame his father's three children weren't enough of a reason to stay alive. But he could understand the patriarch's position: their relationship was co-dependent, and without one another they would be lost; neither compass nor map would put them back on track again. Who would cook for Norman if Helen – or 'Mud' as he nicknamed the mother of his children – went the way of all flesh? The man could just about manage a pot of tea; even then, it would invariably be stewed. And who would do the hoovering or mow the grass if Helen, held to ransom by arthritis and insubordinate hips, was left to her own devices?

Clooney's parents refused to take a cent from him for food or bills. Instead, he treated them to dinners or lunches in nice restaurants, something he planned to do the day after Vonnie immortalised him on canvas.

It was the middle of June, and the weather was balmy, if breezy, so they decided to venture to Cabra Castle in the neighbouring county of Cavan. Here, Clooney's mother loved to sit amongst the hydrangeas and sip an Americano or, if she was feeling naughty, a glass of Sauvignon Blanc.

'Now, Norman, sit down and I'll put suncream on you,' she ordered as Clooney's father was about to make his way out of the kitchen and into the car.

'Do I need it today? It's a bit windy,' Norman protested, his mild OCD rendering him opposed to anything other than water near his skin.

'Are you crazy? Have you a death wish? The wind doesn't protect you from skin cancer! Sit down, or we'll be going nowhere!'

And so Norman reluctantly sat down, unwilling to lose out on a free lunch courtesy of his youngest son.

'You're being unreasonable,' he mumbled under his breath.

After applying cream to his face, just as she would have rubbed lard onto a chicken, Helen demanded that her partner of fifty years raise his hands so they could get similar treatment.

'Ah, Mud, is that really necessary –'

'Norman,' she replied, her decades as a school teacher coming to the fore, 'give me your hands.' Like the obedient schoolboy he still was, Norman meekly did as instructed.

'Right, have you got your scarf?'

'It's June, Mud, not December!'

'Didn't you just say it was windy outside?' she roared, stunned at his recklessness. Her pretty coral blouse contrasted sharply with the fury bubbling underneath. 'And didn't you see in the forecast they are expecting storms in Scotland?'

'Ah, Mud – what's that got to do with us? I know we have many Scottish brethren here in Ireland, but I don't think their weather has much of an impact on us.'

'Didn't the weather forecast say it might travel down to the North? So it could be in Cavan by lunch!'

'Helen, you're crazy this morning!' He always used her real name when she annoyed him.

'Well, I won't be crazy about you unless you wrap that scarf tightly around your neck!'

Clooney suspected his father wanted to wrap something tightly around his mother's neck, and it wasn't a scarf.

'Right, are we ready now?' Norman asked, exasperated.

Helen placed the suncream in her bag in case she needed to reapply later. 'Have you gone to the toilet?'

With that, Norman was out the door.

'Right, come on, Mam,' Clooney ordered. 'I'll look after locking up. You wait in the car.'

He walked down the hallway and stopped in front of the alarm. Through the porch, he could see his parents continuing their health-and-safety spat in the garden. As he opened the alarm cover, his phone vibrated in his pocket: Isla.

'So you're alive! You didn't answer any of my messages yesterday,' he said.

As Isla described the damage done to her house – not to mention her liver – by the party, Clooney punched in the five-digit code. Waiting for the confirmation beep, he thought he spotted something, or someone, in the bushes outside. In fact, since returning to the house the previous day, he had harboured a feeling that somebody was keeping an eye on him.

It's probably just a dog, he told himself, half-listening to Isla's plight. But, unfortunately, there was no five-digit code he could use on his brain, because it was in his head that bells were well and truly going off.

What if the presence in the garden wasn't a wandering canine, as he hoped?

EIGHT

The morning after completing her masterly portrait of Clooney, Vonnie gave another house viewing. The couple hoping their search for accommodation had finally come to an end didn't get a chance to offer much to the conversation, thanks to the self-appointed landlady's incessant chatter.

'He's the first person to get me. To understand me. I feel we are kindred spirits – it's hardly a surprise as he's a Scorpio and I'm Piscean. You know that's a zodiac match made in celestial heaven! He's very well versed in astrology – he's like an encyclopaedia! Water sign this … Rising sign that … We're going to be friends for life. He promised!'

Vonnie, having just returned from Clooney's garden, was a little breathless – how she cursed her defective lungs (another burden she'd inherited from her self-centred mother). She led the prospective tenants into the modest kitchenette, not remotely concerned about the crumb-covered countertops or dirty pots and pans spawning layers of mildew and mould.

'He's a huge fan of my artwork,' she panted. 'Wait till you hear this. He sought me out yesterday to commission an original portrait. I can tell you it was nothing short of an honour, particularly seeing as he's a famous actor.'

'Oh! What's his name? What has he been in?' asked the woman, Patricia, interest suddenly piqued. If they moved in, maybe she would be mixing with the stars of the silver screen! Was it Michael Fassbender, perhaps? Or Colin Farrell?

'Clooney Coyle,' Vonnie replied, nostrils flaring with pride.

'Who?' the couple asked in unison.

'Clooney Coyle,' Vonnie repeated more slowly, disgusted they weren't immediately swooning in ecstasy.

'Never heard of him,' Roger, Patricia's fiancé, replied dismissively. 'Would I know him from anything?'

'He's only the star of *Brú na hAbhainn*! The soap.'

'Is that the Irish-language soap?' Patricia probed, not quite as anxious as her partner to terminate the conversation. 'We've been in Canada for years, so aren't too familiar with Irish television.'

'It was on before we left,' Roger corrected. 'You remember, on TnaG. We never watched it.'

'It's called TG4 now, isn't it?'

Vonnie looked aghast as the pair debated the name of the channel, disgusted at their ignorance and shocking lack of appreciation of dear Clooney's work.

'What is it that *you* do?' Vonnie quizzed, voice now oozing contempt. Judging by Roger's flabby figure, she doubted he trod the boards.

If he did, the elephant would probably crash through the stage, she thought.

'I'm an electrician.'

'Have you ever been on television?'

'Eh no.'

'Hmmph, I didn't think so. Unlike Clooney.'

Patricia prodded Roger, chastising his dismissiveness about this actor with whom Vonnie was clearly besotted.

'Good for Clooney,' Patricia enthused, trying to diffuse the situation. 'I must keep an eye out for him!' Unimpressed as she was by the house and Vonnie's irritating voice, the bride-to-be was worn out looking at properties. This place, while in need of a dramatic transformation, was bargain-basement cheap, which suited her perfectly, seeing as she and Roger were keen to save what they could for their Big Day.

'He is staying in the family home in Meadowbrook for another few days before travelling to Jamaica on behalf of one of
the national magazines. Not content with being a star of the small
screen, he's also a travel journalist. There's nothing he can't do!'

'Is that so?' Patricia replied, eager to keep on the right side of
this strange woman.

'Yes, he's such a sweetheart. They have a bad rep, but Scorpios
have such big hearts. He adores his parents and, in my book, that
tells you all you need to know about a person. The three of them
are about to start lunch in Cabra Castle as we speak.'

'God, you prised a lot of information out of him during your
sitting yesterday, didn't you?'

'Well, he didn't tell me – though I'm sure he would have if
we'd had a little more time. We were busy talking about lots of
things. And gathering dead rats.'

'How do you know he's in Cabra Castle then?' Roger demanded, voice full of sarcasm, choosing to ignore the reference to deceased rodents.

'He posted it on Facebook just now,' Vonnie replied tartly,
disgusted at the disrespect – and in her own home, too! Sensing
another altercation brewing, Patricia suggested looking at the
bedroom.

'You have a look, babe,' Roger said, resolute that he would
never darken the door of the house again. 'I'm just going to run
to the toilet.'

'You're probably going to do a poo, aren't you?' Vonnie barked.
'You look the type – gates always wide open! There's a dingy pub
across the road. You might feel more comfortable there.'

'Right, I'll do that. Then I'll be waiting in the car.'

He left the house, and the artist-as-an-adult led Patricia up
the stairs.

'If you'll permit me to be honest with you,' Vonnie began as she opened the bedroom door, 'you can do so much better than him. I wouldn't be surprised if he were a paedophile, actually.'

'I think you've gotten the wrong impression! Roger's a sweetheart, a real softy.'

'What's his star sign?'

'Sorry?'

'His star sign? I bet he's an Aquarius.'

'Jesus, I don't know. His birthday is at the start of February. What does that make him?'

'An Aquarius.'

'I didn't realise. I know very little about horoscopes and astrology.'

'My Clooney knows everything. Like me. We're very compatible – probably the most compatible signs in the zodiac, actually.'

'Yes, you mentioned. Tell me about Aquarians – what does that mean?'

I bet you're a self-centred Sagittarius – me, me, me! Not even interested in discovering why Clooney and I are compatible!

'Being an Aquarian means he'll murder you,' Vonnie explained calmly, 'and then get pissed off with your mother for not sending him a Christmas card the following year in prison. They're made of ice! Kim Jong-il was an Aquarian – that's all I'll say on the matter. Don't accuse me of not warning you.'

But it wasn't Patricia who needed warning. If anyone did, it was a thirty-five-year-old actor waiting for a table some eighty-five kilometres due north because, following this viewing, Vonnie had a surprise in store for her one true love.

'Friends for life!' she announced suddenly.

'Sorry?' Patricia asked as she felt the firmness of the bed.

'That's what he said to me. "We'll be friends for life, Vonnie!"'

'Er, how nice.'

'Listen, don't think me rude, Pamela, but you're going to have to leave. I have an appointment and we both know we're wasting one another's time. You, I could live with, but not your mass-murdering boyfriend. I'd have to keep a knife under my pillow.'

'I see.'

'But pop into the gallery sometime. It's only €20, as I mentioned.'

'Yes, I'll be sure to make it a priority. Definitely.'

NINE

Many others had had the same idea as Clooney and his parents that Sunday afternoon, and it took the best part of half an hour for them to get a table on the terrace. The grey, nineteenth-century castle loomed behind them. Despite the Scottish weather forecast, the winds had not, thankfully, reached the outskirts of Kingscourt, so Norman was able to relax, scarf-free. Helen kept it close by, however, just in case.

Since Norman had faced death nine years earlier, following a nasty combination of cancer and septicaemia, his beloved wife wasn't taking any chances. Heck, she'd spent eight months travelling up and down from Navan to Dublin on a public bus, visiting him in hospital daily, and she was determined never to go through that again. For Clooney, the silver lining during that dark period had been witnessing his mother's devotion to his father – an answer to the million-dollar question doing the rounds since Moses was a boy: *what is love?* During his father's illness, Clooney had seen, first-hand, what it was.

Ugly and beautiful; devastating and raw.

It was an allegiance.

Loyalty.

In sickness and in health.

His mother had put on a figurative mask and showed no signs of weakness. She'd fed her husband when he couldn't feed himself. She'd comforted him and rubbed his belly when he'd complained of constipation. She'd reassured him repeatedly that he would recover, despite being told by specialists that the prognosis was grim.

And then, one sunny spring morning, he'd been discharged.

Norman's successful recovery had not only been as a result of the medical team, Clooney was sure. It had been partly due to the unwavering support and mollycoddling he'd received from his devoted missus.

Today, it seemed little had changed.

Except for Cabra Castle's menu, which didn't impress set-in-his-ways Norman in the slightest.

'They've no steak?'

'I'm afraid not. How about some nice fish instead?' Helen suggested, browsing the new options on the menu. 'They have plaice and cod.'

'Does either of them come in batter?'

'The cod does.'

'That will do me, Mud.'

'No, I think you should have the plaice.'

'Is there no batter on that?'

'No, but it's better for you.'

Norman, aged seventy-two, folded his arms and began to sulk.

'If you have the plaice,' Helen continued, registering his discontent, 'you can have dessert after.'

Norman's eyes lit up.

'What do they have?'

Helen read through the various sweet options. 'Oh look, Norman: they have a lovely Bakewell tart!'

'No jelly and ice cream?'

'I'm sure if we asked nicely.'

'You're a good woman, Mud, a good woman!' He unfolded his arms. It was going to be a pleasant afternoon after all.

'I think I'll have a glass of wine,' Helen decided, leaning back, pleased with herself.

It seemed fifty years in a relationship had severe side effects, Clooney thought, as he unsuccessfully signalled for a waiter to take their order.

'By the way, I hope you realise you can pay for your own wine and desserts,' he joked. 'I only promised you guys lunch!'

'That's no problem, Cloon; we'll use the money we were going to give you for your inheritance. How about that?'

'By the way, Cloon, how do Isla's curtains look? I bumped into her in Geoghegan's a couple of weeks ago, did I tell you, and she asked my advice. Not that she needed it – she's great taste.'

'Except in her friends,' Norman teased.

'Cloon?' his mother interrupted, putting on her sunglasses. 'Do you know that woman over there? She keeps looking over.'

Clooney turned around, delighted that he was the subject of someone's gaze. Because of the strength of the sun and the fact that he'd left his sunglasses at home, he couldn't make out his admirer. He loved when fans of *Brú na hAbhainn* approached him and told him how much they enjoyed the show – was this another such occasion?

He fixed his shirt. 'I can't see anything but a blur. What does she look like?'

'She has jam-jar glasses.'

Clooney's heart sank. 'I don't believe you …'

'Black curly hair. Stocky build.'

'Wearing what would appear to be her grandmother's cast-offs?' Clooney asked, dreading the answer.

'If her grandmother was a sailor, then yes. It's quite nice actually – you know me, I love uniforms.'

'If I'd known that, Mud, I'd have asked the lollipop man for the lend of his white jacket years ago! Clooney, you might have had more than two siblings!'

But Clooney was too preoccupied with this unexpected turn

of events to berate his father for making inappropriate jokes. He attempted discreetly to steal a glance behind his mother; his heart quickened, his skin moistened; maybe he hadn't conquered his anxiety as well as he'd previously thought.

'Fuck. Pretend you don't see her, Mam!'

'Too late, she's coming over.'

'What?'

'Who is she, Cloon?' his father quizzed.

'She's from Navan; she does some voluntary work in Isla's school.'

'Would I know her parents, do you think?'

But Clooney didn't get a chance to provide his father with any further information because Vonnie stopped in front of the trio, arms outstretched.

'Isn't this a surprise!' she declared in a manner so false, Clooney hoped she'd no designs to follow him into the acting profession.

'Vonnie, how lovely to see you,' he grimaced. 'What are you doing here?'

'You know me; I like to seize the day! The sun was out, so I thought I'd have myself a little adventure, put on the glad rags and spend the day in Cabra Castle! I obviously wasn't the only one!'

Clooney knew that if he introduced her to his parents, the conversation would be unending. His encounters with Vonnie had bemused him over the past few days, and they'd been costly, given the price of admission to the gallery along with the terrible portrait she'd subsequently created. However, now that she'd followed him to Cabra Castle, he knew it was paramount to begin to temper her expectations around their relationship.

'Well, you better get back to your table, sailor,' he encouraged. 'The hotel is so busy today; it'll get swiped if you're not careful.'

'It's already gone,' she said without bothering to check. 'You don't mind if I join you, do you?'

Clooney and his parents died a little.

'Actually, Vonnie, it's a family gathering. I'm just spending a little time with the folks. They're getting lonely in their old age –'

'Oi!' his parents protested in perfect harmony.

'But we might see you later for a drink?'

'Lonely? I don't like to blow my own trumpet,' Vonnie said without a trace of irony, 'but I've been told on many occasions that I'm the perfect antidote to *ennui*. The stories I have! Aren't I right, Clooney?'

She pulled up a chair, and Norman folded his arms again. Not even two desserts would put a smile on his face now.

'We're all ears,' he grumbled.

'That's settled, then.' Vonnie clapped her hands before settling herself in the empty chair. 'You'll have to cover my share of the bill, Clooney. Didn't I only go and leave my purse at home.'

The three Coyles looked at the unwanted guest. How they envied her purse: home alone.

TEN

'I just think the chef could do better.'

Vonnie instructed the waiter to return her chicken curry to the kitchen, saying it was cold, even though the steam emanating from it was akin to an Icelandic geyser. The exasperated waiter smiled politely and indulged the request.

'You'd think a place with this reputation would get the basic requirements right, wouldn't you? I mean, if I wanted something cold, I'd have ordered sorbet. Or an Aquarian.'

'I have to say, I've never found any fault with their food,' Helen shot back. The diplomacy for which she was renowned was being tested. 'Maybe they are just a little swamped with the number of people here. I think they have a couple of weddings to contend with as well.'

'I don't mean to be rude, Hannah –'

'Hel–'

'But I don't think that's a good enough excuse, particularly when I'm paying so much for it.'

'You mean *we're* paying so much for it,' Norman corrected, hunger pangs getting the better of his natural courtesy.

'I think we're going to start while you wait for yours, Vonnie,' Clooney announced, moving the conversation forward.

'Really? I'd prefer if you'd wait. I hate eating on my own. People looking at me, food falling out of my mouth, slurping, chewing – stop! I hate it!'

The trio looked at each other.

'Wait? We'll do no such thing, Vonnie,' Norman snapped,

already shovelling a few chips into his mouth. 'Otherwise, the hungry birds will be swooping in.'

Vonnie was far from impressed and made a point of showing her displeasure by aggressively rearranging the cutlery on the table in front of her.

'You two start,' Clooney instructed his parents, 'I'll wait. My salad won't go cold.'

'What way did you come here, Vonnie?' Norman asked, his humour becoming more upbeat. The food was proving revitalising. 'Out by Wilkinstown?'

'I went through Kells.'

'You shouldn't have gone that way, Vonnie. You probably added an extra ten minutes to your journey. The best way from Navan is through Wilkinstown –'

'I assume Clooney told you I have an art gallery on Watergate Street,' she interrupted, having little interest in road routes. 'It's still early days, but I have big ambitions.'

'Is that so?' Helen politely replied. The speed at which she was guzzling her Sauvignon Blanc suggested to Clooney that she wasn't falling for the charms of the new arrival, despite her jolly outfit.

'Clooney's eldest brother, Cormac, is an archivist in the Musée d'Orsay in Paris,' Norman said, making a valiant effort to put Vonnie in her place following her rude interruption of his travel recommendations. 'Have you ever been? You might pick up some tips.'

'I don't need any tips, thank you very much. As Clooney will attest, my gallery is unique. Does Connor …'

'Corm–'

'… create work like me? As an adult, I'm an artist.'

'You beat him there, Vonnie,' Norman conceded.

'I thought as much. I assume Clooney showed you the painting

I created of him? Actually, I assume it's going above your mantel-piece. Your horrible print of dolphins is only fit for the scrapheap.'

'How do you know we have a print of dolphins?' Clooney asked.

'You should come in to the gallery sometime,' Vonnie conti-nued, deftly returning the conversation to safer topics. 'You'll see my talent in all its glory. Admission is €25.'

'It was €20 yesterday.'

'Inflation, Clooney. Blame the government.'

'Will we receive a discount, now that we're paying for your lunch?' Norman needled, strongly suspecting such a gesture was unlikely.

Clooney noticed again how uncomfortable Vonnie became when the topic of spending money came up. She fidgeted with her napkin. He had guessed she lacked generosity when it came to her personal finances – Isla had said as much – but hadn't realised the degree until now.

'I think I'll check what's keeping my food,' she eventually said. 'It's beyond a joke at this stage. I trust you won't be leaving a tip on my behalf.'

Without waiting for a response, she disappeared into the hotel. Clooney looked at his parents, face awash with remorse.

'I'm so sorry. I don't know what to say.'

His mother remained tight-lipped: she was of the persuasion that if one had nothing good to say, one said nothing at all. Norman had no such reservations.

'She's like one of the rogues from those J. B. Keane plays,' he said, licking a dollop of ketchup from his fork. Keane was one of the few playwrights Norman was familiar with, having grown up in the West of Ireland – a place the scribe archived in his work, not always in a positive light.

'Norman! Put that fork down, or you'll slice your tongue.'

There were times Clooney felt his parents could have come straight out of a J. B. Keane play themselves.

'I met her at Isla's party the other night,' Clooney explained, 'and I felt sorry for her. I think she's just really, really lonely. As you can tell, she hasn't the best social skills.'

'You can say that again, Clooney. Mud, I'm going to see if they can bring out my dessert now.'

'Can you not let your dinner digest first?'

But Norman had no interest in hanging about chatting. He never had. 'Tide and time wait for no man, as they say,' he argued before racing over to a waiter.

'Clooney,' Helen said, her voice full of kindness, 'you've always had a soft spot for those less fortunate than you, and it's one of your best qualities …'

'I know what you're going to say, Mam.'

'Be careful; that's all. I think you're right about Vonnie. She's lonely and in need of company, poor thing. But people like her can become attached very easily. She's what, fifty?'

'Forty-three, I'm told.'

'That's over four decades worth of unwanted love she has built up, and now she's going to direct it all at you, the first person to show her compassion or interest. And what's more, you're good-looking –'

'Would ya stop …'

'Charismatic.'

'Am I?'

'And an actor with a national profile.'

'I do have a couple of fans, I suppose.'

'Cloon, be nice and kind but, for your own sake, exercise a little caution.'

Before he could respond, the lady of the hour returned, trailed by a waiter carrying the kitchen's second attempt at her lunch. He put the plate in front of her, but his body language suggested he would have liked to smash it over her head.

'If this isn't up to scratch,' Vonnie warned, 'this sailor will be informing the captain of the ship that we won't be returning again.'

Helen, who planned to be back in Cabra Castle every sunny Sunday from here on in, threw a please-be-careful look at her youngest child, before finishing off the remainder of her wine.

'I'll have another glass,' she said to the waiter as Vonnie groaned, apparently dissatisfied with what she had just tasted.

'Actually,' Clooney said, 'make that a bottle.'

ELEVEN

Vonnie waited.

It was Friday mid-morning, and the usually lively Kenny's pub where she sat was empty. Earlier, she'd called the principal of the school and told her she was under the weather. As it turned out, this wasn't entirely a lie; Vonnie was sick and tired of waiting for the manager to appear. Incidentally, she'd expected a little more compassion and sympathy from the school but had been left wanting. Sometimes she felt she would be well within her rights to pack it all in – see how they felt then!

The lone barman had said his boss would be down shortly, but ten minutes had passed and there was still no sign.

'What do you have there?' the barman enquired as he polished wine glasses, killing time before the lunchtime crowd arrived.

'It's a painting. My own.' Vonnie's knife-like tones made it clear she had little interest in speaking to staff. 'It's of someone extremely famous, and if your manager has any sense, it will soon be hanging on the wall there for everyone to appreciate.'

'I see. Who is it?'

'Clooney Coyle.'

'Oh yeah, I know Clooney. God, I've seen him in here in some state over the years. I hope your painting captures some of that drunken madness. You'd never think it when you meet him sober! He's calmed down a lot though, hasn't he? His partying, I mean. Sure ye barely see him out and about anymore.'

'I actually see him all the time,' Vonnie mumbled under breath.

'Do they still call him "Mirror Boy"? By Jaysus, he always

loved gawking at himself, the vain fucker. Not the worst looking in fairness. He's not my type because, you know, he's a fella, but each to their own!'

'Haven't you other things to be doing?' Vonnie was fast growing tired of this exchange. 'Like forming a personality?'

'Would you call Clooney famous?' the barman considered, reaching for a bag of lemons. 'I've seen him on the telly a few times, ads and stuff, but I wouldn't call him famous. He's hardly the Irish Brad Pitt.'

Vonnie clenched her fists. Just as she was about to jump to her feet and shove those bitter lemons where the sun doesn't shine, a group of lively women entered. Her colleagues from school.

Where the fuck was my invitation?

Spotting Vonnie, the teachers' laughter died down, resulting in an awkward stand-off. It was left to Isla to break the ice.

'How she's cutting, Vonnie? Ye in for an early beverage? I always knew ye had a thirst on ye!'

'I'm not,' came the icy reply.

'Lunch?'

'I'm here on business, actually, Rhonda.'

'Rhonda? Who the fuck is Rhonda?'

'I don't mean to be rude, but the only name I need to remember is Clooney. You might know him – he was at your dull party.'

'Clooney? Yeah, I know him alright. He happens to be my best friend. Since we were in playschool, in fact.'

Vonnie's jaws clenched; her palms began to sweat. Isla's flowing gypsy skirt was teal and her hair golden blonde, but all the artist-as-an-adult could see was red.

'Well, Rhonda, it seems like your time has passed because I'm the only friend he wants in his life at the moment. He told me so the other day.'

'Knock yourself out, Vonnie – you can have him. He gives me

fuck-all of his time anyway these days, too busy jet-setting across the world!'

'Show some respect, Rita,' Vonnie hissed, inching closer. 'Maybe he travels the world so he can get away from you – you and your toxic ways! You made a show of yourself the other night – drunk as a skunk.'

'And d'ya know what, Vonnie? Me and the gals are planning to be just that right now, to celebrate the summer holidays. Isn't that right, everyone?'

Vonnie battled to hide her envy at the camaraderie between the group of teachers, knowing she would never be a part of it. Before she could show any further signs of weakness, the middle-aged manager finally appeared behind her.

'I believe you've been looking for me?'

Vonnie composed herself, turned her back on her colleagues and walked over to the manager, artwork in hand.

'I've been waiting quite some time if I'm candid,' she complained as she placed the covered portrait upright on the table. 'But we won't get into that now. Are you the manager?'

'Guilty as charged.'

'You're certainly guilty of crimes against fashion,' Vonnie said, staring at the woman's oversized, unflattering black pants and lime-green blouse. 'But I'm not here to share my sartorial expertise. I've more important matters to address.'

With her free hand, Vonnie removed the brown paper and threw it to the ground, ignoring the manager's cold gaze.

'Ta-da!' she exclaimed, bowing her head in advance of the congratulations that were sure to follow. 'By the looks of things, business isn't too brisk for you at the moment, so I'll offer a generous discount and sell it to you for €800. Do we have a deal?'

The manager examined the work in front of her. She might not have known her Rembrandt from her Renoir, but having cleaned the pub's toilets for years before her current managerial position, the woman most definitely knew what shite looked like.

'Is this some joke?' She enjoyed an excellent relationship with her colleagues – perhaps this was their latest attempt at humour?

'Yes,' Vonnie solemnly replied. '€800 for a portrait of local man and celebrated soap-star Clooney Coyle is a joke, but, as a savvy businesswoman, I'm well aware that times are tough economically, so I have to be prepared to undersell myself.'

The manager looked at the portrait again. It consisted of blobs of paint, feathers and glitter.

'Did your child do this?'

'What?' Vonnie cried, disgusted. How exhausting to be surrounded by so many Philistines. 'I made it. Earlier this week.'

'I see.'

'I had the honour of Clooney's presence in my gallery across the road. He said we are going to be friends for life. He isn't back in Navan for long, so I was very fortunate he afforded me so much of his precious time. The sweetheart is one of the biggest supporters of my work and commissioned me to do a portrait, which I did. Then I felt so inspired that I created this – a companion piece – on Monday night, the day after having lunch with him and his parents. They invited me to Cabra Castle. I'm like one of the family now, his father said.'

'Isn't that just lovely.' The manager was beginning to suspect that the woman standing in front of her might be struggling with mental health issues; she needed to tread softly. 'Thank you so much for coming to us and allowing us to look at your work ...'

'But?'

'But we don't have a budget for, em, art at the moment. We've recently completed a refurbishment, so things are quite stretched for us. I hope you understand.'

Vonnie did not understand.

'Congratulations on your achievements,' the manager conti-nued, 'and I'm delighted you've made such lovely new friends.' She put out her hand, and when Vonnie didn't reciprocate, smiled and headed off in the direction of her office.

Vonnie stared after her. She couldn't believe what had just hap-pened. Her face flushed and cheeks reddened. She spotted one of the newly polished wine glasses on the counter.

All I'd have to do is smash it and slash the bitch's face. It would be no more than she deserved. Yes, Vonnie decided, *that's precisely what I'm going to do.*

She carefully placed the portrait flat on the table and rolled up her sleeves. There was urgent business that needed her attention. The unappreciated artist went towards the counter and grabbed the glass before storming in the direction of the manager's office. It had been many years since she had felt such rage. Before mov-ing to Navan in her early teenage years, there had been rumours in the village in which she grew up that Vonnie, tired of being engulfed by her mother's long illness, had disobeyed the Fifth Commandment and shoved her down the stairs.

'Blame her cheap moccasins!' Vonnie had repeated over and over again when questioned by those around her. 'Those slippery soles are a deathtrap.'

The extensive autopsy carried out following the accident indicated the lack of faith police and medical experts had in Vonnie's version of events, but the results had eventually come back as 'inconclusive'. No charges were ever brought, but those who knew Vonnie knew that when her temper was roused – as it currently was – those in her path needed to be battle-ready.

That wagon will rue the day she dismissed this magnificent portrait of my darling man!

Vonnie mounted the six steps that led to the next level and raced down the oppressive, burgundy-painted corridor. But her fury left her blind to a couple of empty kegs, and she tripped, falling face-first onto the floor. She released the wine glass, which smashed into smithereens around her. One of the shards sliced her forehead. But Vonnie was oblivious to the river of blood escaping from her face, for the tumble had knocked her out cold, a state in which she would remain for the best part of half an hour.

When she awoke in Navan hospital, the only person she wanted to see was her one true love, Clooney. But by then he was heading for the other side of the world and the azure blue Caribbean Sea.

He had escaped.

But only temporarily.

TWELVE

'Would you like another Martini, sir?', the air hostess whispered to Clooney. The high jinks that invariably occurred on this particular transatlantic flight had led the airline to implement a strict one-drink-only policy. But this hostess, with her you-only-live-once attitude, was happy to forgo the rules for her favourite passengers, and she'd taken a shine to Clooney early on the flight after he'd praised her new fringe.

'D'ya know what, my love? I'd murder another! It's not every day you find yourself travelling to Jamaica.'

'Your first time?'

'That it is. It's been a dream of mine since I was yay-high. And I've my big brother, Cormac, to blame for that.'

With a few drinks in him, Clooney tended to get a bit sentimental. He was the youngest in the family and Cormac the eldest by some ten years. Long before the Kardashians monopolised the letter 'K', Helen and Norman had embraced the letter 'C' for their three children – they liked the alliteration with Coyle.

Cormac.

Casey.

And last, but by no means least, Clooney, named after his father's favourite singer, Rosemary Clooney.

Cormac had introduced the baby of the family early to the giants of the cultural world – men and women who'd excelled in a variety of fields: cinema, stage, art and literature. While his contemporaries were giving football magazines, jerseys or board games to their brothers, Cormac had gifted Clooney *The*

Noël Coward Diaries for his twelfth birthday: a collection of musings from one of theatre's most celebrated dramatists. But it hadn't been the anecdotes about Frank Sinatra, the Kennedys or the Beatles that had grabbed Clooney's attention, it had been Coward's captivating descriptions of his adopted home: Jamaica.

According to his vivid accounts, when the stage icon wasn't entertaining the world's glitterati at Firefly, his house on the west side of the island, he'd been whiling away hours in the Jamaica Inn, a luxurious resort in Ocho Rios. When the young Clooney had rifled through the pages of the book from the confines of his comparatively dreary bedroom (enlivened by Madonna's distinctive voice on the tape recorder, urging him to get into the groove or cautioning her father not to preach), he'd been immediately transported from Navan to the other side of the world. He had vowed that one day, he too would visit the Jamaica Inn and savour its stunning views of the Caribbean Sea.

During the first few years of his professional career, Clooney had realised that such ambitions would have to be parked. His bank balance was so meagre that many mornings were spent with his hand down the back of the sofa in the hope of finding some lost change to cover the bus journey to an audition. He could barely afford the €2 ride to the city centre, let alone acquire the means to transport himself across the world. And even if he had put his strong breaststroke to good use and swum the Atlantic, he was more likely to rest his head under a banana tree than at the Jamaica Inn.

But Clooney was not the type to abandon dreams – particularly not on account of anything as vulgar as cash. He debated whether to align himself biblically with a millionaire, or become a travel journalist and write about his experiences in glossy magazines and national newspapers. The former option never materialised, so the actor decided to pursue a parallel career as a journalist instead. Much to his surprise, he'd made a great success of it.

In the first couple of years, he'd visited some of the world's most exciting cities, from Istanbul to Chicago, Reykjavík to Warsaw, but following in Mr Coward's footsteps to Jamaica had continued to elude him. Until one morning he'd received an email on behalf of the Jamaican Tourist Board, inviting him to visit. And now he sat aboard a busy flight, enjoying a Martini and expressing his profound gratitude that the world had conspired in his favour. He felt a little salty discharge present itself around his eyelids, a reminder not to overindulge his fondness for onboard hospitality.

'This will be my last tipple on this flight, my love,' he informed the kind air hostess, 'so you keep your distance, d'ya hear? Unless you're coming over for a juicy gossip! Or to show off your new haircut!'

Clooney also didn't want to undo all his recent gym work; he was determined to roam across the island's famed powder-white sands confident and free from any pesky self-consciousness.

Yes, he decided, as he took another sip, this was going to be a week to remember.

True enough, in seven days, Clooney would have been able to stand in front of any judge in the land and swear that that was precisely what it had been.

However, thanks to his new 'friend for life', it was to be memorable for all the wrong reasons.

THIRTEEN

'Look, I'm not one to make wild accusations, but I'm certain one of the doctors touched me inappropriately while I was unconscious.'

Vonnie, sporting a large bandage across her forehead, sat in the back of a car, a suitcase by her side.

'You're a woman,' she said to the driver, 'you know what I'm talking about when I mention the word "instinct". That's all I'll say on the matter.'

Vonnie's recovery would have been a lot more successful if she hadn't been hell-bent on discharging herself from hospital prematurely. She'd little interest in listening to the medical staff advise her to get as much rest as possible following the accident in Kenny's, ignoring their concerns that the knock she'd received to the head had the potential to be quite dangerous. She'd been on the verge of a hunger strike ('And if you think what Bobby Sands did to the walls was bad …') before her calls for freedom were heeded. Vonnie had things to do and places to go (and a lawsuit to file against the owners of Kenny's), and she'd been resolute that an unnecessary sojourn in Saint Mary's Hospital, Navan, wasn't going to stand in her way. Besides, over her forty-three years she'd had her fill of hospitals.

And doctors.

And specialists.

And shrinks.

She'd spent much of her childhood in consultation rooms, becoming increasingly exasperated by the inability of the people around her – parents, teachers, 'experts' – to listen when she told them she didn't want to take medication or pursue various treatments, whether of the tried-and-tested variety or new and alternative approaches.

'I'm fine! Just leave me alone.'

She had become adept at switching off when the professionals bandied about new diagnoses:

'Depression.'

'Bipolar.'

'Schizophrenia.'

'Neurocognitive disorder.'

'Personality disorder.'

The unpleasant possibilities appeared never-ending, and at last, as a young adult, Vonnie had decided enough was enough. She may not have enjoyed full control of her mental faculties, but she had the power to take control of her life, something she was determined to do without the interference of supposed do-gooders – chiefly her mother. ('Such a shame Mammy fell down those steep stairs in the former family home – clumsy till the very end!' Vonnie would often comment. 'The poor dear probably even tripped while approaching the pearly gates of heaven, headbutting St Peter in the process! It's a good job I take after Daddy.')

'You wouldn't mind speeding up a little,' Vonnie demanded. 'I don't want to miss my flight.'

'What time is it boarding?' the driver enquired.

'Four hours, but one must be prepared for all eventualities.'

Vonnie was surprised by how light she suddenly felt. Usually, she would have demolished any driver going slow enough to be overtaken by a crippled tortoise, but at that moment, such was her excitement, she was fit to do like Mount Etna and explode. After being painfully separated from her darling man for two whole days, they were soon to be reunited.

'Have you ever been to Jamaica?' Vonnie queried although

she'd no intention of listening to the reply. 'I haven't, but I always trusted that the day would come when an opportunity would present itself.'

'You're going on your own, fair play to ye. Not every single woman would feel –'

'I'm meeting my boyfriend there,' Vonnie firmly corrected, as a wide beam spread across her haughty face.

'I didn't realise …'

'Yes, he's my toy boy. Aren't I a terror! I should know better at my age, but he is smitten with me!'

'Good for you, girl.'

'His name is Clooney Coyle, and he's a famous actor.'

'He sounds familiar.'

'Yes, he is very well known.'

'No – do you know who I'm thinking of? George Clooney. I loved him in *ER*. Did you use to watch it? I don't suppose you know him?'

Vonnie could feel her blood boil, but she quietly told herself to resist the urge to thump the woman in the back of her bony head.

'The only Clooney I know is my Clooney,' she replied with impressive composure.

'What's he been in? Has he worked with Steven Spielberg or anyone famous like that? Otherwise, I probably wouldn't know him.'

Vonnie squeezed her moist hands. How dare this floozy be so dismissive of her boyfriend's career. The absolute cheek! Did she not realise how difficult it was to earn a living from the acting profession, and how only the very best and most determined carve out a career in the field? He was a leading man on a national soap, for goodness' sake!

'Have you ever heard of *Brú na hAbhainn*?' Vonnie queried, her face an unsavoury mix of smug and irritation.

'No, can't say I have.'

Vonnie twisted her knee deeper into the back of the driver's seat – a welcome release of her growing frustrations.

'I think that says more about you and your evident lack of culture. You probably never heard of James Joyce either.'

'No, I have! Are they related?'

Vonnie did not even dignify such stupidity with a reply. She looked out the window and narrowed her focus on the airport in the near distance. Aeroplanes crowded the skies above: some landing; some taking off. She could hardly wait for the moment she boarded one of them – what a pleasant surprise Clooney would get!

'I didn't catch your name,' Vonnie said, double-checking that she had her passport.

'I've told you about four times.'

'Right, well then, Ruth –'

'Amy.'

'Aileen – I'm sorry I didn't get a chance to show you around the house, and even though I'm grateful you offered me a lift to the airport –'

'I didn't offer –'

'I don't think we would work well as housemates. I'm sure you understand.'

'I see.'

The car approached Terminal One. Vonnie had offered to cover the cost of petrol when they left Navan, but she now hoped that amidst the commotion of getting her luggage, with the car wedged in between impatient buses and taxis, the promise would be forgotten.

'I hope you find somewhere soon,' Vonnie disingenuously wished as she shut the boot. 'Safe home. Oh, my bad – you don't have one.'

'Wait, you said you were going to give me –'

'Must dash!'

With that, Vonnie disappeared through the revolving doors, almost knocking two shocked pensioners and their suitcases to the ground. Amy looked on, speechless. Well, almost.

'What a stupid c–'

Beep!

Amy turned towards the furious bus driver behind her and gave him a salute of the one-fingered variety.

'Never mind needing somewhere to live, I need a fucking drink,' she exclaimed out loud, speeding off to find the nearest pub.

FOURTEEN

'Shaken not stirred.'

According to Renardo, the hotel's handsome, dark-haired manager, the famous James Bond line was first coined in the Jamaica Inn. Thanks to the diaries of Mr Coward, Clooney was well aware of the hotel's status as an artists' retreat since the 1950s, but it wasn't until he and his fellow jet-lagged journalists received a tour of the sprawling, Colonial-style seaside property, that he realised the full extent.

'It was a hot day, not dissimilar to what we're currently experiencing,' Renardo explained, his voice as colourful as the hibiscus flowers growing nearby. 'Ian Fleming and his friends were desperate to cool down, so they decided to have their Martini shaken on ice. The shaker was so cold, their hands even stuck to it! And so, the refreshing Martini was born.'

Renardo led the small party along the pillared corridor and into the wood-panelled bar, bestrewn with artwork and ornate furniture. Much to Clooney's delight, the manager popped behind the bar and began gathering the utensils needed to create the famous tipple.

Attractive and accommodating!

The Navan man could sense the energy in the group was flagging – understandably so following a nine-hour flight from London, not to mention the well-intentioned but gruelling yoga session the tourist board had organised on one of the beaches en route to the hotel. He was optimistic that a dash of hooch was the very thing to, in this case, literally, break the ice.

'Isn't it a wonder Bond could drink that and still save the world,' Clooney joked as they watched the manager pour the various potent ingredients into the shaker. 'When I have a couple of those, I just want to go to bed. And preferably not alone.'

His light-hearted quip received a more enthusiastic response than it deserved. On these press trips, Clooney played the role of the chatty clown – a part that was easy to assume given his dual profession as an actor. He'd discovered that journalists often tended to be more comfortable and authoritative behind a computer, and so he'd taken it upon himself to lure them out of their shells by disarming them with highfalutin' anecdotes and scandalous tit-bits about his life. This approach was particularly successful when the journalists weren't Irish, as was the case here in Jamaica. The other three were from England – refined and, initially at least, reserved; a stark contrast to Clooney's gregarious personality. On one trip, a journalist had questioned whether his carry-on was all an 'act' – a way of hiding in public.

'You give the impression of being an open book, but maybe you're just steering everyone away from your true self?'

Whatever the underlying reason, Clooney had been adamant that every group needed someone willing to inject a bit of life into proceedings. Otherwise, idioms about 'dull' and 'ditchwater' would run riot.

Everyone received a welcome glass of the iconic refreshment and after the first sip – whether due to the alcohol or the cool indoor temperatures – Clooney noticed everyone's guard coming down.

'I have a connection to 007,' Clooney continued. 'Pierce Brosnan is from my hometown, Navan.'

'So we know who to turn to in case of an emergency,' Renardo joked.

'Then I'd better stick to the water!'

Renardo pretended to swipe Clooney's glass. 'More for us!'

The forced laughter and introductory tour continued, and Renardo deftly guided his guests into the reading room next door. What struck them all most weren't the books on the shelves but rather the framed photos on the walls and various tables. Marilyn Monroe and Arthur Miller, who had celebrated their honeymoon in the hotel, looked ecstatic and ridiculously in love. The ghosts of Errol Flynn, Katharine Hepburn, Vivien Leigh and Winston Churchill loitered. Clooney decided that the emotions that currently overwhelmed him weren't on account of the stiff gin and vermouth he sipped but a response to the humbling fact of sharing a space with so many deceased icons – people who'd once shaped the world. If he discovered Madonna had holidayed there, he'd be ready to meet his maker. He had to pinch himself.

Is this all a dream? Am I really a guest of the Jamaica Inn?

'Do you have anyone famous staying at the moment?' a cheery, middle-aged journalist called Alexandra asked, lured out of her shell by the cocktail.

'Yes,' Clooney interrupted, 'us!'

'Exactly,' Renardo agreed, smiling. 'Every guest is a VIP at the Jamaica Inn.'

'Seriously, though – anyone famous?' Clooney whispered while also taking the opportunity to share a flirtatious glance and risk a cheeky squeeze of Renardo's toned arm, perfectly showcased by his crisp white shirt.

'Actually …'

The word roused everyone's interest. Was it Angelina Jolie? Beyoncé and Jay Z? Or, better again, the Material Girl herself?

Please let it be Madonna, Clooney prayed, knowing he was pushing his luck while also hoping he might spot her infamous conical bra somewhere amongst all the bikinis on the beach.

'A former British Prime Minister was here until this morning – but that's all I'll say on the matter.'

If the group had had a few more drinks, they might have released a collective sigh. As it was, they were too polite and merely forced a smile.

Renardo ushered them back out onto the terrace. They strolled past the main section of the hotel, painted a signature colour scheme of white and Wedgwood blue, and continued onto the golden sands below. Thick straw umbrellas and white deckchairs were neatly arranged all along the private beach, with a small handful of kiosks dotted about the place to ensure guests remained hydrated. In front of them was the view that had taken their breath away on arrival.

The majestic Caribbean Sea.

Much as the world celebrated its colour and translucence, Clooney concluded that no photograph or footage he'd previously seen had done it justice. Surrounded by such calming waters, was it any wonder Jamaicans were so friggin' relaxed and chilled?

'I'm sure you're all looking forward to taking a dip, which you're free to do at any time,' Renardo said, noticing how entranced everyone was by the stunning views in front of them, 'but we also have a snorkelling expedition to Devil's Reef planned for tomorrow. In your bedroom, you'll find a more detailed itinerary that we put together with the tourist board. I hope it will be to your liking.'

Not one of the journalists could imagine anything about this week-long trip that wouldn't be to their liking. Certainly not Clooney.

Although he soon would.

FIFTEEN

Clooney was the last of the quartet to be shown to his room, or if he was to be precise – as all journalists should be – his two-storey cottage.

'Oh my good fucking Lord!'

'You like it?' Renardo asked, confident of a positive response.

'No, I think it's hideous, buddy, and I want an upgrade immediately.'

Two young staff members accompanied the pair. One carried Clooney's luggage; the other provided him with more refreshment. Job completed, they disappeared to attend to other duties, leaving their boss and new guest alone.

'Wait until I send pictures to Isla – she'll be ragin'!' Clooney joked admiring the delicate, antique furniture perfectly positioned across the living room area.

'Isla? Your girlfriend?'

'She wishes!'

Not wanting to over-analyse why Renardo had enquired about his relationship status, Clooney explored the rest of a property that could easily have graced the pages of *Vogue* or *Vanity Fair*. As if the plunge pool in front of the cottage wasn't impressive enough, the sea views beyond the French doors stood the risk of being arrested because they were obscene! Better yet, this section of the Caribbean seemed to belong to him alone. As he stood in front of the terrace, the setting sun looming large above him, Clooney's limpid gaze followed the steep path and discovered it led to a private cove below.

'I want to stay forever,' he whispered to Renardo, standing behind him.

'People ask me what I love most about being general manager here,' Renardo said, 'and I always say it's the reaction on our guests' faces when I first show them their rooms. Although I have to say, you've managed the best one yet.'

'You're an absolute gem of a man ...' Clooney replied, trailing off when he realised he'd been too excited to catch his host's name when they were initially introduced. 'I'm sorry, you'll have to forgive me,' he confessed, 'but could you remind me of your name? I was a little distracted earlier, as you can imagine.'

'Renardo. And when you're not being referred to as Navan's second James Bond, yours is Clooney, like the actor?'

'I get that a lot. It's definitely more common as a surname, but my dad was never one to follow the rules. He was a fan of George's aunt, Rosemary. After my mother, he always maintained she was the most beautiful person in the world.'

He obviously never met you.

Clooney realised he was flirting and ought to rein it in. Yes, he'd gotten a bit of colour earlier that day and knew he was reasonably presentable. And no, there weren't any wedding rings on any fingers, but statistics pointed to the fact that Renardo was probably straight, and Clooney didn't want to fuel the unfair stereotype that all gay men were sexual predators. Neither did he want to make the man uncomfortable. Especially as he had blessed him with the best accommodation on the property.

'Clooney,' Renardo repeated to himself. 'It's a handsome name. Strong. Your parents named you well.'

Was there a spark between them, Clooney wondered, or was Renardo simply doing his job and making his guest feel extra special? Clooney's friends often accused him of believing that everyone fancied him. 'Mirror Boy' they called him, claiming he worshipped his reflection at every turn. What his friends didn't realise, however, was that when Clooney looked at himself, he rarely admired his reflection. Instead, he'd focus on the features he felt were unsightly. Such self-criticism happened more frequently in recent years, ever since his youthful appearance had abandoned him for an alternative and, he considered, less attractive version. But even in his 'prime', he, like so many in the acting industry, had been held to ransom by insecurities. Being an actor wasn't a profession in which to lack self-esteem. When his first acting job had aired on television, Clooney had entered a deep depression. His nose had appeared too crooked, his body too skinny, his skin too blotchy. His looks quickly became an obsession. Now, at thirty-five, what he wouldn't give to look like that crooked, skinny, blotchy, younger self! Today, his pesky insecurities told him that he didn't possess the assets to be the object of anybody's desire, least of all the muscular Adonis in front of him with the dark, curly hair and warm, almond eyes.

Yet …

'Upstairs … I should take a look upstairs,' an unusually tongue-tied Clooney eventually remarked.

'Oh yes, I hope it's to your liking.'

'If it's not, Renardo, I'll be demanding a room change!'

Jesus, Clooney – knock it off and learn some fucking chill! Like the locals.

He wandered up the stairs on his own, leaving Renardo behind him to take a call.

The white bedroom and adjoining bathroom – both nearly the size of tennis courts – warranted as many plaudits as the rest of the cottage.

Is that an outdoor shower I see?

Clooney jumped onto the bed, exhausted from the transatlantic journey, but also roused by his adventure. It was close to six o'clock and catching forty winks would be just the ticket right now, especially as there was a drinks reception planned for the evening. But no.

You'll sleep when you get back to Ireland, buddy, now get yourself into that pool outside.

As he pulled himself away from the bed and put on a pair of swimming trunks that he'd fished out of his suitcase, he heard Renardo, below, give a joyous exclamation. Clooney promptly made his way down the winding stairs and, back in the living room, saw the man fist-pump the air, like a character in a 1980s movie.

'Good news?'

'You could say that! My younger brother just received his exam results – he passed and is now officially a doctor.'

'Fair play to him, that's amazing. He obviously got the brains in the family!'

Clooney could see the news had overwhelmed Renardo, and he thought he could understand why. Life as a guest in this luxurious hotel wasn't exactly representative of the rest of the island. Surrounded by such wealth and decadence, it was easy to forget that Jamaica was still a developing country where education wasn't as readily accessible as Ireland. Becoming a doctor must have taken Renardo's brother a lot of blood, sweat and tears.

'My family doesn't have too much money. So my sister and I took second jobs. To support him. It's been worth it. Would you mind giving me a little hug, Clooney?' Renardo asked, fighting back tears.

Being an actor meant hugs and kisses with relative strangers were the norm, but Clooney knew this wasn't the case for the majority, especially amongst men, so the request took him by surprise, especially as he was now wearing just a rather short pair of trunks to cover his modesty. But instead of reading too much into it, Clooney decided to oblige his new friend on this special day.

'Of course, come here.'

Renardo wrapped his strong arms around Clooney and rested his head on his shoulder. It was a tender moment, and Clooney chastised himself for attempting to sully it by questioning the fellow's motivations. After a few moments, he started to break away from the embrace but noticed that Renardo wasn't quite finished. Ten seconds later, he continued to hold the Irishman in his grasp.

He's a good hugger, that's all! Clooney told himself.

When Renardo finally ended the embrace, he stared into Clooney's eyes. It was an intense look, which could have been interpreted as an extension of his happiness at his younger brother's success, or …

'Hey, guys!'

Clooney and Renardo turned towards the French doors. Behind the voile curtains, the three other journalists were busy inspecting the pool and the view below. The pair shared an awkward giggle before separating.

'Pretty impressive, lads, don't ye think?'

As Clooney joined the others, all pinching themselves, he stole a final glance at Renardo, disappearing down the side of the cottage towards the reception area. How this Navan man would have liked a little *zsa zsa zsu* in his life. It had been some time since he had last enjoyed intimacy with anyone.

If he'd known who was then halfway across the Atlantic, Clooney might have paid a little more heed to the old adage: *be careful what you wish for.*

SIXTEEN

It had only been twenty-four hours, but as the small band of journalists finished ackee and saltfish on the breakfast terrace, fuelling themselves in advance of the snorkelling and water sports to follow, they bantered together like fast friends. Usually, Clooney found there was at least one in every group who was a bit of a gobshite, but that wasn't the case here. Alexandra, a delightfully eccentric lady originally from Greece; Teddy, a solid and devoted family man; Pippa, an unassuming and soft-spoken photographer with an enthusiasm for black lipstick – the previous night had revealed that not only were they all proficient raconteurs but, more surprisingly, they were also excellent listeners.

This morning, despite operating on less than five hours' sleep and battling slight headaches, the dynamic continued. Dressed in swimming trunks and a sleeveless T-shirt, Clooney wolfed down the yummy fish and, as he cleared his plate, was struck by how open and honest the conversations were. There was one common theme: nobody was bulletproof, and nobody pretended to be. Far from it.

Battles with depression were discussed.

Struggles with cancer were shared.

Grief.

Heartbreak.

Self-esteem.

Even Clooney, who rarely allowed anyone to see him as weak or vulnerable, talked about the anxiety that had dominated much of his twenties.

'Someone would only have to say my name and I'd start sweating,' he recalled as he poured himself another cup of tea. 'I think I was the only actor in Ireland who prayed their agent *wouldn't* call them with news of an audition. The "no-thank-you" responses so quickly began to outweigh the "see-you-on-Monday" variety, and I lost self-belief.'

These unexpected revelations surprised the others. Clooney had shown himself a natural leader, and the idea of him going to war with confidence was both striking and, in a strange way, refreshing.

A loud whistle sounded from a nearby boat, interrupting the intimate disclosures.

'I'm not a great swimmer,' Pippa confessed as they gathered their belongings. Her funereal swimming gear perfectly reflected her mood.

'Well, there's no pressure on anyone,' Renardo assured them as they made their way across the hot sand. 'You can simply stay on the boat if you'd prefer.'

'I'll give it a go.' Pippa was determined that the fears she faced were not going to hold her back.

'Bravo! I think today is going to be another wonderful day for us all,' Clooney predicted, linking arms with Pippa as they waded through the waters towards the boat.

SEVENTEEN

Vonnie shuffled about the deck, dressed head to toe in scuba diving gear. A large mask covered her sunburnt face, while the snorkel in her mouth prevented her from calling out, 'Surprise!' when Clooney boarded. And if it hadn't been for this same rubber apparatus, her jaw would have dropped to the floor at the sight in front of her. Sitting beside her darling man was some repugnant young goth who, if the worried look on her face was anything to go by, could have done with a Xanax or two.

The island's newest arrival was sure Clooney wouldn't have done anything so ungallant as aligning himself with another in her absence, so the blame, she decided, must rest on the shoulders of this brazen harlot. Beneath her diving gear, Vonnie's skin broke out in a furious rash, something that often happened when she became outraged. Her grim demeanour was in stark contrast to the fun and frolics taking place opposite her. Without an iota of shame, Clooney placed his arm around the young woman and squeezed her tightly. Carefully avoiding the gash on her forehead, Vonnie set the goggle straps above her ears so that she could listen in. How she hoped that her true love was telling this ugly bitch that any designs she may have had on him were futile because his heart belonged to another.

'You will be absolutely fine, my love,' she heard him insisting, followed by a kiss on the girl's temple. 'We'll all stay with you for the entire expedition, and if at any time you want to return to the boat, we will do that. Okay? And don't forget, I'm from Navan —'

'Hometown of Pierce Brosnan!'

'Exactly. I'll protect you.'

Maybe she was still shaking off jet-lag, but Vonnie was sure that Clooney hadn't told this shameless usurper to –

'Fuck off!' she inadvertently roared.

Every passenger on the boat turned to face the source of the profanity. (Yes, they were en route to a place called Devil's Reef, but surely language should be more family-friendly?) Blessedly, the sports gear Vonnie wore afforded her anonymity, allowing her to escape being reprimanded. Not that she cared what anyone said to her right then; she was far too concerned with trying to keep her fragile heart in one piece.

During the long flight over, she had allowed her imagination to run wild, weighing up all the different outcomes their reunion might produce. She knew there would be tears, but had foolishly assumed they'd be tears of joy. She had also believed that Clooney's arm would be doing some draping, but over her bare shoulders and not those of another.

If she likes having hands around her neck, I'll be more than happy to accommodate her desires, Vonnie decided. *Yes, that's exactly what I'll do.*

She leaned against the boat's railings, delighted she'd devised the bones of a plan to free herself from those earlier, unpleasant feelings. While she couldn't see her skin, she was confident her rash was already subsiding.

You see, doctors of the world, there are many more effective ways of promoting happiness than pills and potions.

She closed her eyes and, as the instructor announced the details of their outing to Devil's Reef, felt the sun kiss her face and body.

It's been such a long time since I've ventured on holiday; I'd forgotten how much fun they can be.

Knowing the importance of warming up before exercise, Vonnie clenched and unclenched her fists.

I must make sure I take trips like this every year!

EIGHTEEN

The journey from shore to Devil's Reef hadn't been as relaxing or enjoyable as Clooney had hoped. Not only had he torn his poorly tailored trunks when hoisting himself up onto the boat, but he'd also been overly enthusiastic when it came to securing his life jacket. He could hardly breathe. At least he was confident it wouldn't abandon him in the water.

'Do ya see the sea's slight change of colour about fifteen metres in front of us, mon?' the guide asked, his demeanour utterly laid back. 'That's the shallow reef, so be sure to swim in and around that area.'

He pointed towards a gigantic chart that hung on the wall with numerous images of fish.

'Before ya get into the water, mon, take a quick look, so ya'll know what ya'll be swimming beside – barracuda, moray eels and snappers will be common ones.'

'Are any of them dangerous?' Pippa stuttered, unaware that the real threat to her safety came from a human a couple of feet in front of her, not the many exotic fish below.

'Mon! We haven't had an issue in the ten years we've been doing this. Reeee-lax!'

Clooney noticed that Pippa was anything but relaxed. Her cheerful demeanour had wholly abandoned her. He understood what it was like to be overwhelmed by anxiety. He also felt he knew the reason she was so conflicted – Pippa wasn't here on her own clock, she was representing a magazine and felt duty-bound to partake in all activities. He stood beside his new friend and placed a hand on her arm.

'My love, nothing is worth getting this distressed over. We all have things we're fearful of. If someone asked me to play rugby, I'd probably bawl my eyes out and run for the fuckin' hills. But that's okay because there are plenty of things that I can do – just like you. Didn't you say last night that you weren't a great flyer? And haven't you just travelled halfway across the world? That's no mean feat, I'll have you know. So if this isn't something you're comfortable doing, don't berate yourself – you have already accomplished so much on this trip, and I'm sure there will be lots of other exciting things that you can take part in before we return home.'

Pippa looked at Clooney and smiled.

'You talk an awful lot of shit, don't you, hun?'

'I have a degree in it.'

'Right let's do this – but promise you'll stay close to me.'

'So long as you promise to sing for us this evening – don't think we didn't hear you warbling to yourself at the buffet this morning.'

'Deal!'

Clooney took the young woman by the hand and joined the fast-moving queue towards the ladder that had been the undoing of his purple trunks earlier that morning. Renardo and the two other journalists had already made their way overboard and were floating on the surface, waiting for them. Alexandra was waving frantically – she was the type of person who wanted everyone to share in any happiness she felt, although judging by the triumphant flapping of her arms, happiness might have been an inadequate description of her current emotions. Clooney wanted to leap off the boat and take part in the fun, but he'd responsibilities towards a shivering Pippa beside him.

'You're gonna have a wonderful time, mon!' the guide guaranteed as he assisted the various passengers down the ladder. 'And if you're not too confident, just swim close to the boat – you can come back on board at any time.'

She nodded. Clooney noticed that Pippa was now implementing some of the breathing techniques they'd learned in the yoga session following their arrival the previous afternoon.

'You've got this,' he whispered encouragingly.

Pippa braved a smile and carefully lowered herself into the water. The life jacket ensured that she remained on the surface, and once she realised she wasn't going to go the way of the *Titanic* and sink to the bottom, she discovered the sensation was, in fact, quite pleasant.

'Wahoo!' she shouted, thrilled she hadn't given in to her fears.

'Wahoo!' Clooney echoed, equally thrilled.

Renardo, Teddy and Alexandra swam towards them, and they formed a small circle, clutching each other's hands.

'Ready for some snorkelling, guys?' Teddy enquired.

'Let's do it,' Clooney answered on behalf of the group.

From the boat, the guide gave them an encouraging round of applause.

'Don't worry; I'll keep an eye on y'all!'

Unfortunately, he wasn't the only one keeping an eye on them.

NINETEEN

At school, Vonnie had never excelled in anything related to physical education. Netball, running, even walking to the dustbin – the girl was an utter disaster.

Before throwing the first shot, she'd hit herself in the face.

Before moving a muscle, she'd pulled one.

And before taking her first step, she'd been out of breath.

While her counterparts had claimed cabinets teeming with medals and trophies, Vonnie hadn't so much as a wooden spoon to her name, because she quickly stopped taking part altogether, damned if she was going to allow herself to be humiliated so cruelly by her classmates. The youngster just had to concede that she'd no talent when it came to sport.

On land that was.

The village she'd lived in before moving to Navan barely had a road to call its own, let alone a swimming pool, so nobody knew Vonnie could easily have auditioned for a role in *The Little Mermaid*, such were her underwater talents. It was only by chance, during a trip to Mosney Holiday Camp, that she'd discovered her aquatic gifts. It wasn't so much that she could complete a length in record time; it was that she was so unconcerned with living even then, that in no time at all she could effortlessly remain submerged in water for minutes at a time. For the duration of her two-week stay, ten-year-old Vonnie had spent every possible moment in the swimming pool, happily toying with life and death.

These days, Vonnie was no longer equipped with the same skills as her younger self, but she could remain underwater for longer than most. As she lowered herself into the Caribbean Sea, she knew there was only one person who had to remain longer beneath the surface than her, and that was the unprincipled slut who dared to have designs on her darling man.

Initially, when the guide had given her the swimming apparel, Vonnie had been somewhat miffed. She'd squandered a large part of her savings on booking this last-minute holiday and hoped she might at least get something resembling a tan to impress Isla and the rest of the bitches back in Navan. But the restrictive mask and wetsuit were not conducive to such a goal. However, as soon as she realised the beautiful anonymity these afforded her, she scolded herself for being so unappreciative.

Clooney, her victim – *Petulia, is it?* – and the other journalists swam close to each other like a co-dependent shoal of fish, so Vonnie knew that to succeed, she needed to distract them by creating a diversion. While she thought of a solution, she decided to dip her head underwater – after all, she'd paid the equivalent of €35 for this snorkelling trip, and was determined to get her money's worth.

What a sight!

She hadn't been sure what would greet her below the surface, but upon seeing the magic at play, her heart skipped a beat. She'd seen a handful of aquariums in Chinese restaurants over the years, but nothing had prepared her for this. From right to left and left to right, the most extraordinary selection of fish glided past. Turtles happily swam alongside blackball sponges. Beside them, she could make out staghorn corals, sea fans and jackfish.

Is that a nurse shark I see? Hello, bogas! Hello, snappers!

Together, their colours were so bright and vibrant, it was as if they'd each consumed a rainbow for breakfast. Their shapes and sizes varied, as did their speed and direction, and Vonnie doubted that even the most advanced computer in the world could have succeeded in counting them. And that was saying nothing of the actual reef below, which could easily be described as an underwater rainforest. The golden branches fought for attention with colourful pops of coral, and it was all so otherworldly that Vonnie wondered if it was fake.

Like Petulia's grotesque boobs.

Speaking of ... Just as she was about to descend further towards the reef, momentarily seduced by its beauty, she spotted the harlot clutch her darling Clooney's hand. That was it! Any notions Vonnie had had that this outing was for enjoyment purposes vanished, and her focus and steely determination returned.

With no time to lose, she swam briefly in the opposite direction and honed in on an older woman. She pinched her bare thigh as tightly as possible while simultaneously raising her head above the surface and shouting:

'SHARK!'

Within a split second, pandemonium ensued. Groups quickly broke apart – every man and woman for themselves. Blessedly, her beloved turned out to be just as gullible and yellow-bellied as the others. She spotted him breaking his grasp from the trollop. Screams sounded above Vonnie as she swam towards her intended victim. The confusion amplified to such a degree that the predator had to remind herself that the nurse sharks below were harmless and that she – like everyone else – was perfectly safe.

Her target floundered in the water, bobbing up and down. Whatever limited skills this Petulia or Poppy person had as a swimmer had quickly abandoned her, and she battled to move even so much as an inch closer to the boat. With every additional cry, the young woman thrashed the water, foolishly wasting the energy she needed to return to the boat when –

'Gotcha!'

Vonnie grabbed the tart's life jacket before descending a good metre underwater. Thinking she was the shark's next victim, Pippa impressively freed herself from her life jacket – although she was far from safe. The aspiring murderer simply grabbed onto Pippa's chubby ankles instead, before dragging her further below the surface in the direction of the reef: the ideal place to discreetly tie her prey to something secure.

Vonnie had no issues when it came to sufficient oxygen levels, but she was hopeful that Piper or Pipette's noticeable decrease in thrashing meant that this boast was unique to her. As she pulled the now near-lifeless body under the reef, Vonnie retrieved some cord that she'd earlier pulled from her life jacket. All she needed was twenty seconds or so to complete her task, then her relationship with Clooney would be free from threat.

Keep steady, Vonnie, she told herself, adrenaline pumping through her veins. *Your mission is almost complete.*

She grabbed Pippa's wrist with one hand, and, with the other, began wrapping the cord around it. Satisfied that she'd securely fastened it, Vonnie then began tying the cord around a piece of the reef that conveniently jutted out from its main body.

Five more seconds, girl, just five more seconds. Keep your focus.

She successfully fixed the cord around the reef, but the coral broke almost immediately. Vonnie suppressed a frustrated scream and began tying it to another section. She completed the task, but there was no time for celebration because the next moment, two divers entered the scene, blundering through the cord and undoing all of Vonnie's hard work.

What the fuck?

Judging by the speed with which they were lugging Pippa's unconscious body towards the surface – and safety – it was clear to Vonnie that they were not on her team. And remembering the unique, ballerina-like way her darling man moved, she soon deduced that one of the people sabotaging her perfect plan was Clooney, and the other was the 'mon' from the boat.

The absolute bastards!

Knowing when to cut her losses, Vonnie bolted from the scene of the crime. If it hadn't been for the blasted snorkel in her mouth, she would have released a roar that could have competed with a tropical storm.

If I didn't love him so much, she fumed, *I'd kill him for ruining everything!*

TWENTY

Night had fallen so Clooney and the group – including a delicate but thank-God-I'm-alive Pippa – couldn't fully appreciate the lush scenery that surrounded them as the bus travelled through a steep, mountainous region. What they could appreciate, however, was Pippa's ability to bounce back after her near-drowning experience; in fact, it was she who'd insisted the itinerary not be altered (Xanax probably influenced this don't-let-the-buggers-get-you-down stance).

The rocky terrain did little to quieten the hunger pangs they all felt; the day's nautical drama had left them in need of refuelling. They were wiped out, physically and emotionally.

Once everyone realised that miraculously, Pippa hadn't gone the way of Natalie Wood, and the subsequent euphoria had quietened down, questions came, fast and furiously.

'What happened?'

'Who screamed "shark"?'

'Where did the cord around your wrist come from?'

For her part, Pippa could barely remember anything about the ordeal except the sensation of being pulled down towards the reef after she'd abandoned her life jacket. Clooney also proved to be an unreliable witness. This poor man's Pierce Brosnan had been out of his depth – in every sense – and, in truth, had scant experience of being a hero, aside from assisting the odd octogenarian with their shopping. Diving twenty-five feet below water and preventing his new friend – who he'd promised to protect – from meeting a grisly end had been well outside his skill-set. There had been nothing elegant or straightforward about the rescue. It had been manic, chaotic and confusing. Yet despite the blurriness of the ordeal, he had a bad feeling.

Was there somebody else involved?

The plan for the evening was a meal in a restaurant called Zimbali, a stunning, mountain-top retreat that, according to Renardo, celebrated all things natural and had little interest in sticking to menus.

'Each day,' he informed them as they emerged from the bus, 'their chefs prepare meals using the freshest ingredients available, which are then served on the porch, overlooking the farm.'

African drumming provided a soundtrack for guests as they dined, and was well underway as a famished Clooney and the gang sauntered down the walkway towards the central quad. Once again, he felt as though they were in a film, and hoped this time it would have a happy ending.

'Clooney?' Renardo tapped him on the shoulder. He let the others continue into the restaurant before asking, 'Are you alright?'

'Me? I'm fine, of course. It's Pippa I'm concerned about.'

'Nothing like this has ever happened before. I hope it doesn't ruin her experience with us.'

'We'll just have to make sure it doesn't.' Clooney readily accepted the challenge – ensuring team morale was undoubtedly in his wheelhouse. 'Plenty of rum will also help!'

Renardo double-checked that the pair were alone.

'I'm so glad that you're here,' he said, placing his hand on Clooney's cheek.

'As am –'

'Oi! Where are you two?' roared Alexandra, eager to get the party started.

Reluctantly, they joined the rest of the group, with Clooney receiving an I-see-what-you're-up-to glance from his Greek friend across the table. She'd enquired earlier in their journey if she'd been misinterpreting the 'frisson' between the two of them. Clooney had staunchly denied any such thing, but the look she now gave him suggested that those protestations no longer fooled her.

'Have you been here before, Renardo?' Clooney probed, realising as soon as the words escaped his mouth how risible his attempts at banter were. Renardo's caress moments ago had thrown him off his game. 'I mean, we're not the first group of journalists you've taken here?'

'I'm afraid not. It's one of a few destinations off the beaten track where we like to bring our guests. As you can see, it's very popular.'

Clooney looked around. He counted about eight tables, all in use by travellers – some delighting in the unique, rustic setting; others trying to swat away the mosquitoes intent on enjoying their own evening meal. One lady appeared so resolute in remaining bite-free that she even wore a veil-like net that covered her entire face. Clooney could not determine her age or anything else about her but had an eerie notion that this was a woman who didn't like to be trifled with.

A bell sounded from the kitchen, which doubled as the dining area.

'There's going to be a cooking demonstration,' a beautiful, heavily pregnant Rastafarian woman announced. 'Hands up who's a vegetarian?'

Clooney and the others finished off their drinks and made their way from the quad to the seats inside.

'Don't let me drink any more of these,' Clooney whispered to Renardo, 'otherwise, I won't be responsible for my actions.'

'More cocktails over here!' Renardo instantly shouted at one of the waiters. 'Besides, I can't imagine anything bad happening in your compan–' But before he could finish his sentence, Renardo felt a sharp dig in his back. Pained, he looked around, but there was nobody there.

Probably just an over-eager guest fighting to get a good seat, he presumed, not allowing the incident to irritate him. *Someone harmless, I'm sure.*

TWENTY-ONE

Always one to find fault, Vonnie thought the drumming too loud and the portions too puny – especially considering the hefty price tag. She conceded that the starter – some type of grilled chicken dish – was remarkably tasty, but if she were to give it a critique, she'd have said it was far too small. She wasn't in good form and wanted to distract herself by chomping down on food – *lots of it.*

Luckily for her, the pregnant hostess had instructed guests not to use mosquito spray anywhere near her, so the much-bitten man beside Vonnie had fled to the yard to douse himself in the stuff. If only he'd thought about protecting his food, though, because in his absence Vonnie swiped the remainder of his chicken without batting an eyelid. She wiped any evidence from her mouth and replaced the veil covering her face. Incidentally, the veil wasn't to prevent the winged irritants from having their wicked way with her – it was to add a measure of drama when she made her big reveal to Clooney. Almost twelve long hours after she'd initially planned.

Vonnie was annoyed that her earlier plan to annihilate the loose woman had proved unsuccessful, but remained satisfied that the near-death experience had been sufficient to cut Penelope down to size and diffuse the threat of any deluded romantic inclination she might have harboured for Clooney. However, as she'd readied herself to make the big announcement of her presence earlier in the courtyard, Vonnie had observed that her darling man was now the focus of some broad-shouldered local's interest.

This is relentless. It's like pulling up weeds from the garden – no matter how often you do it, they keep reappearing. Just like these debased tarts trying to steal my man!

As the waiters served the second course, Vonnie glared at this brute who now had octopus-like arms draped around the object of her desires. Utterly bereft, she stabbed the prawn that sat on a bed of lettuce in front of her and wolfed it down whole. As a child, her late father had always praised the benefits of seafood, particularly for the brain, so she thought it fortuitous that the chef was unwittingly providing her with the support needed to concoct a fresh plan to eradicate her new rival.

Watching Clooney and Renardo giggle together, she wondered if she'd been duped by Clooney back in Navan. Actors were known for their silver tongues and tended to say things that weren't entirely accurate. But she was sure their interactions had been free from embellishments and were, like the food she continued to devour, 100 per cent authentic.

Friends for life, he'd vowed in her gallery. *Friends. For. Life.*

Remembering those precious words, she decided it had been Prudence and now this current creep who were taking advantage of Clooney's friendliness and goodwill. What else could he, the perfect gent, say or do when these red-blooded admirers brazenly threw themselves at him?

As she continued to study the action in front of her, Vonnie realised that this probably wasn't going to be the last time her relationship with Clooney faced challenges by unscrupulous hangers-on, like this man who …

What the fuck?

… was currently kissing Clooney on the lips!

Her heart pounded like one of the drums nearby. She wasn't sure if her mind was playing tricks on her. What on earth was happening? This scenario was the exact antithesis of how her romantic Caribbean escape was supposed to play out! Clooney should have his arms wrapped around her, and not this horrid guy – even if he was toned and muscular and dreamy.

Time to put an end to this fucking silliness once and for all.

This was war. It was time to reclaim her territory. Vonnie spat out the remaining seafood, grabbed her knife and upturned the table in front of her. She crossed the restaurant, but in an attempt to drown out the noise of the plates and glasses smashing to the ground, the drummers amplified the sound of their beats. A drunken American mistook this as the start of a musical interlude between courses and, seeing Vonnie jump to her feet, got up and grabbed her by the hand and began spinning her around the makeshift dance floor as if she were a rag doll.

'Get off me, you fucking fool!' she roared, but it was no use – the drums played so loudly that she would have needed a microphone to be heard. Worse again, the American's cronies thought a bit of a bop was the perfect way to work off the initial courses, and joined the duo on the floor.

'Wahoo! Let's get this party started!'

As Vonnie was thrown from one sweaty drunk to another, she accidentally let her knife fall to the floor, which was then quickly retrieved by one of the vigilant waiting staff. Before she could recover her weapon, Vonnie spotted Clooney and the parasite saunter onto the floor and throw a few inappropriate shapes. She noticed a lightness in her darling man, something that she had not seen before. He looked …

Happy.

Vonnie pushed the inebriated redneck away from her. How she'd have liked to have stormed out of the restaurant at that very moment, but the gal had paid for a further three courses, and, frugal to the bone, there was no chance she was going to see her hard-earned money go to waste. Instead, with admirable composure, Vonnie returned to her table, which had been quickly set to rights by the staff – although such was the weight of her heavy heart that she almost needed help from one of the tractors outside in the farm. Consumed with melancholy, Vonnie swiped some wine from the table behind her and took a large gulp – few things can fortify a weary soul like a beautiful glass of Merlot, she mused. Revived, her gaze swiftly returned to the two lovebirds, busy tripping the light fantastic.

That local chap had better enjoy his last night on earth, she thought to herself. *Because he'll soon be strutting his stuff with Saint Peter!*

TWENTY-TWO

The following morning, Renardo told the group they were heading to paradise. He didn't realise that, in his own case, he might have been speaking literally.

'Mayfield Falls is one of Jamaica's most majestic treasures, located in Glenbrook, Westmoreland,' he'd earlier informed the adventurers as they navigated steep, windy roads. He'd also guaranteed that the taxing, two-hour journey would be worth it, enhanced by stunning views along the way – although within moments, all the journalists bar Clooney had dozed off.

If anyone deserved a siesta, it was the Irishman as, thanks to Renardo, Clooney had had very little sleep the night before. But despite the fatigue, he currently felt more energised than ever. While the rest of his comrades snatched some shut-eye behind their sunglasses, Clooney gave his new lover his full attention.

'We'll get a chance to wade through the waterfalls,' Renardo continued, 'and enjoy the health benefits of the natural minerals.'

'After all that rum last night, we need all the health benefits we can get!'

Renardo intertwined their hands.

'You'll understand why the Falls are such a favourite with locals.'

'And it's easy to see why locals are such favourites with visitors,' Clooney teased before chancing a kiss. 'You've come into my life at exactly the right time. Like a guardian angel. I thought I'd lost … you know … my interest.'

'You could have fooled me last night.'

A loud snore from Teddy behind them interrupted the moment, although Clooney hoped there would be many more moments to come. It had only been a couple of days, but he felt confident this wasn't the usual holiday fling that litters cheap paperback novels. In fact, he was positive it was …

Love.

Could he persuade Renardo to visit him in Connemara, for instance? Or what about saying a fond farewell to the Emerald Isle and uprooting to this heavenly Caribbean island?

Calm down, mate!

His friends would have charged Clooney with being a romantic softy – a trait that had often sabotaged potential relationships with more easy-going, not-looking-for-anything-serious lovers – but even by his giddy standards, mentally things were accelerating at quite the velocity.

'Slow down here,' Renardo instructed the driver as if reading Clooney's mind. They reached the Falls' unassuming entrance. After a few yawns and a stretch or two, the entire gang, led by Renardo, carefully descended a series of steep, slippery steps. There had been storms that morning and the distinctive smell that lingers after rainfall only enhanced the feeling of being at one with nature. All around them were varieties of ferns along with an exotic array of wildflowers, and as they sauntered towards the reception area, Clooney couldn't help but stare at Renardo. Having spent his entire life chasing love, he'd finally been given a taste of what it was like.

Who cares if things are moving quickly? This feels bloody fantastic!

He linked arms with Pippa and Alexandra, who were walking together in front of him.

'It doesn't get much better than this, girls. Sure it doesn't?'

They entered the reception area, a large log cabin where staff gave them the swimming shoes required for their trek up the waterfalls.

'Forgive my smelly feet,' Teddy apologised as he removed his filthy runners. 'I didn't have time to take a shower this morning.'

But malodorous body parts were of no concern to anyone; a rubbish truck could have unloaded its entire rancid contents, and they still would have been in heaven, such was the beauty of the verdant landscape surrounding them.

'Are you guys ready?' a bubbly group leader asked as she ushered them towards another series of wooden steps. 'More importantly, are you ready to get wet?'

'Your prayers are answered, Teddy – you'll get your shower after all!' Clooney quipped as he dipped his feet into the water, which was, much to his delight, surprisingly warm.

'Everyone needs to be careful as we turn this corner – the rocks can be quite slippery,' the leader continued as they slowly made their way up the river. 'Once you arrive on top of the main rock, I want everyone to wait for each other and then, together, we will all jump into the pool below.'

The pool she referred to was one of many dotted throughout the river, some of which, Clooney noticed, produced lots of natural bubbles.

'I imagine that if you're tense in any way,' Clooney said to Renardo, next to him, 'this place would work wonders for stress.'

Renardo offered him his hand. 'It's wasted on me today – I've never felt more relaxed in my life. Thanks to you, my dark, handsome Irishman!'

'Ah, would ye stop!' Clooney replied coquettishly. 'But don't! Handsome, you say? Tell me more!'

The leader stood to the side of the group.

'Are you ready, guys? One! Two! And three!'

With that, Renardo and the four journalists threw caution to the wind and jumped into the pool below them – even Pippa, who, having faced death square in the face, was determined to live life to the fullest degree. (Whether it was her continued use of Xanax that inspired such a spirited approach to life remained to be seen.)

When they re-emerged from the water, a cacophony of hoots and hollers followed.

'This is the life!' Teddy yelled in his crisp English accent. 'I wouldn't change this for the world.'

'Neither would I,' Renardo agreed as he draped his arms around Clooney before placing a gentle kiss on his sunburnt cheek. 'Nothing could ruin this magical day.'

'We'll see about that.'

Renardo looked towards the rest of the group to see who had made that sinister comment. But it appeared everyone was busy splashing happily about, so he decided he'd imagined it. Although, if Teddy hadn't jumped on his back just then and dunked him underwater, he might have heard the sound of footsteps among the trees behind him.

TWENTY-THREE

Vonnie had been waiting for her moment all morning. She hadn't known precisely where the group's itinerary was taking them and had been careful not to be noticed when trailing them in her rental car. Now, as she hid behind the trees, she mouthed a 'thank you' to the Good Lord above for providing her with a suitable venue to carry out her deed. Embarrassingly, she'd failed twice over the past twenty-four hours, but now He was presenting her with another opportunity.

Like her darling man, Vonnie hadn't gotten a wink of sleep the night before, but for different reasons. When she and the group had returned to the Jamaica Inn, this woman-on-a-mission had shadowed the lovebirds along the beach, watching them give each other hugs and piggy-backs. Vonnie had wanted to vomit, and when she returned to her bedroom, the poor girl had done precisely that – although she hadn't been sure if it was on account of the sickly sweet sight she'd just witnessed or the copious amounts of shellfish she'd devoured earlier.

Giddy stomach calmed, Vonnie had then collapsed onto her bed but had tossed and turned for the entire night. Her mind had whirled in anticipation of the following day's mission – her heart skipping many beats at the thought of being free from the threat currently wreaking havoc between her and her one true love.

As she stalked the group from the safety of the woods that framed the river, she was thrilled that her fatigue was not holding her to ransom. She supposed it was the adrenaline kicking in. In different circumstances, the gal felt she'd have enjoyed the adventure Clooney and the others were taking part in – she envied the camaraderie amongst them, having never been part of a group. Not even her cousins had allowed her to play with them when they were younger because she was so 'weird and smelly'.

Clooney is the only group I need now. Friends. For. Life.

She could tell that some were more confident than others at diving off rocks or swinging from trees, and admired their patience and how they supported those who were less so. There were few instances in Vonnie's life where she could recall someone having her back or rooting for her. Apart from her late father, nobody had ever told her she had talent.

Except for Clooney.

Nobody had ever said she had a purpose in this world.

Except for Clooney.

Nobody had ever made her believe she was beautiful.

Except for Clooney.

She was relieved when the group paused at yet another pool where they vanished underwater and appeared to swim through some tunnel at the bottom of the riverbed; it afforded her a moment to catch her breath. She rested on a rock and scanned the area for inspiration as to how best to kill this pest who refused to leave her one and only alone.

The means suddenly revealed itself.

Renardo emerged from the water and raced up the pathway on the other side of the river. Vonnie jumped up and trailed him along the opposite side. He grabbed a camera from a bag before climbing onto an extremely high rope-bridge.

Extremely high – as in perilous, should one fall from it.

'Look at me and say cheese!' he called out to the group below him from the centre of the bridge.

He's such a gobshite, Vonnie thought to herself as he bossed the group about, instructing them where to stand and ordering them to smile and say cheese. In a few moments, thanks to the rocks below, Renardo would be ill-equipped to smile because all his teeth would be dislodged from his gob and disappearing into the surrounding river. The rest of his skull wouldn't be in good shape either, she suspected.

'Smile everyone!' Renardo repeated.

Vonnie was not going to insult the opportunity by letting it slip by, so she whipped out the knife she carried in her satchel, ran up the steep route towards the bridge, hid behind an accommodating bush and, with admirable skill, cut the four ropes that secured it to the wooden beams.

Speaking of smiles, the biggest imaginable hijacked Vonnie's face as she watched Renardo plummet to the rocks below. How she wished she had the means of recording his short but pathetic cry of terror. She would have listened to it on loop! If only she'd had time to snatch the camera from his grasp, she'd have loved to have taken a photograph of the bloody mess as a keepsake.

This Jamaican adventure had just leapfrogged over Mosney Holiday Camp and climbed to the top of her Best Holiday rostrum!

TWENTY-FOUR

Clooney had once had a wonderful acting coach in college – a cranky, middle-aged dame from England with little interest in sugar-coating her feedback during classes. If an improvisation had been shoddy or a performance found wanting, she would yell out, full-voiced, 'Bollocks!'

Like the rest of his classmates, Clooney had been the recipient of her tough-love criticism on many occasions, but there was one particularly lousy improvisation that remained vivid in his memory.

The car crash.

The exercise was simple: Clooney had to sit in a chair and imagine it was a car seat. He then had to 'drive' – and crash into a tree. It didn't need to be the full-on, near-fatal variety of crash, just enough to frighten him. Having been fortunate enough to have avoided any such situation in real life, the then seventeen-year-old had called, not just on his imagination, but on the many films and television shows he'd seen. From what he had remembered, they all included more than a hint of tonsil-throbbing screams. Yes, Clooney had decided, he'd scream and shout and scream some more! He'd commit to the moment and belt out a fine roar. That would surely impress his audience.

Following his intense performance, however, his tutor had called out the word that Clooney and his comrades dreaded most:

'Bollocks!'

'What did I do wrong?' Clooney had quizzed, confused as to why he hadn't received a dozen red roses and a standing ovation.

'One day, Clooney, when you're faced with a near-death experience, you'll realise why that performance was utter bollocks.'

It took him eighteen years to understand what his tutor meant.

Watching the bridge on which Renardo stood collapse, sending his lover crashing onto a rock beneath him, Clooney hadn't screamed or shouted or wailed as he'd done during the improvisation. He hadn't dashed over to the bloodied body. He hadn't looked skyward, pleading with the gods above to come to their rescue.

He'd frozen.

For what seemed an interminable moment, Clooney had remained rooted to the spot without a single sound. The shock of the incident had enveloped him entirely, and it would take a full five minutes for the disaster to even register with him. When the screams from the others had eventually awoken him from his stupor and he'd fully absorbed that his beautiful man had been killed, he could only manage a single word.

'Bollocks.'

PART TWO

TWENTY-FIVE

'Anything else?'

'No thanks, just these bottles, *go raibh maith agat*.'

There were only two shops in the Gaeltacht fishing village of Spiddal where Clooney could buy alcohol. He still couldn't drive, and so, when he uprooted to wild and rugged Connemara on the west coast of Ireland for six months each year to film *Brú na hAbhainn*, he was compelled to live close to both the set and the village because everywhere he went, he had to go by foot.

Not only did this restrictive, vehicle-less arrangement isolate Clooney from his friends and family in the aftermath of the tragic accident in Jamaica two months earlier, it was also proving to be a nightmare when attempting to discreetly purchase wine in a misguided attempt to tackle the grief that engulfed him.

Today, he bought three bottles. He knew the usual two wouldn't be enough.

'Thanks again,' Clooney said to that day's cashier as he took his change and started walking the thirty-minute journey back to the house where he lived alone.

When he had returned for the season a couple of weeks earlier, he had been determined that his self-destructive habits wouldn't become the talk of the village. He'd wanted neither attention nor sympathy. But neither had he wanted anything to get in the way of his newfound alcoholism. So he had devised a system when acquiring his daily stash: he alternated between the two shops and frequented them at different times, knowing there would be different cashiers behind the till.

Concealing his daily drinking habits from the local community meant nobody fully realised his life was in free fall.

Clooney passed the beach – the mighty Atlantic Ocean in fine fettle, creating lively waves and entertaining surfers. The sun had brought out the masses, happy to either embrace or ignore the growing winds. He briefly rested on a bench and watched families swim, build sandcastles or top up on summer tans. If sense had prevailed, he'd have cast aside the booze and joined in the merriment, but he wasn't remotely interested in getting his life back on track; there was far too much comfort to be obtained from his current, chaotic, messy existence.

When he'd returned to Connemara weeks earlier, he'd allowed his gym membership to expire while his fridge and cupboards had remained mostly undisturbed. Being sober, healthy and clear of mind would have required him to address the fact that he'd seen a man, one whom he might have loved, die before his eyes. He had no desire to return to the scene of the tragedy. He didn't want to recall how the happy sight of Renardo on a footbridge above him had become so horrific.

So violent.

So brutal.

So heartbreaking.

Clooney shuddered, crossed the busy road and continued home, determined to forget the specks of Renardo's blood that had splashed across his face. He was even more resolute in his decision not to journey back to the night before the accident when the lovebirds had shared a romantic and tender time.

So far, he hadn't revealed details of the incident to anybody – not even his parents or Isla were aware of what he'd experienced. Every time the memories bullied themselves into his mind, he'd simply take another drink.

And another.

And another.

As he traipsed along the footpath, passing a picture-perfect cottage and narrowly avoiding an exchange with the village gossip, he felt his phone vibrate in his pocket. He retrieved it and saw that Isla had sent him *another* message:

> *I hope you're not ignoring me, m'dear! Good news – first day back at school and I think we've finally gotten rid of Vonnie … the wacko was a no-show! Still lol-ing at you giving her so much of your attention at the start of the summer! You're lucky you escaped when you did – I'm just after hearing a rumour that she killed her ma when she was a teenager! Wouldn't put anything past her, the rascal!*

Vonnie.

Clooney had almost forgotten about her. He promised himself he'd reply to Isla later. Or tomorrow. Or next week, perhaps. Today just wasn't a good day for him – in fact, it was proving particularly problematic. That morning, he'd filmed some innocuous scene in which his character, Pól, discovered his flatmate had forgotten to put the milk back in the fridge.

No tears had been required.

No emotion.

No vulnerability.

All Clooney had to say was: 'Try to remember to put it back in future.' But the ghost of Renardo crept up on him out of nowhere and, without quite knowing what was happening, Clooney had begun wailing uncontrollably. The rest of the cast and crew had looked on, admiring his commitment to the role (while also making a mental note to keep all dairy products secure in the Green Room fridge). Even when the cameras stopped rolling, the tears had continued with no signs of stopping.

'There's no point crying over spilt milk,' one of the boom operators had joked, although the dig he then received from the costume mistress suggested there were a few who suspected something was amiss with the actor.

When quizzed about his trip to Jamaica, he had replied, 'It was a great holiday, I had a magical time.' If he'd taken them into his confidence, they would have surely rallied around him and supported him through this difficult period. But Clooney had no interest in wasting his tears on their kind shoulders.

He just wanted to drink and numb the pain.

That was why he was so frustrated at his unnecessary meltdown on set. He knew that some of his close friends on the show would have picked up on his over-the-top performance and would soon be starting to ask questions.

Fuck!

He placed the key in the door of the chalet and as he yanked it open – he turned around briefly and scanned the near-abandoned roads, fields and woods that surrounded his teeny-tiny house. There wasn't another property visible to the naked eye. He was alone. Just himself and his three bottles of Sauvignon Blanc.

Bliss.

He threw his bag on the floor in the hallway and snatched a glass out of the cupboard in the kitchen before slumping on the couch. His lodgings were simple and well constructed. The wooden floors were a particular highlight, although the grey, faux-leather sofa, while comfortable, was ugly and cold to the skin. But interiors were the least of his concerns just then.

Yes, he was embarrassed by his unravelling earlier that day, but as the first sip of wine glided down his throat, that incident, along with the one from two months earlier, slowly began to fade away. He wrapped a blanket around himself and decided that, for the fourth night in a row, he would refrain from eating. The wine was proving to be far more sustaining than the stews or curries he had rustled up in previous years.

Clooney pulled the net curtains to one side and peered out the window. For the first time, he noticed how unseasonably early the leaves were beginning to fall. It was only late August after all; usually it was another month or so before nature unceremoniously stripped them of their armour. The wind he'd noticed on his walk home appeared to be growing in strength, which was possibly causing the leaves to unfasten and flee prematurely. There had been talk on set that a storm was brewing – 'Make the most of the sun while you can!' – but he had no interest in bringing the bins in from outside.

Little did he realise that the real danger came in the form of a new guest currently checking into a B&B down the road. Just like the storm making its way across the Atlantic, this woman was a real force of nature. She was worse than a storm.

She was a hurricane.

TWENTY-SIX

Clooney sat slumped in the make-up chair. The harsh lights were unflattering on the best of days, but even if the room had been pitch-black, he knew that the effects of his daily drinking would still have shown up. The three bottles he'd devoured the night before didn't have the good manners to conceal their flagrancy. Clooney didn't care; for the first time in his thirty-five years, the pride he took in his appearance had abandoned him.

Up until now, he'd arrogantly believed that, like a good Agatha Christie novel, he was deftly able to conceal secrets. This morning, as Maud lashed on the foundation, full of vim and vigour, he realised his body was letting the side down and displaying his indiscretions for the world – well, *Brú na hAbhainn*'s weekly audience at least – to see. In the space of two months, Clooney had aged about five years, and in his scant moments of sobriety and self-awareness, he wondered what he would look like come Christmas if the lifeline he desperately needed continued to elude him.

His expensive moisturisers went untouched; deodorants, face mists, aftershaves all went un-spritzed. Bags had taken up permanent residence under his bloodshot eyes while his cheeks and nose were ruddy like Rudolph. Pimples littered his jawline and only for the fact that he'd brushed his teeth twice that morning, he'd have sent his fellow actors into a coma with the bang of booze emanating from his mouth.

Thankfully, the make-up team was the personification of discretion and didn't allude to the fact that this once-handsome leading man had begun to resemble something from a Hammer horror. That was why actors held the make-up department in such high regard; they did far more than simply apply powder to cheeks. With a bag of tricks that concealed the indiscretions presented on their swivel chairs daily, they doubled as the actors' protectors; shielding their dirty secrets.

'We haven't heard yet whether we're going to be called in tomorrow,' Maud said as she applied an extra layer of concealer beneath Clooney's eyes. 'If we miss a day's filming, the schedule is going to be upside down.'

'What's tomorrow?' he asked robotically, his raspy voice reminiscent of one of the local elderly fisherman.

'The hurricane! Haven't you heard? Met Éireann has upgraded it from a storm. Everyone is talking about it. Didn't you hear the news?'

Clooney had turned on neither a television nor a radio in quite some time, so 'no' was the simple answer to that particular question.

'Why wouldn't we be filming?' Clooney probed. The television industry was notorious for filming no matter the weather. *Brú na hAbhainn* had often filmed sunny summer days in minus temperatures in February, with the cast wearing nothing but shorts and T-shirts – everyone trying not only to remember their lines and hit their marks but also hide the goose-bumps riddling arms and legs.

'All the schools are going to be closed. Government buildings, public transport, shops, restaurants – the works. Winds are expected to be as high as 200 kilometres per hour. The Taoiseach is calling a state of emergency and has demanded that everyone stay indoors.'

'Right,' Clooney replied, his interest suddenly piqued at the prospect of having a day off mid-week – and being instructed by the government to stay indoors, no less. (The number of bottles he could get through!)

'People aren't taking it seriously,' she added. 'I heard that surfers are planning to go out because the waves will be colossal. Their recklessness boggles the mind!'

'Has it got a name yet, this storm?'

'It's a hurricane. And yes – Cassandra.'

Cassandra: the Greek mythological figure cursed to speak true prophecies that no one believed.

Since he first learned to talk, folk had accused Clooney of sometimes being economical with the truth to give a story a kick. And indeed, if a dog attacked him in an alleyway, didn't it sound more exciting and dramatic to say there had been three? But he'd never told an untruth. An exaggerated version of the event, yes, but not an outright lie – no matter what his friends might say. Even so, they often doubted him. And because of this, he'd always felt an affinity with the Greek prophet. Now, reflecting on all the people Maud claimed weren't taking the forecasters' reports seriously enough, he wondered whether Cassandra would get a chance to avenge herself on all the doubters.

A couple of minutes later, one of the stage managers popped into the make-up room and told him that there was a new extra on set that morning claiming to be his 'wife'. Clooney concluded that, unlike Cassandra, somebody was telling a lie.

TWENTY-SEVEN

Vonnie hadn't been certain what type of treatment would greet her as she made her debut as an extra on *Brú na hAbhainn*, but she hadn't anticipated such a grim welcome. Rather than being gifted a bouquet of roses or allocated a private dressing room, as she'd imagined, some young stage manager grunted at her to take a seat in a tiny, damp corridor with a group of strangers who'd more interest in playing silly computer games on their phones or reading newspapers than complimenting her magnificent outfit.

'The look I was going for was mid-career Liberace,' she said of her teal mink cape trimmed with fake rhinestones. 'Don't you all think I look fantastic? I hope I'm not overdressed.'

'You do realise that this is a rural soap, not *Dynasty*,' a sour-faced woman called Anne said from across the corridor. 'And, by the way, that's my husband's seat you're sitting on – he's just popped to the toil–'

'Glamour isn't limited to the bright lights of city life,' Vonnie shot back. 'But judging by those hideous dungarees you've insisted on wearing, you clearly didn't get the memo.'

'You'll probably start sweatin' under the lights, wearing so many clothes,' Des, a kind elderly man, warned Vonnie as he finished a crossword. 'There's not much ventilation on set. Don't worry, though, that hurricane that's brewin' will bring the stench of silage from the farms nearby, so no one will know if ye smell or not.'

Vonnie's face contorted. Such vulgarity. 'Won't I have an assistant? Someone to bring me an ice-cold refreshment or fan me down?'

'Here,' Des said, handing her his tattered newspaper. 'Ye can cool yourself down with this if ye need to. And if you want tea or coffee, you'll have to go to the canteen, which is down the steps on the other side of the set.'

'There must be some sort of confusion,' Vonnie began to protest.

'There's no fuckin' confusion, you stupid bitch!' Anne shouted, irritated by this would-be diva's ridiculous demands. 'Do ye think you're bloody Charlize Theron?'

'She wishes.'

'Just a friendly word of advice then, Charlize,' Anne continued, leaning forward and pointing her finger. 'You're an extra. Nothing more, nothing less. At one o'clock, you'll receive fifty quid for your services. Before then, you're going to be spending most of the morning waiting here with the rest of us, so, unless you want me to fuckin' smother you in that ridiculous coat, I'd zip it! And get off my husband's seat!'

'Anne, there's no need to be cruel,' Des chastised. 'The woman is new – just like you were once – and doesn't know how it all works. Be patient.'

'Here we go again! Mr Nice Guy, sticking his nose in. Mind your own business, Des.'

'Don't you dare speak to Derek like that,' Vonnie chimed in, her days of indulging bullies well and truly over.

'Who the fuck is Der–'

'And while we're being open and transparent, Alice, if I had your hideous haircut, I wouldn't haven't left the house. I wouldn't have even left the bedroom! Or, at the very least, I'd have put a black bin bag over my head. Although your skanky roots would probably still shine through. Not to mention your horrible personality. The likes of Oprah Winfrey and Mother Teresa warned us about toxic people like you. I'm surprised I've been able to keep down my breakfast, to be honest. So do us all a favour, and *you* zip it!'

Anne looked incredulously at her pal sitting next to her.

'Besides,' Vonnie continued, delighted that her authority in the group was now firmly established, 'you probably all aren't aware that I've special status here on this show. I'm the wife of the leading man, Clooney Coyle!'

Anne and her friend exchanged another 'what-the-hell?' look before bursting out laughing. Des, who, at eighty-four years of age, had encountered his fair share of eccentric people, smiled. 'That's nice, love.'

Vonnie didn't care for the negative atmosphere in the corridor any longer, so decided to head down to the canteen and get that cup of tea. She needed comforting after such an unpleasant encounter with that boorish Ariana person and her ugly dungarees.

'I'll bring you back a couple of digestives, Dermot,' she whispered, rising to her feet. 'Don't croak it before I return though, otherwise I'll probably scoff the lot and I'm on a diet. I don't want to be like all those other women who let themselves go after walking up the aisle. Like that Annette one over there. Although how anyone asked her to marry them in the first place is beyond me. Stevie Wonder, was it? Ray Charles?'

Vonnie freed herself from the claustrophobic corridor and the insufferable woman, and emerged into the fake village sets that were so familiar. She passed the pub, the shop and then the café, and couldn't resist kicking one of the doors to see if it was real or not. The sore toe that followed proved it was, very much so. Not that the pain mattered – she was far too consumed by the fact that the announcement about her relationship status had been so poorly received. Of course, she and Clooney weren't officially married – yet – but she'd always been a firm believer in the power of visualisation and manifestation, and a book she'd read on the flight back from Jamaica recommended that everyone should behave as if their dreams had already been realised. She'd even made space for Clooney's belongings in her wardrobes at home (well, she'd allocated him a small press in the shed out on the terrace).

Vonnie turned a corner and crossed another part of the set, not caring in the slightest that in doing so, she was interrupting the filming of an exterior scene. She made her way down a steep flight of steps – ignoring the objections of an irritated floor manager – and wondered whether she and Clooney would have time later that day to pop into the nice department store she'd spotted en route to Spiddal. Maybe they would have a sharp suit for Clooney to wear for their upcoming nuptials? She didn't need anything from the racks herself – the bride-to-be had recently acquired a large stash of costumes that were so fabulous, Liberace's wizened bones would be turning green with envy!

Where will we go on our honeymoon, I wonder? Surely an actor of his calibre has money to burn. So long as it's not Jamaica again – too many bad memories. What disrespect he showed to our relationship over the summer. Although, I'm not one to hold grudges – so magnanimous, me!

It had undoubtedly been an eventful few months since Isla's party. No wonder she suddenly felt a little fatigued.

Yes, I could murder a cup of tea right now.

Within a few hours, it would be more than hot beverages she'd want to kill.

TWENTY-EIGHT

'Okay, Clooney, you – or should I say Pól – is going to take a deep breath before opening the letter,' Fiach, the director, instructed. 'After you read the contents, you can react as you see fit – delighted, excited, disbelief, whatever you think. Then I want you to walk over to one of the extras –'

'Where will they be sitting?'

'They'll be somewhere here,' Fiach replied, pointing towards the side of the restaurant, 'then deliver your line –'

'"We've won!"'

'Exactly, and then, what do you think, maybe a hug?'

'Something like that. Let's see what the extra is happy with.'

'Cool, let's do a quick rehearsal for camera before bringing them in, will we?'

'Sure.'

'Hey,' the director whispered. 'Is everything alright?'

Fiach had asked Clooney three times that morning whether he was 'alright', which irked the actor considerably. It meant that despite Maud's Trojan efforts, the alcoholic cracks in his armour were beginning to show.

'Grand, why? Don't I look alright?'

'Yeah,' Fiach fibbed. 'There's a dose going around, so be sure to take care of yourself – especially with that storm coming.'

'Hurricane, I'm told.'

'Now for ye – be sure to neck back the Vitamin C at every chance.'

Vodka and orange juice sounded to Clooney like the perfect elixir at that very moment – an ice-cold Screwdriver.

'Hey,' Fiach joked, as he walked off set towards the monitor in the room nearby, 'I hear your wife is in the building. You kept that one quiet, ye dirty dog!'

'Ye know me; I'm a very private guy.'

In truth, Clooney hadn't the foggiest idea who was telling all and sundry that she was his 'wife'. Since he joined the show, many of his pals had come to stay – very few could say no to a weekend in the stunning wild west of Ireland – and the non-actors amongst them usually jumped at the chance of being an extra for a few hours, especially Isla. Maybe it was one of them, surprising him with a visit and stirring a bit of trouble in the process?

Oh, God, that means they're going to want to stay, he suddenly realised, heart leapfrogging into his mouth. *Please, let it be some old dear who likes the show and is getting a bit carried away with the occasion. If she wants a kiss on the cheek, that's grand, just don't let it be somebody who wants to stay and talk and laugh. What with the blasted hurricane that's promised, they'll be here for a fucking eternity.*

Anxiety, Clooney's old foe, was at its worst during drinking splurges. As he rehearsed the scene, his mind was ablaze with worry about being forced to play reluctant host to an uninvited guest. What excuses could he make?

Sorry, a hurricane is coming so you'll have to get back to your home as quick as a wink!

I'd love for you to stay, but it's a bit of a man-cave at the moment and not in any fit state to welcome guests. My mother will kill me if I let so much as a rat into the house!

My bad – didn't I tell you that I'm in the throes of a depression and on the verge of being medically classified as a fucking alchie because my lover fell to his death before my very eyes a couple of months ago, and it took me two full days to get his blood and guts off my face, hair and clo–

Before he could finish brainstorming the various excuses, the door from the corridor opened, and in sauntered someone

Clooney would have walked right past if Isla's message the day before hadn't reminded him of her existence.

'Vonnie?'

She sashayed over, arms open, and landed a big kiss on his trembling lips.

'Is that wine I detect on your breath, darling man?' she chastised. 'Now that Vonnie is here, there will be big changes, mark my words! Speaking of words, where's the director? I should get a few lines in this scene. I've been practising my *Gaeilge* for weeks.'

She was more than welcome to Clooney's because, at that moment, he was rendered speechless.

TWENTY-NINE

'And action!'

Pól stands behind the counter, casually pouring two glasses of red wine. He seems to be in a different world altogether. Clearly, there's something on his mind. A waitress looks on, impatiently. The restaurant is unseasonably busy, and they are understaffed. Pól is not helping matters by being distracted and preoccupied.

Wine poured, he goes to place the bottle in the fridge. Seeing this, the waitress rolls her eyes and coughs loudly, which rouses Pól from his stupor. He looks at the waitress – she points at the bottle of red wine in his hand and whispers, 'Only white goes in the fridge.' Realising his error, it's now Pól's turn to roll his eyes towards heaven. He laughs to himself before returning the bottle to its rightful place on the shelf.

After he hands the two glasses to the waitress, his attention turns to the letter in his breast pocket – the source of all his anxiety. He ignores a customer who is waving at him close by, gesturing to request the bill, and hides behind the till. Following a series of deep inhalations, he finally opens the envelope and scans the contents. His face is a mixture of fear and excitement. The viewers should be in doubt as to whether the news is good or bad.

Beat.

Pól releases an ecstatic cry. After years of waiting and trying, his ship has finally come in! The entire restaurant falls silent – they look towards him. They appear confused. Realising that he has created a scene, he gestures apologetically. The customers return to their meals and conversations. Pól slowly walks towards the kitchen – his strut is majestic. It's beautiful seeing him so confident and happy. He stops beside a woman eating on her own, toying with her phone. He bends down and pecks her on the cheeks before exclaiming, 'We won!'

Pól continues in the direction of the kitchen, but the woman stands up and grabs him by his jacket. She then lands a full Hollywood kiss on his lips, rendering Pól completely stunned.

'And cut!'

Fiach raced onto the set for the eighth time. As a director, he'd always prided himself on being able to keep his composure, but that was before this infuriating extra entered his life.

'Vonnie!' he barked, clutching the back of one of the chairs to prevent himself doing something he might regret, 'I'm not sure how many more ways I can tell you this: DO NOT STAND UP AND KISS CLOONEY! Just let him give you a little kiss on the cheek – and that's it, okay?'

'I did tell you that as an adult, I'm an artist, so I have a good instinct for these things. I feel my character would seize her moment and take her chances with him,' Vonnie insisted. 'Look how handsome he is.'

The old Clooney, a fool for compliments, would have basked in these words; the new Clooney, however, was too busy storming off the set to be flattered. He'd already demanded that Vonnie be removed or replaced, but because they'd filmed so much already, Fiach unwisely decided they would ignore this woman's inappropriate behaviour and her inability to take direction, and persevere.

Now, some thirty minutes later, everyone was regretting that decision.

'I completely understand your point, Vonnie,' an exasperated Fiach continued, displaying the patience of a diplomat while wondering how many years he would get for assaulting an extra. 'And I am very impressed by your passion and enthusiasm, but I must insist you do as I request. Allow Clooney to give you a little kiss on the cheek – AND THAT'S IT! Okay?'

'But –'

'No fucking buts, Vonnie. That's it!'

Devastated, she forced a nod before helping herself to a few of the chips on the plate in front of her.

'And please, stop eating the props.'

In a final act of defiance, Vonnie fished a handful of food from the plate and shoved it into her mouth, happily allowing scraps to fall from her mouth as she munched. Who was this person who dared to stand in the way of her and her true love?

Munch.

Munch.

Munch.

Fiach, calling upon every ounce of composure he had left, took a deep breath and returned to the monitor.

'Is himself ready? We'll go from his walk to the kitchen before he kisses her on the cheek, okay?'

Clooney, who'd reluctantly been coaxed back on set by the floor manager, threw his director an 'I-swear-I'm-going-to-fucking-kill-her' look.

'Join the queue,' Fiach mouthed. 'First positions! And action!'

Pól crosses towards the kitchen. After five years of playing second fiddle to everybody, he's finally relishing his moment in the sun. He stops by a lone customer – he can't resist and gives her a little kiss on the cheek before continuing on his way. He gets to the door, and just as he's about to push it open, the customer shouts, 'Wait!' She jumps to her feet, roughly removes the clip from her hair, shakes her head from right to left – her curls free at last – then marches towards Pól, grabs him and lowers him onto her knee, Hollywood style, then lands a big smacker on his lips.

'AND CUT! CUT! CUT! CUT! FUCKING CUT!'

THIRTY

Clooney started running. He was panicked, fearful. Through the violent winds and rain, he could see the shutters of the petrol station come crashing down. Cassandra had, as always, been accurate in announcing her devastating might. The difference was that now everyone believed her.

Brú na hAbhainn had stopped production early. Drivers had deserted roads, and businesses – including the three pubs and two shops where Clooney could buy his much-coveted liquor – were battening down the hatches. It was six o'clock but appeared much later thanks to the dark clouds.

'Wait!' he roared to one of the station's employees, but his pleas fell on deaf ears – not even this classically trained actor could compete with the conditions currently creating chaos across the Emerald Isle. Rather than continuing to shout and bring on a sore throat, he decided to put his years of cross-country running to the test and tore down Main Street before hopping over the station's side wall. The downpour, increasing in force by the second, left Clooney's visibility compromised and, as he landed on the ground, his foot hit a stray tyre shield that had freed itself from some vehicle, leading him to fall flat on his face.

You have got to be fucking kidding me!

Focused on the task at hand, he gamely ignored the blood that trickled from his nose and sallied forth. With a face drenched with an unsightly mixture of rain, sweat and now blood, Clooney arrived at the entrance and banged on the blasted shutters while looking skywards for a miracle. He'd no interest in spending the night alone with his thoughts. He needed alcohol. And, following the unpleasant morning with that psychotic woman, plenty of it.

No response.

He banged a second time, and then a third.

Nothing.

Please, don't do this to me …

Then he had a brainwave. He raced around the side of the building to where he knew the staff would be on the verge of leaving. He planned to use his charm to convince them to return inside and fetch him a bottle of Sauvignon Blanc.

Possibly three.

He was on first-name terms with the majority of them, so he hoped his request would be fulfilled. He stood by the door and waited. It was only when he heard the rattle of the front shutters, followed by the roar of an engine that he realised that whoever was on duty had fled by the main entrance, not the usual side one.

'Fuck!'

Clooney returned to the front where his suspicions were sadly confirmed. He watched as the car disappeared into the storm, and with it, his final chance of getting a drink. There would be no alcohol tonight, he reluctantly conceded, unless he fished out some of the cleaning products from under the kitchen sink – an idea he hadn't yet wholly dismissed.

Inconsolable, he ventured along the pathway towards home; the violent winds thrust him forward, proving helpful for once. On a fine day, the journey between set and home took thirty minutes; today, it was half that.

Fifteen minutes extra sitting home, alone and sober, he thought as he made his way up the winding bothareen off the main road. *Maybe I could ask one of the neighbours for the loan of a bottle?*

Now that he'd thought of it, his friend Jess had recently opened a craft beer brewery with her husband – she was sure to have a few bottles up for grabs. While on paper the couple could have been referred to as his neighbours; in reality, they were about a ten-minute hike away. But aside from a couple of derelict houses that hadn't enjoyed a burning fire for many years, they were the closest people to him.

Good job there's never been an emergency, he'd thought a couple of times over the years.

Having decided to abuse his neighbours' hospitality, Clooney's mood now rose to the heights of the mischievous clouds above.

Tonight's going to be a good night after all!

He decided to drop his bag home first, but as he passed the pine trees that obscured the view of his chalet, he noticed a car parked in the driveway – a red Renault. He didn't recognise it – was it one of his comrades from *Brú na hAbhainn* unexpectedly popping over for a cup of tea? He didn't think it belonged to his landlady, who might have called over to ensure her property remained upright. He wondered if it was related to the hurricane – maybe the electricity or phone lines were down, in which case, perhaps the unwanted visitor was from EBS or Eir. But he'd heard there were warnings for everyone across the country to stay indoors, warnings which, he imagined, included such workers, so he quickly discounted that possibility. Besides, their vehicles would be more official-looking than the car parked in front of him. Whoever it was, Clooney wanted them gone post haste.

Or maybe they could give me a lift to Jess' house? Drinking could start earlier.

As he made his way up the driveway, leaves and twigs swirling around him, his phone began to vibrate in his pocket. It was his landlady. Maybe she could explain the presence of the unknown vehicle.

'You're a dark horse,' she teased. 'You never told me you were married to a woman!'

Clooney decided it must be Cassandra and her violent ways that were preventing him from hearing the lady correctly: surely she hadn't suggested he had a wife!

'What did you just say, my love?'

'That you have a wife! And here you were telling us you were gay! Sure I'd have loved to have introduced you to my niece – if only I'd known. Although you aren't single, I suppose … Not that it would have mattered to Noreen. Well, it certainly hasn't in the past, if you catch my meaning.'

Clooney's throat tightened. Knots formed in his stomach.

My wife – oh, Jesus Christ, please tell me this car doesn't belong to … It couldn't, could it?

Refusing to accept the inevitable, he prayed that his landlady – a self-proclaimed technophobe – had allowed her mobile phone to get the better of her again. He would have needed the assistance of a mathematician to tot up the number of times she'd accidentally called him or texted him over the years.

'This is Clooney – are you sure you've called the right person? You probably meant to ring –'

'Your wife! She arrived at our house about thirty minutes ago and I gave her a spare key. She's probably waiting for you inside.'

Clooney's throat tightened and his stomach began doing a *ceilí* dance.

'Keep safe you tw–'

Without another word, Clooney hung up and continued cautiously to the front door. He rummaged through his soaked backpack for the key, ignoring the blood from his fall that now partially covered his clothes and face. After shutting the front door behind him, he walked into the small hallway and dropped his bag on the floor. The heat was on and there was a strong smell of cooking wafting from the kitchen. He took a deep breath and opened the door.

There, standing in front of the oven, still in the Liberace-inspired costume, but now with an apron draped over her fake mink coat, was Vonnie, his 'wife'.

'Just in time for dinner!' she announced, placing condiments on a terribly decorated table – the centrepiece was the lid of the dustbin, upturned, filled with damp leaves gathered from outside. 'I hope you're hungry. I've made tripe. And risotto.'

Clooney remained rooted to the spot, desperately trying to string a sentence together.

'What ... Why?'

'Don't mind your jibber-jabbering: go and wash your hands. And face. I hope that's not blood I see. I haven't time to be your nurse in addition to your personal chef. What am I saying – of course I do. Let me know if you need help – I can even lick that blood off your face if you need me to! And I'm only half-joking!'

Without knowing what else to do, a shell-shocked Clooney limped obediently to the bathroom.

THIRTY-ONE

Vonnie had always prided herself on her ability to rustle up a delicious meal at short notice, and even though the local stores in Spiddal didn't have all the ingredients she needed – 'What do you mean you haven't heard of porcini mushrooms? And you don't have fresh saffron? Honestly ...' – she was confident the food sitting in front of them now wouldn't have looked out of place in a Michelin-starred restaurant. Others might not agree, but that didn't matter a jot to her. And how she was able to set the scene. Outside, the hurricane destroyed everything in its path; inside, with the help of background music and a couple of candles, peace and tranquillity – two essential ingredients for a night of romance – reigned supreme.

Or should that be 'rained' supreme? the domestic goddess quipped to herself, peeping outside the window.

'I've left the receipts on the shelf over there,' she told Clooney, joining him at the table. 'It's only fair we share the bills, don't you agree? Considering I had to go to the shop and slave over the cooker for the past hour, shall we say an 85/15 split?'

'Sorry, but –'

'No, you're absolutely right – I used your electricity, so we have to factor in those expenses as well. How about 83/17? Yes, I believe that's fair. Although,' she mumbled under her breath while sprinkling a pinch of salt over her risotto, 'most gentlemen would insist on footing the entire bill – particularly a soap star like you.'

'What? I'm not a soap ... That doesn't matter – what does matter is what you think you're do–'

'What I'm doing? I'm eating! Before the food goes cold. And you should be doing the same. Quick, tuck in,' she barked before devouring a mouthful of risotto.

Vonnie's attention soon drifted from the food to her darling man sitting opposite at the long rectangular table. She held her tongue and decided not to reprimand him for failing to bring her any flowers or chocolates – nobody was perfect after all. Instead, a blizzard of questions raced through her mind.

What will his favourite part of the meal be? How will he express his satisfaction to me? With kind words or, preferably, an empty plate and demands for seconds?

She'd been dreaming of this moment for as long as she could remember: cooking for her one true love! Such was her excitement, it took her an age to realise that Clooney's face was so contorted, it bore a striking resemblance to the offal he toyed with.

'Is everything okay, Clooney? I know you Scorpios are notoriously difficult to read, but I suspect that something is wrong. Pisceans are very intuitive, you see. What is it? Tell Vonnie.'

He grunted.

'Aren't you hungry? Please don't tell me you don't have an appetite; you have no idea of the effort that went –'

'We need to talk, Vonnie.'

'Of course! We have all night to chat and, judging by those noises outside, we won't be going anywhere in a hurry! Maybe we can play cards or charades – or sing a selection of our favourite numbers from the musicals.'

'Dear God.'

Vonnie's instinct to remain polite and courteous was being challenged. The social etiquette for which she knew she was famed was rapidly disappearing into thin air – like most of the garden furniture outside, she suspected.

'Vonnie, what are you doing here?' Clooney blurted out,

slamming his fist onto the table.

'Visiting you, silly! That's not an issue, is it?' She picked up her knife, delicately gliding her finger along the edge. 'Is it?'

'My love, you are a dear friend,' Clooney continued, his tone dramatically altering, 'and I am delighted that you feel so comfortable around me that you're happy to visit. Uninvited.'

'Why didn't you invite me then?' she attacked, her grip tightening on the knife.

'Was that your expectation? I hadn't realised.'

'What's all this talk about expectations? You sound like one of those horrid new-age hippies.'

'Do I?' he replied with a smile – a fake one, she could tell. 'Do you mind if I get a glass of water? My mouth and throat are a little dry.'

Vonnie nodded. She kept a close eye on him as he reached for a glass in the cupboard above the sink. She caught him throwing a glance at the door – was he going to do what every other person in her life had done?

Run out on me?

Judging by the chaos outside, she didn't fancy his odds against Mother Nature.

'Well, why don't you tell me exactly what you want from me?' he questioned after he'd emptied the contents of the glass and returned to his seat. 'And why you've been telling everyone that you're my –'

'Firstly,' she interrupted, 'I want you to eat your dinner. Every last morsel of it.'

'But,' Clooney argued, pushing the plate away from him, 'I'm not hungr–'

'EAT THE BLOODY FOOD!'

Obediently, Clooney picked up a fork and did as she demanded.

'Yum,' he said after swallowing a mouthful.

'FAKE! You don't mean that! Do you?'

'I do! It's delicious.'

'It is, isn't it?' she agreed, and by way of stressing her point, devoured what remained on her plate. 'Do hurry up. I'm dying to try the delicious dessert I made.'

'What is it? Death by Chocolate?'

'How did you know?'

'Just a guess, I suppose.'

'Ah no, it's not. It's jelly and ice cream.'

THIRTY-TWO

'I spy with my little eye, something beginning with …'

'I have to go to the bathroom,' Clooney interrupted. 'All that delicious food wants out!'

'There's no need to be so vulgar – do you think a lady wants to hear such coarseness? Any more chat about the inner machinations of your bowels and I'll be straight out that door.'

If Clooney had only realised it was that easy to get rid of her, he'd have tapped into his obscene side much earlier.

'Quick! I have a fabulous *I Spy* that begins with "W".'

Witch.

Weirdo.

Whack job.

Clooney slipped into the bathroom and locked the door behind him – more out of habit than for protection, as he suspected the flimsy piece of metal would be no match for this second-rate Annie Wilkes of *Misery* fame. He sat on the side of the bath – the white wall tiles along with the vase of lavender on a glass table in the corner offered him a moment of calm. But just a moment.

'Hurry!' Vonnie yelled from the living room.

Clooney knew he had to act quickly. Back in Navan, he'd thought Vonnie was harmless, but as the various scenes had unravelled that day, he began to remember both Isla's and his mother's cautions.

Always listen to Mammy, he joked to himself, placing a hand in his pocket to double-check his phone was still there. It was.

He debated calling the gardaí, but then decided against it.

They'd enough on their plates tonight. The entire country was being ripped apart by Hurricane Cassandra; they didn't have time to contend with a paperback domestic between an actor who was a sip away from being admitted to the Betty Ford Clinic and his delusional 'wife', whose only crime was being a little too enthusiastic about the relationship. She hadn't broken and entered, he reminded himself – the landlady had let her in – and the thinly veiled threat with the knife could be dismissed as nothing more than a harmless gesture. After all, who doesn't run their finger along a sharp blade before using it to cut food?

Maybe you're paranoid, Clooney, he told himself. *This is why alcohol is 'the libation of Lucifer' – as Granny used to say. It leaves you jittery and overly suspicious. Go back in there and have a pleasant, adult conversation –*

'Get the fuck out of there this minute!'

Such was the surprise of Vonnie's attack from the other side of the door that Clooney unbalanced and tumbled into the bath.

'What kind of host do you call yourself? I drove for over three hours to get here, and this is the thanks you give me? If you didn't want to play *I Spy*, you should have just said. I'm not the type who forces others into doing things they don't want to do.'

The histrionics soon gave way to pounding and kicking. Clooney fished his phone from his pocket, and just as he began to punch in 999, he realised the handset was in the same state Vonnie seemed to want for him.

Dead!

That's impossible! It was fully charged about an hour ago.

He prised open the back of the phone and realised it had been the victim of foul play: the battery and SIM card were both missing.

She's good; I'll give her that.

The thumping and kicking continued, and Clooney knew he

had mere moments to escape this vile situation. There may have been twisters, tornadoes and cyclones outside, lifting the roofs off houses and trees from the ground, but it was guaranteed to be paradise in comparison to the predicament he was currently in. He finally accepted the gravity of the situation.

He was in danger – real danger.

'Open the door! Open it NOW!'

Clooney attempted to lift himself from the bath, but the wet surface meant his movements were more like those of a fawn than a sober, thirty-five-year-old man. He grabbed the towel rail but not too vigorously; he didn't want to yank it from the wall entirely and then knock himself out by banging his head against the edge of the bath.

Although there might be some value in playing dead, he considered. *Maybe an unconscious body would appeal to her protectiv–*

'I'm going to kill you, you bastard!' she roared, the door almost off the hinge. 'I can't believe I've let someone use me like this! Well, it will be the last time, I promise you that, Clooney Coyle!'

He decided to put an end to his ridiculous cogitating and get the hell out of Dodge – while he still could. Energised by a blast of good old-fashioned adrenaline, Clooney quickly pushed open the window. Even though he no longer possessed the slim physique of his earlier years, back when his diet, like that of so many penniless thespians, consisted of cups of coffee and cigarettes, he still managed to squeeze his way out in the nick of time. It was about ten o'clock and nearly pitch-black. As soon as he landed on the water-logged ground below, a knife came flying. If it hadn't been for the strong gales wreaking havoc around him, it would undoubtedly have entered his skull. Murder was an act this woman was familiar with, he deduced, bolting from the house.

What had Isla said about Vonnie killing her mother?

Clooney didn't have a car; Vonnie did, so he knew that to

outsmart her, he'd have to avoid the roads and keep off the beaten track. While the country was currently and collectively cursing the weather, he decided the hurricane was to become his ally. Yes, thanks to the winds and lack of daylight, Clooney couldn't see an inch in front of him; but neither could she. He knew the area; she didn't.

As he stumbled down the driveway and out of his garden, he decided upon a route: make his way to his neighbours' house but, rather than take the road, venture across the fields. He'd no torch and stood the chance of disappearing into a hole or drowning in the now marsh-like terrain, but it was the best chance he had. Clearing the gate, he landed in the first field and, quite literally, hit the ground running. But this good start wasn't to last. As suspected, the usually solid earth was akin to a swamp, and as Clooney tried to move forward in the direction of Jess' house, his feet kept sinking. That, coupled with the winds and rain punching his face, made the task ahead of him Everest-like.

Keep going, Clooney! You have no choice.

He could hear the engine of Vonnie's car start in the distance. Rather than venturing deeper into the field, the escapee decided that he needed to alter course and, instead, run along the edges where the surfaces were slightly more secure – with the added benefit that the tall hedges might hide him from Vonnie's vision. He retraced his steps.

Beep! Beep! Vonnie sounded the horn: she meant business.

Blessedly, the ground beneath the hedges hadn't, in fact, been subjected to the same treacherous conditions as the rest of the area. Slightly stooped and out of sight, Clooney made a good run for it. Behind him, the clang of Vonnie's Renault grew louder – a realisation that only spurred him on to sprint faster. Discounting a couple of stumbles here and there, Clooney was convinced he was well on his way to safety. For Vonnie to be any danger to him now, she would have to get out of the car and give chase by foot. Should she do that, he decided, he'd lure her into the centre of the field where the mud would surely stop her in her tracks. But before he could congratulate himself on his brilliantly conceived plan, he heard the sound of something that didn't appear to want company in the field.

A bull.

You have got to be kidding me!

THIRTY-THREE

Vonnie didn't even wait for the door to open before storming into Jess' house.

'Where is that pathetic, deceiving little toe-rag? I know you're harbouring him. He's a fugitive! Hand him over, or I won't be held responsible for my actions.'

If it weren't for the fact that Jess was weighed down by a large crate of empty glass bottles, she would have pushed this intruder back out of her house. While she was less than five foot and her thin frame didn't appear too threatening, she had been grafting every hour of the day in her micro-brewery located on the other side of Connemara, and her newly formed biceps were not to be underestimated. That said, the possessed trespasser in front of her, drenched from head to toe and carrying at least three knives, was not to be underestimated either. Aware of her weaponless state, and the fact that her children were mere metres away, Jess decided on a more diplomatic approach to resolve the unexpected and unpleasant situation.

'Sorry, who are you and who are you looking for? You seem to be upset and lost.'

'You can say that again – I've lost my marbles over this double-dealing monster!'

'I'm sorry to hear that, but who is this person you're talking about?' Jess asked, cautiously placing the crate on a small wooden table beside her. Without drawing too much attention to herself, she rolled up the sleeves of her oversized cream Aran sweater. She wanted to be ready if the scene got ugly.

Uglier.

'Soap star Clooney Coyle! I'm his wife!' Vonnie roared, her eyes scanning the property for clues of his whereabouts. 'Although I have a good mind to call it all off this very moment!'

The penny finally dropped for Jess. She'd received a phone call earlier that day from her pal Anne, who was desperate to have a gossip about some deranged woman who had sauntered onto the set of *Brú na hAbhainn* claiming to be Clooney's paramour. Apparently, she'd created more chaos than Hurricane Cassandra.

'I know Clooney, of course,' Jess said calmly, 'but why do you think he's here? He's not. He's only been to the house once, and that was a couple of years ago for our Christmas party. And even then, he didn't stay long.'

Vonnie inched closer to her, lifting her collection of knives – the silver blades glistened under a chandelier that hung from the ceiling. 'And where was my invite to that festive soirée? It sounds right up my street. I'd have even dressed up!'

Jess quickly concluded that this woman was more unhinged than Anne had made out. 'I suppose we didn't know you at the time.'

'And now that you know me, would I get an invite? Of course I wouldn't – nobody ever wants to be in my company! Not that that mattered since Clooney swept me off my feet. But seeing as his true colours have now been revealed, he'll feel the weight of these feet as they come crashing down on his skull. Right, enough pleasantries – *where is he?*'

Vonnie stormed the quad-shaped hallway, searching cabinets, under chairs, behind potted plants. Jess took the opportunity to arm herself with a couple of glass bottles from the crate, preparing herself for combat.

'Clooney, where are you? I know you're here – I can smell your cheap aftershave. There's no escape!'

'Who's Clooney?' A small child, Teresa, stood at the door leading to a kitchen area, a half-eaten slice of cheese in her hand.

'My lover that's who!'

'Why is he here?'

'Because he's a poor man's Marcus Junius Brutus, stabbing me in the back. But you see these?' she asked, waving the knives in front of the girl. 'I will avenge Julius Caesar! I will avenge Vonnie J. Gallagher!'

Jess quickly stood in between the angry intruder and her daughter. 'I promise you; Clooney is not here. Now, please leave.'

'He is! I can smell him for heaven's sake. I don't know what's the stronger odour – his hideous cologne or his cowardice.'

Jess gripped the bottles more tightly but still hoped to resolve the situation amicably. The last thing she wanted her five-year-old daughter to see was a bloody brawl in their hallway. 'You might be getting confused with Teresa's IBS. It smells like she ate a big slab of cheese, even though she knows fine well she's intolerant to dairy. Am I right, Teasy?'

Teresa lowered her head, ashamed. 'I'm sorry – I just wanted something to chew while watching the bull and the man stare at each other in the field. Like popcorn in the movies.'

'Which man. Which field?' Vonnie probed.

Jess tried to persuade her youngest not to reveal any additional information, but it was no good. Teresa was too distracted by the pains in her stomach to take hints.

'The one next door.'

Delighted that she had been given a precise location for the whereabouts of her prey, Vonnie smiled. She leaned over to the girl and whispered, 'You want me to sort your mam out for ye while I'm at it, Teasy? Then you'll be able to eat as many Easy Singles as you like!'

But before Teresa could give a response, a loud human roar

sounded from outside. Vonnie knew immediately who the wimp responsible for the shrill, high-pitched tones was.

'I've gotta go! You can give me your answer later, Teasy. Call me!'

And with that, she disappeared from the house as abruptly as she'd entered. Her knives weren't going to use themselves after all.

THIRTY-FOUR

Through heavy rain, Clooney could just about make out the black, horned beast. Despite the limited visibility; it was clear to him that the bull felt there was only enough room for one in this particular field. Moments earlier, the actor had unsuccessfully attempted to scare his new rival away by roaring. Now, the pair held still and faced each other.

One was ready to pass out.

The other was ready for war.

There was no sign of Vonnie. Normally, this would have given Clooney much comfort, but in his current predicament, he longed for an ally – even of the psychotic, knife-wielding variety. Without moving a muscle, Clooney mentally raced through his options. He could attempt to jump over the hedges, but they weren't low enough for him to comfortably clear them – the last thing the poor lad wanted was to be entangled in the middle of thorny branches before being gored to death by his current enemy. He could run back to the closest gate, but worried he wouldn't be quick enough or might be the victim of another fall. Instead, Clooney settled on his third option.

Rather than escaping sideways or backwards, he decided to go upwards.

He quickly identified the nearest tree, thrashing in the wind close to the road, some fifteen metres away. It was no oak tree, granted, but given the circumstances, it would have to do.

The stand-off continued and seeing as the bull was warming up by taking a series of deep inhalations, Clooney decided to follow suit – a few final breaths to fuel him along on this, the most treacherous part of his journey. Over the past few months, he'd vacillated between life and death, uncertain whether he'd any interest in persisting with the former. Now that the choice was being taken out of his hands, he realised how much he wanted to give this living and breathing lark another go. If he survived this horrid night, he vowed, he would sort himself out once and for all.

One, two, he silently counted, *and three!*

He darted towards the tree with the bull in close pursuit. The animal's roars were an excellent match for those nature currently created around them, so Clooney, getting a little carried away, joined in and shouted louder than he'd ever done before.

'Argh!'

'Whaa!'

'Motherfucker!'

About two metres from the tree, Clooney took a final breath before calling upon his inner eagle. He leapt through the air, landing slap-bang in the middle of the trunk. Just as the bull was about to ram his head against his target's feet, Clooney grabbed a branch above him and pulled himself up. The world fell away around him and he dangled in the wind – mere inches kept his lower body from being gored by the field's more powerful resident.

Clooney didn't know how long he could continue hanging from the tree. He looked up towards the other branches – even if he was able to pull himself up, none of them appeared strong enough to hold his weight for longer than a few moments. To add insult to injury, the bull had now transformed into an arcade pinball machine, firing himself against the trunk over and over again.

What the fuck am I going to do?

In his panic, Clooney failed to hear the car return. It was only when the headlights illuminated his sorry situation that he realised there were now three at this spontaneous outdoor party. Vonnie emerged from the car and stood close to the hedge, which dipped low at that point, her hands positioned on her waist.

'You thought you could escape, did you?'

'Look, Vonnie, this isn't the right time to talk ab–'

'I think this is the perfect time.'

The bull was working hard at his goal of getting the intruder out of the field by repeatedly headbutting the trunk. As the tree lowered towards Vonnie, Clooney noticed that she was armed with not one but three knives.

'Vonnie, we can talk about this like adults. Remember all the –' he could hear the tree's roots freeing themselves from the soil, '– good times we had.'

'I do! That's why I visited you here in Spiddal. And if it weren't for Cheesy Teasy, my new partner in crime, you'd have escaped for good.'

'Who's Cheesy Teasy? It doesn't matter. Let's focus on those good parts of our friendsh–'

'Before Cheesy Teasy, you were the only person who ever listened to me. You never ignored me or laughed at me. You've no idea what that's like, being the butt of everyone's jokes.'

'But I do, Vonnie – I absolutely do. I grew up in Navan during the 1980s. Do you know how difficult that was for an effeminate boy like me?'

'You weren't bullied; someone with your personality and confidence.'

'Is that what you think? My personality and supposed self-confidence were formed as a result of being taunted daily. I had to form an armour to defend myself.'

'You're lying.'

'I'm not, I promise you. You see, we are far more alike than –'

But Clooney didn't finish his sentence. The bull had decided that he had drier and more exciting places to be, and with one final charge, he put an end to the silliness once and for all. The unsteady tree, along with the man hanging from it, came crashing down with a bang and a wallop.

Say what you will about bulls, but this fella had an excellent aim, for the tree landed directly on top of the second intruder in the area.

Vonnie.

PART THREE

THIRTY-FIVE

'You look absolutely fabulous, Tony. Have you lost weight?'

'Would ye fuck off! I'm about twice the size since we last met. Speaking of which, you look very dashing – that navy jacket is very flattering on you.'

'Do you think? Jesus, I feel I look like the wreck of the *Hesperus*!' Clooney fibbed, knowing his faux protestations would only lead to additional praise from his agent. And what of it? He deserved a few flattering words, given his physical and mental transformation over the past twelve months.

The pair hurried down a busy Nassau Street, dodging passers-by while keeping their banter going. 'You really do look good, kiddo – very good. I wish I had your discipline these days. Or any day for that matter.'

'What are you talking about?' Clooney draped his arms around Tony's shoulders. 'Many's an editor would happily put your handsome face on the cover of their magazine!'

'Which magazine, *Farmers' Monthly*?'

'I wouldn't turn my nose up at that – especially considering how a bull saved my life.'

'I know you didn't just compare me to a bull!'

Over the years, Clooney and Tony had enjoyed not only a great professional relationship but also a great personal one. Every time they met, they'd try to outdo one another with over-the-top compliments – usually related to weight loss or complexion. For better or for worse, it was their shtick, and it made them giggle. Tony represented some of the leading talents in the country, but he'd have been hard-pressed to find anyone whose company he enjoyed more than Clooney's – or who was as vain!

'Come on, let's go in or we'll be late,' Tony said as he held open the door to the offices of the publisher Manoscritto.

'Ladies first,' the budding author replied tartly.

As they announced themselves to the receptionist, he thought how fitting it was that Manoscritto's offices were on Nassau Street, beside his Alma Mater, Trinity College, and directly above the menswear store where his first-ever film had been made – a twenty-minute short called *GPO* that was about seventeen minutes too long and set against the backdrop of the Easter Rising.

While it wasn't the 1916 Proclamation, the book deal Clooney was on the verge of signing felt revolutionary. Never in his wildest dreams had he thought he'd be a published author. When his teenage self had first sashayed through Trinity's front arch to begin acting training, his focus had been extremely linear: he'd wanted to tread the boards and nothing else.

'You make a plan,' he said now to Tony, reflecting on his surprising career shift, 'and then God pisses his pants laughing.'

'Hopefully it will be us doing the laughing today. There are a couple of tweaks I want to make to their contract – nothing serious, just a few wrinkles I want ironing out.'

Clooney couldn't help but admire his agent. Diplomatic yet demanding, charming yet disruptive. It was what made him such a good agent. And, a few months shy of sixty, he really did have perfect skin – despite years of practically eating Rothmans cigarettes.

'Guys, I hope I haven't kept you waiting.' Lucy emerged from her office, fixing the belt on her grey pleat skirt. Her jet-black hair and smoky mascara belied her sunny disposition. 'It's pandemonium here this morning. I won't bore you with the details. Come on in.'

'You've a remarkable view,' Clooney observed as he took a seat next to the window of Lucy's large office overlooking Trinity's cricket lawns, more beautiful than ever with the sun falling on newly cut grass. 'And I'm surprised how quiet it is in here, despite all the traffic outside. I'd say it's a great place to people-watch. You must see all sorts of shenanigans!'

For someone trying to present himself as an exciting up-and-coming scribe, Clooney was highly aware of how bland and vanilla he sounded. He should just start talking about the weather and show himself the door! When he was younger, he'd felt awkward about silence, so rabbited on in almost every situation, regardless of how inappropriate – libraries, funerals, during sex … The chatterbox had gotten better over the years, but only marginally.

'Clooney, we love your book,' Lucy gushed, obviously uninterested in engaging in small talk, 'and we think there's a large audience who'd be excited to hear your unique story.'

Clooney and Tony shared a smile.

'Tell me,' she continued in a conspiratorial hush. 'Have you seen or talked to Vonnie since that night?'

'No, thankfully,' Clooney answered. Even though he had written an entire book based on their brief but explosive relationship, every time her name came up in conversation or her image bullied its way into his mind, he shuddered. As Tony and Lucy discussed some of the practical aspects of the deal, Clooney's mind couldn't help wandering to where Vonnie was now, and how her recovery had been since that stormy night when he and the tree had crashed on top of her. At the time, doctors had said she would be unable to walk for several months – and, even then, only if she committed to an intensive physiotherapy programme.

'She's fortunate the tree didn't fall on her head,' one of the doctors had told Clooney in the hospital, 'otherwise, she wouldn't be here today.'

Over the following months, Clooney had wondered whether she would get in touch with him, or if she might be hiding in the bushes with night-vision goggles. Thankfully, his fears had proved unfounded.

So far.

'Right, time to sign, Clooney.' Lucy handed him a pen. 'And then, how about some Champagne to celebrate?'

'That sounds heavenly,' Tony beamed – few people in the world enjoyed a glass of bubbles more than this chap. Clooney would usually have shared his passion, but he hadn't touched a drop in about ten months and wanted to keep it that way. Alcoholism wasn't a good colour on him – was it on anyone? In the end, the decision had come easily. There had been no significant announcement to make about his abstinence or AA meetings to attend. With a hangover, his grief for Renardo worsened; without one, he could get on with his life and get things done. Like writing his first book. And it felt bloody fantastic.

'Right, where do you want my autograph?'

THIRTY-SIX

'Don't forget to sign the visitors' book,' Vonnie instructed as she stood in the doorway, blocking the electrician's exit from the gallery. She sported khaki combats and a tank top, topped off by a wine beret – a nod to her combative state since the accident. She may have been down, but she certainly wasn't out. 'And feel free to say something gushing about my work.'

'I'm in a bit of a rush, actually,' came the polite reply.

Vonnie raised her bejewelled walking cane in the tattooed man's direction to indicate that she wasn't asking, she was telling.

'Okay, what will I write?' he complied, anxious to avoid a scene.

'Jesus, do you want me to do everything for you? Look around – what do you see?'

The electrician hadn't noted the junk and scribblings on the walls until now; he hadn't much interest in those sorts of things.

'Pictures? Doodles? What do you call them? Sculptures?'

'That's right, they spurn definition, don't they?'

The electrician nodded politely.

'But what is it you see in the work? Describe them to me.'

'I'm sorry; I'm not good at this type of thing.'

'For the love of fucking God,' she roared before hobbling over to the image that stood proudly in the middle of the main wall. With the help of her cane, she pointed towards it, every inch the exasperated school teacher forced to simplify a lesson for more challenged pupils.

'Is this a man or a woman?'

'A man. I think.'

'Good! You're not as stupid as you look.'

'I really need to be going –'

'Don't move a muscle!' She slammed her cane against the floor. 'Next question: is he happy or sad?'

'Sad, I think.'

'And how do you know that?'

'Because he's crying, I suppose.'

'And is he crying normal tears?'

'Sure.'

'So you're telling me that you cry red tears?'

'I don't really cry. Maybe when Celtic lose.'

'And are those tears red?'

'No, I suppose not.'

'Then how in the name of God are his tears normal, huh? Tell me?'

'They're not.'

'They're not. Good! Because his tears are –'

'I don't know what you mean.'

'Blood! His eyes are bleeding. Is it not patently obvious?'

'Er, why are his eyes bleeding? Does he have some disease?'

'Because a hammer has crushed his skull – don't you see?'

The electrician stepped a little closer to the painting (although still keeping distance between himself, this scary woman and her threatening walking aid). 'Ah yes,' he replied after noticing the implement hidden behind what appeared to be a scattering of dry porridge oats. 'Why is there a hammer in his skull?'

'Because, my good friend, he's a hairy bastard and that was the very least he deserved!'

'What did he do?'

'How long do you have?'

'Not long, actually.'

'You see this walking stick?'

He nodded anxiously.

'I need it because of him. He nearly killed me.'

'Really? Do the police know?'

'They won't do anything because he's famous.'

'Wow! Can you tell me who he is? Only if you want to, of course.'

Vonnie staggered over and leaned in close to his ear. In conspiratorial and covert tones, she whispered, 'Clooney Coyle.'

'Who?'

'He may have won the battle, but I am going to emerge victorious in the war.'

'What are you going to do?' the electrician pressed, suddenly captivated by the vengeful woman standing opposite him.

'That's for me to know and you to find out. And mark my words, you will find out!'

Bored now by the exchange and anxious to rest her legs, Vonnie disappeared into the storeroom in the corner.

'When you invoice me,' she called out to him, 'don't forget to deduct €10 for the art lesson.'

THIRTY-SEVEN

'Do you see that house over there, Cloon – to the side of those trees?' his father asked from the driver's seat.

'I do,' Clooney politely replied, ignoring the fact that he had heard this story every time they passed this particular stretch of road.

'I bet you don't, Isla.'

'I don't think so, Mr Coyle.'

'"Norman," Isla, please. How long have we known each other?'

'Sorry. Old habits.'

'We were coming back from the All-Ireland Final in 1996,' Norman continued, delighted that he had a captive audience. 'How old were you then, guys?'

'If it was September, I would have been fourteen,' Clooney answered.

'I'm a couple of months older – as this fella always reminds me – so I'd have just turned fifteen.'

'Do you remember it, Mud?'

'I do. Now, Norman, keep an eye on the road. These roundabouts are vicious.'

Clooney, dressed in navy chinos and a red velvet jacket, looked out the window, wondering why his father insisted on taking the old road from Navan to Dublin via Clonee, rather than the quicker motorway route.

'It was rainy, Cloon – wasn't it, Mud?'

'Sorry for cutting in, Dad. But why are you going this way? Would it not be better to take the motorway?'

'There's no traffic at this hour of the day, Cloon, so I guarantee we'll reach Dublin at the same time, and then we'll go through Ballsbridge and out to Donnybrook. We'll be there in no time.'

Clooney took a breath. His father had just presented a ridiculous proposal that meant their journey to RTÉ's studios would take at least thirty minutes longer than if they had remained on the motorway before joining the Stillorgan dual carriageway.

'I don't mean to be rude, especially considering you're driving, but the other way is much quicker.'

Isla squeezed his hand; she could see he was irritable – understandable given the occasion.

'Well, this way is quieter, I suppose,' his mother chimed in, revealing the real reason for the scenic route. 'We have plenty of time, so relax, Cloon!'

Clooney reminded himself that his parents were in their seventies and that he needed to adjust his expectations of them; it was unfair to assume that competing with cars that whizzed up and down motorways at over 120 kilometres an hour would appeal to them. And his mother was correct – they did have plenty of time. Due to his father's insistence on being early for everything, they'd left a good three hours ahead of schedule.

His parents had just returned from a stint in Nice. They'd stayed in the same hotel as always and dined in the same restaurants – an approach that was mind-boggling for Clooney. He always searched for new experiences; but he also accepted that he was in the prime of his health and not, like his parents, contending with the various consequences of advancing years, such as arthritis, volatile blood pressure or cranky backs and knees. At this stage of their lives, they'd earned the right to do things their way.

'Do you know what, this way is a much better idea,' Clooney fibbed.

'So can I finish my story now?'

'Please do, Dad.'

Clooney needed the distraction. Just a few short weeks after signing his first book contract, his publisher had managed to secure him an interview on *Friday With ...* the iconic Irish television staple that enjoyed the status of the world's second-longest-running late-night talk show, trailing only America's famed *The Tonight Show*. Simply put, it was a national institution.

Since the early 1960s, *Friday With ...* had heralded the start of the weekend for every household in Ireland. Commentators often credited the show as being the catalyst for social and cultural change in the country. All the hot-potato topics were aired and analysed, often resulting in blushes for guests and viewers.

Sex.

Religion.

Divorce.

Homosexuality.

Abortion.

Rape.

It wouldn't have been an overstatement to say that the chat show had dragged the country kicking and screaming into modern times.

When he'd first received the news about his appearance, Clooney couldn't believe it. After dancing on the spot for a few moments, anxiety had quickly set in: he would be sitting in front of over a million viewers – including all his parents' friends and his own colleagues – talking about his work. Since then, a kaleidoscope of pesky butterflies had taken up permanent residence in his stomach with no sign that they might decamp anytime soon.

'Isn't that a good one, Cloon,' his father prompted, concluding his story about the puncture and the subsequent rescue by the owners of the house to the side of the trees.

'I loved it,' Isla said, noticing that Clooney was busy drying his sweaty palms on the car seat.

'Mud, I often wonder whether they still live there or not.'

'Ah, Norman, I'd say they're dead by now,' his wife, ever the realist, opined. 'They were about eighty at the time.'

'Meath people are a good breed, Mud! Sure isn't that nun – what's her name? Sister Agatha? – over 120 or thereabouts?'

'Well, if you want to live to 120, keep your eyes on the flippin' road, Norman. My glasses are in my bag in the boot – I can't see the signs. Can you, Cloon?'

'Mud, the best thing you can do now is keep quiet and relax. I know this route like the back of my hand.'

'I know that – that's not what I'm saying. The roads have changed so much over the past couple of years. We don't want to end up in Galway!'

Clooney's mother's imagination was a thing of wonder.

'Mud,' Norman said firmly.

'Right, okay, I'll keep my mouth shut!'

As they drove on in silence, Clooney took comfort in the fact that in the run-up to this nerve-racking interview, he'd been living the life of a saint, with a diet that would have impressed even the most fastidious nutritionist. He'd declined all of Isla's tempting invitations to share a couple of bottles of vino – alcohol was very much in his past. Now, he just needed to keep breathing and creating happy thoughts.

'Mud, this time last week, were we in Ventimiglia?' Norman asked. 'Every time we go to the South of France, Isla, we pop over the border into Italy. We like to get bang for our buck and visit as many countries as possible!'

'Sounds dreamy. Mrs Coyle, I love the soap you got me from Fragonard.'

'Delighted to hear that, Isla.' Helen looked at her watch.

'They're an hour ahead over there, which would make it about six o'clock –'

'Cloon, you know France is an hour ahead?'

'I do, Dad.'

'Glad to hear that we didn't waste our money educating you,' Norman joked with a smile.

'If it's six o'clock there,' Helen continued, 'we were at the train station, weren't we? What time was our train back to Nice? Five past or ten past?'

'Five past, I think, Mud.'

'No, it was ten past,' she corrected. 'And do you know how I know?'

'Go on.'

'The train to Milan was five past and remember we had to ask those two teenagers smoking on the platform.'

'That's right. Nothing wrong with your memory!'

Clooney caught his mother giving herself a little proud nod in agreement.

'Cloon,' she added, 'you would have been very impressed with your father's French on the trip. He can now even ask where the toilet is – and be understood.'

'Is that so?' Clooney said, pleased that his anxious mind was being distracted from what lay ahead. 'Let myself and Isla hear you so, Dad.'

Clooney's father had never been afforded the opportunity to learn foreign languages in school, so when he retired, he'd decided to join a French class in Navan, and he adored it. Of course, his accent was *affreux* but, bless him, he had the all-important enthusiasm, and at this stage of his life, that was more than enough.

'*Où sont les toilettes?*' Norman declared, delighted with himself, although it sounded more like '*Oooe sont less toilets?*' if one were to be critical.

'*Magnifique!*' Clooney replied encouragingly. 'It's almost as though you're a native.'

'I was transported to France there for a moment!' Isla added.

'Not bad for an old-timer like me, huh?'

'You can say that again, Dad!'

'Oh, Mud, d'you know who's dead? I'll give you a clue – you gave her Communion at mass three or four weeks ago.'

As his parents discussed the sorry demise of the second cousin of one of their former neighbours, Clooney and Isla shared a knowing look: parents! He then turned his focus to outside the window and took a moment to reflect on all the success he had recently achieved, and congratulate himself for being able to turn a hairy period in his life into something remarkably positive.

It was, he thought, a new chapter; the perfect idiom considering he was on the verge of releasing his first book. Those dark days were in the past.

Or so he thought.

THIRTY-EIGHT

'I've good days and bad days. Today was a bad one.'

Vonnie lay sprawled across the couch in her living room, her cats resting in between her legs. Her new housemate, Monica, was forced to drag an uncomfortable chair in from her bedroom, having been told that there was 'no room' on the long three-seater. The television was on in the background. Even though the young Italian student nurse had expressed an interest in watching the various programmes as a way of improving her English, Vonnie felt that the only voice that deserved to be heard that evening was her own.

'It's getting up and down those steep steps that cause me the most difficulty. What a curse that my little gallery has such an awkward location. You must come in one of the days – I'll even give you a student discount. Five per cent off.'

'I would like that very much,' Monica said. The Venetian had yet to make any friends in Navan so readily embraced the idea of injecting her social life with an activity or two.

'Should you be drinking that?' Vonnie stared at the bottle of wine her housemate had just placed on the table.

'Why shouldn't I?'

'How do I put this sensitively? Your happy pills. The ones rattling in your handbag.'

'How do you know they are happy pills?'

'I checked, of course. You can't take any chances these days with those you live with. You could be Myra Hindley for all I know.'

'Who?'

'Never mind. Speaking of murders,' Vonnie continued, 'don't kill me but I'm afraid that you're going to have to cover the household bills this month on your own.'

On the verge of unscrewing the cap of her wine, Monica returned the bottle to the table. This wasn't a time for merriment.

'I don't understand. We share them, no?'

'Not this month.'

'Is there a reason? You mentioned not this when I was moved in.'

'I didn't want to make you feel uncomfortable, Melissa. You see, my last remaining grandmother died earlier this year, and she had one ambition in life, and that was to build a beautiful patio in the back garden. Unfortunately, she never got around to it because a heart attack killed her in seconds.'

'I thought it was your father who wanted the patio.'

'Who are you, Mona, the bloody FBI? My granny also loved nothing better than dirtying her hands in the soil, I'll have you know – and it gives me great comfort knowing that those very hands, as well as the rest of her withered body, are currently covered in the stuff out in St Finian's Cemetery.'

'You must miss her.'

'I do, very much. Which is why I have no choice but to fulfil her dream for her and build the patio in her honour. You know, maybe get one of those benches with an engraved plaque on it saying something like, "Here sits Granny – join her! Although her conversation may be a bit 'wooden'."'

Vonnie giggled, but her cheeriness was cut short when she realised Monica wasn't laughing.

'Rude,' she mumbled.

'That's a beautiful gesture – your *nonna* would have been happiest, yes?'

'She would have been "happy", yes. Remind me to invoice you for English lessons, by the way. Anyway, my tribute comes at a price, so I need to save my money. That's why I won't be able to pay the bills.'

'Well, I'm not sure if that's fair.'

'It is fair. Very fair. Sure, I am hardly here, Melissa.'

'Neither I am! And you have showers every day since I moved in two weeks past. And you use the hairdryer, no? And the dishwasher and washing machine. And the lights – you switch them on to see things, no? And the television, and the –'

'All right, Monica, there's no need to rabbit on.'

'Rabbit? What do you mean?'

'It doesn't matter. Anyway, that's the way it is, so if you don't like it, you can move out, and I'm sure you don't want to be doing that.'

'I am very sorry, but I don't have –'

'Be quiet!' Vonnie ordered, the television suddenly demanding her attention. 'What the …'

There in front of her was the person she hated more than any-one else in the entire world, stingy Monica aside.

Clooney Coyle.

Almost without taking a breath or blinking an eye, she watched, dumbfounded, as Harry Swing, the presenter of *Friday With …* announced that on the couch that night would be a host of exciting guests, including a soap-actor-turned-author who was getting ready to release a new book about his real-life experiences with a stalker.

'I don't believe it.'

Vonnie's phone began to sound.

'How dare he!'

She ignored the ringing and listened intently as Mr Swing explained that the show would start after the news, meaning in about thirty minutes. He also mentioned that the first section would be dedicated to selecting Ireland's entry for the Eurovision Song Contest, which meant that if Vonnie took the motorway and then the dual carriageway, and turned a blind eye to the odd red light en route, she could just about make it to the RTÉ studios in time.

Monica, who was already in a foul mood, couldn't tolerate the sound of the ringing phone any longer and picked it up to see who was calling her housemate.

'Here,' she said as she passed it to Vonnie, 'it's your dead *nonna*.'

'Tell her I'll call her back!'

With that, Vonnie disregarded the limitations of her compromised mobility and made a beeline for the front door, grabbing not only Monica's unopened bottle of wine as she left but also the small container of 'happy pills' from her handbag.

'Sorry, *sorella*, it's only right that we give our old pal a couple of presents to celebrate his succe–'

'Get your own fucking pre–'

'If he thinks he's going to humiliate me on national television, he's another think coming!'

THIRTY-NINE

In the green room, Clooney was relieved to discover how relaxed he now felt. It helped greatly that one of the other guests on the show was an old friend, Debbie Leigh, and amongst her many qualities was an ability to have a laugh and keep things light.

'Do you like my dress?' she asked confidently, knowing it wouldn't have looked out of place on a Milanese catwalk. 'It's got pockets!'

'Them rags! My love, I wouldn't use it to dust my knife collection,' Clooney replied with a cheeky glint in his eye.

'Speaking of knives, is it any wonder that mad yoke tried to kill ye – I've half a mind to finish the job for her myself.'

Clooney had worked with Debbie a few years earlier on a television pilot that had included, amongst other things, a top prize of a million-euro house. It was an ambitious concept, and the pair enjoyed great chemistry together, but the format had proved too expensive and never made it beyond the initial episode. In quieter moments, Clooney had reflected on this project and wondered whether he had what it took to be a television presenter. Debbie made it look so effortless (the wagon!). Well, in about twenty minutes, he was going to get a glimpse into how successful or unsuccessful he might have been with live television.

'Any tips for tonight?' he asked Debbie, who was busy putting the final touches to her make-up.

'You know that old chestnut about being yourself?' she said, pursing her lips to ensure the lipstick was evenly applied. 'In your case, do the exact opposite!'

'God, you're vicious tonight!'

'You'll be grand, doll – enjoy it. Love the outfit by the way. The red makes you look very dashing.'

Clooney smiled, noticed by Debbie.

'I don't think I know anyone who loves a compliment more than you, doll!'

Before he could defend himself, a knock came at the door. One of the show's runners, complete with an impressive headset and gift bag, popped his head into the room.

'Debbie, you're up in about five. Clooney, it will be about thirty minutes before your turn – the Eurovision segment went on a little longer than we anticipated. Jesus, that auld one can talk some shite, can't she? Just take it easy until then, alright?'

Thirty minutes, sitting alone, working himself up into a frenzy did not sound to Clooney like an opportune time to take things easy. He hadn't even been able to persuade Isla to leave the studio audience and join him backstage – nothing came between that girl and the Eurovision Song Contest.

'Here,' the runner added as he handed Clooney the gift bag – in it, a bottle of wine, decorated with a pretty ribbon around the neck. 'This might relax you. Although just a glass!'

Clooney accepted the Pinot Grigio. First, he praised the show's generosity, providing guests with such gifts. Then he reminded himself how great life had been, alcohol-free, over the past few months. Yes, he knew he'd be able to have one glass and leave it at that, but did he need it?

It might help me take the edge off the nerves, but do I want to be that guy who's dependent on things like alcohol to succeed?

During those horrible weeks following Renardo's death, Clooney had needed his daily bottle (bottles, rather), but he was proud to say his dependency had proved passing and, under the circumstances, justifiable. Tempting as the tipple in his hand looked, he decided that a little meditation would produce a more positive outcome.

'What are you waiting for? Go on, open it and pour me a cheeky glass,' Debbie ordered. 'My throat's fucking banjaxed at the moment. The joys of being a mother to two sets of lively twins!'

Clooney, happy to be the barman rather than the punter, walked over to the refreshment table, removed the cap, not noticing it had been tampered with, and grabbed a glass before pouring his pal a generous measure.

'Here you go, my love,' he said as he handed it to her. 'Get that into ye.'

But there wasn't time for Debbie to get anything into her, for a second knock sounded at the door. It was showtime.

'Leave that lovely looking glass of vino on the table, doll, and I'll have it as soon as I've charmed the pants off Harry!'

'Don't be too fabulous,' Clooney warned, 'I have to go on after you, remember!'

After that, the actor-turned-author sat alone. Remaining on his feet, he paced the floor for a few moments. Slowly but surely, anxiety began to rear its ugly head again, and he felt his mouth dry and his stomach tighten. He was working himself into a frenzy.

You've got this, Clooney, believe in yourself.

He tried to avoid looking at the glass of wine boldly winking at him a few metres away.

Don't Clooney, don't.

He turned away.

Don't.

He attempted to focus on a vase of flowers.

Well ... he rationalised, *maybe just a sip or two. It would be rude, after all, not to at least sample the producers' thoughtful gesture.*

If his nerves hadn't been so boisterous, Clooney might have noticed a little card attached to the ribbon. And the message scrawled across it would have left him filling out a restraining order rather than his glass:

'*Truce? Love, Vonnie.*'

FORTY

Clooney stood behind a partition and listened to Harry list his credentials. The introduction was so gushing, Clooney's mother could have written it: an actor on TG4's flagship series, *Brú na hAbhainn,* who became the *objet d'amour* of an overly enthusiastic fan, which resulted in a dramatic showdown during Hurricane Cassandra.

Speaking of his mother, he could just about make her out through a crack in the partition. The old gal was brimming with a perfect mixture of nerves and pride. His father had his eyes shut tightly, unable to bear the excitement of the moment. Isla, sandwiched in between them, was busy looking around the audience in case there was someone famous close by. She couldn't resist a celeb!

I'm going to make all three of you proud, Clooney vowed. *I promise.*

The Navan man was seconds away from appearing in almost every household in the country. He was delighted he'd had the good sense to take a couple of mouthfuls of the wine; his nerves had evaporated entirely. In their place prevailed a striking confidence and vitality that he was sure would help him during the interview.

Not cocky, though – no one will like that, he reminded himself.

Were he feeling critical, he might have argued that the wine was a little on the bitter side, but to do so would have been ungrateful, particularly given how much it had fortified him.

'Ladies and gentlemen, please give a warm welcome to my

next guest, Clooney Coyle!'

Emboldened by the enthusiastic applause – led, he was sure, by Isla and his parents – Clooney strode out onto the studio set full of swagger.

'Hello, everyone!'

After giving the audience a gentle wave, he shook Harry's hand and took his seat on the couch. He hadn't tripped up and face-planted the ground – one of his many worries – so everything appeared to be going swimmingly. So far.

This is my night; this is my time.

Memories of all those failed auditions – worse, all those non-existent invitations to audition – faded away. As did all the horrid experiences with tyrannical theatre directors that had almost led to him giving up the profession and becoming a shepherd on some remote hill.

Everything had been worth it.

He decided that every hurdle over the years had presented itself for a reason – to empower him and make moments like tonight all the sweeter. The book was the start of a new phase in his life and, by God, he was going to grab the moment with both hands.

'Clooney, you have quite the tale to tell,' Harry began. 'I read an advance copy of your book in one sitting – actually, on the train from Galway to Dublin. I couldn't help but be taken aback by the lengths this woman – who shall remain nameless – went to in her bid to woo you! That was quite a dicey encounter in Connemara last year. I laughed at the irony that the word "Spiddal", where the incident took place, comes from the Gaelic word *ospideal*. As everyone knows, that means "hospital" – and the place your pal ended up that night. I'd say you're thankful for the help of that temperamental bull!'

'Shyou chan shay that again, Harry.'

'What was that, Clooney?'

'Shyou chan shay that again, Harry.'

What is happening? Why can't I speak correctly? Maybe those blasted nerves haven't high-tailed it after all. Maybe nobody noticed. Keep going!

'Itsh hash been a very eventful twelve monchs.'

'Indeed,' Harry responded, concerned that the moment was proving too big for his guest. Or was that the way he usually spoke? Surely of all people, an actor should have proficiency with diction?

'Shthank you sho much for reading it and for your swheet wordsh.'

Am I drunk? Clooney asked himself, his heart racing.

Is he drunk? Harry and the rest of the country collectively asked themselves.

'People tink acting ish a glamoroush profeshion,' Clooney continued, reminded of that old theatre adage that no matter the circumstances, the show must go on. 'But shometimes, itsh can be dangeroush.'

His slurring was getting worse. He felt his cheeks redden; his hands moisten. He was losing control of his movements.

Why the fuck did you take those mouthfuls of wine, you moron! he scolded himself as he battled to remain upright. A heavy tiredness was beginning to take over him. Not only was he contending with unsteady speech, but he was also fighting to stay awake. He could hear his mother's distinctive cough in the audience – a clear warning to get his act together.

'There's one part of the book I was particularly taken by,' Harry, the consummate professional, continued, trying desperately to keep the interview moving forward.

'Yesh? Whish parsh ish jat?' Clooney asked before trying to instruct his hands to remain by his sides. Why were they unbuttoning his shirt and trousers?

'It's the part before the ambulance arrived and – wait till you hear this, guys,' Harry said, turning towards the audience. 'Clooney had to give his stalker mouth-to-mouth resuscitation – something she turned out not to need. Even in her sorry state, with a tree having almost crushed her to death, she took her chance and gave this fella a big, romantic kiss. If nothing else, we can hardly criticise her for not seizing the moment! What are your thoughts on the woman now, a year later?'

Harry returned his focus to his guest and let out a gasp when he saw Clooney naked.

'Oh dear – feeling a little hot under these lights, are you, Cloo– and now he's dancing for us! Wiggling his … his, em, John Thomas!'

'Fire! Emergency evacuation! Everyone out!' Isla desperately and unsuccessfully tried to divert the audience's attention from her best friend and the horror show that was unravelling.

Harry decided to put an end to the entire affair. 'Maybe we should "wrap this up" before we get shut down by the censors – what do you say, Clooney?'

There was no reply.

'Clooney?'

Still no reply.

'ZZZZZZZZZZZZZZZZZZZZZ!'

'Ladies and gentleman, I think our guest must be so exhausted promoting this great book that, following his little naked performance for us, he has fallen asleep! At least, I hope that's the reason – I trust it wasn't my boring questions!'

The audience burst into fits of laughter. All apart from three. Isla and Clooney's parents. They burst into floods of tears.

'Maybe we'll have him back on the show when he's managed to get some sleep. Speaking of tired, that's me off to my own bed. Thank you so much for joining me tonight. And congratulations to our two lucky competition winners – I hope they will send us postcards from their respective holiday destinations. Good night and thank you!'

And it was goodnight and thank you to Clooney's career.

FORTY-ONE

The traffic in Navan was usually horrific, and on this particular Saturday morning, things were no different. Children were being dropped off to their various activities while parents did the weekly shopping. The town, framed by the majestic River Boyne, had the potential to be a truly beautiful destination, but, like so many other places in Ireland, urban planning had meant channelling all energies and resources into making space for cars, cars and more cars.

This vehicular situation was a particular bugbear for Vonnie, but as she sat sandwiched between a Volvo teeming with irritable teenagers and an empty hearse, she smiled. She could have remained static there in the middle of Kennedy Road for the entire day, and her high spirits would not have faltered. Today, her horn remained silent, and gentle whistling replaced her usual bolshiness. She even found herself waving at the group of teenagers who had tormented her for years, throwing rubbish up at her gallery window on a near-hourly basis.

'Beautiful day, isn't it, fellas!' Vonnie cheerfully shouted, rolling down her window, almost regretting the revenge she'd previously enacted on them with the assistance of some dead rats.

It seemed her mood was contagious; traffic suddenly began moving, and as she drove into the shopping centre's car park, a rare free spot awaited her.

Lovely.

After parking her rusty Renault, Vonnie reached into the back seat and picked up a couple of bags and a small box. Today, she felt there was no need for her cane; the small darts of pain she continued to experience around her knees when she walked unaided were of no consequence to her any longer. Even if another tree crushed her body once again, her blitheness would have been unruffled. She emerged from the multi-storey and sauntered along the side of the shopping centre.

'Hi, Dolores,' she called out to one of the parents she recognised from school, getting a name right for once in her life. 'Stunning day, don't you think?'

'I suppose it is,' came the response – although the speed with which Dolores disappeared into the shopping centre suggested that the mother of two was uninterested in communicating with such an unhinged woman (if the rumours were right, of course).

Vonnie gracefully crossed the busy road and passed Supermac's and an off-licence before arriving at her destination: the charity shop. The premises was alive with activity, which was only great, Vonnie thought – so much money raised for those in need! She made her way to the till, and while it would usually have irritated her to find it unmanned, today she leaned against the counter and patiently waited. What was the rush? If she had her way, this day would never end. She was on the verge of having a mooch through some of the railings to see if there were any potential costumes on offer when an elderly lady arrived.

'Sorry for keeping you, dearie,' the septuagenarian said as she battled with a selection of clothes hangers. 'Have you something to drop off?'

'I most certainly do,' Vonnie replied, 'and there is no need to thank me either.'

'What do we have here?' The assistant rummaged through the belongings and hauled out a selection of men's clothing – beautiful items, at that – along with a handful of magazines and newspapers. She also found a stack of DVDs including some *Brú na hAbhainn* boxsets.

'This is very generous of you,' the woman gushed. 'Where did you get all these lovely things?'

'Some things I bought online.'

'Oh.' The assistant sounded impressed; she could barely use her phone, let alone purchase items on a website. 'Even the clothes?'

'Nope. His washing line.'

'Is that the name of a new shop? I can't keep up these days!'

This charity shop had often been the recipient of people's rubbish – tat that was fit for the scrapheap alone – but this stash was most welcome. 'And what are these?'

'Photographs of my former lover.'

'They are very well taken. Professional.'

'Yes, he was an actor. Not very good, I'm afraid.'

'Oh, dear. He looks familiar – would I have seen him in anything?'

'Were you watching *Friday With* … last night?'

'Of course I was. Wait – is this …? It isn't …'

'It most certainly is.'

'His poor parents. His mother taught one of my grandchildren. They must be so ashamed.'

'We all are.'

'I think the only place for these photographs is in there,' the lady said, pointing to a nearby bin.

'You said it, sister!'

Vonnie turned to leave but stopped.

'I almost forgot,' she said, taking her purse out of her bag, 'I also wanted to donate. Life is so good for me at the moment, and I wanted to share my happiness.'

'That's a splendid outlook. Thank you very much.'

Proudly, Vonnie revealed a €20 note.

'How's this for a start?'

'An excellent start, I must say!'

Vonnie held it out to the woman but found that her hand refused to let go. The assistant tried to prise it from her without much success.

'Actually,' Vonnie said, 'maybe I'll donate another time. I think I've given enough for one day, don't you?'

FORTY-TWO

Sporting dark sunglasses and a peaked cap, Clooney waited for Tony in a small sandwich café in Portobello. The humdrum location suggested by his agent was extremely revealing; the pair had enjoyed many long lunches together over the years, always starting with the wine list. Here, the most exciting beverage was a double espresso. Not that Clooney wanted a drink – he needed Valium; double Valium.

He hadn't eaten a morsel in three days, not since the public humiliation. And he was sure his appetite – along with his dignity – wouldn't return for quite some time. He sat in the corner, hands on his stomach in a futile attempt to calm the crippling pain he'd endured ever since waking up the morning after the night before.

Despite his efforts to remain incognito, Clooney knew he was the recipient of a few pitying and disapproving looks from other customers scattered about the café. He hadn't switched on his phone since the night of the interview – he couldn't bring himself to face the humiliation. Tony had had to call his parents to arrange the meeting.

Clooney had no concrete proof that he was an international laughing stock, but he suspected that should he turn on his phone and pay a visit to any social media site, the clip of him drunk, wiggling his willy and falling asleep on primetime television would be doing the rounds. Such moments were what Facebook, YouTube and Twitter were made for.

Aside from relaying the message from Tony, his parents had barely spoken a single word to him. His mortified mother had been especially silent. She remained in her dressing gown and drew the curtains in every room in the house – they were a family in mourning after all. His father had been more philosophical and had even joked that Clooney wouldn't be the first person inebriated on national television, and, so long as there was alcohol to be consumed, he wouldn't be the last.

'This is just a blip,' he'd assured him the afternoon following his appearance. 'You'll overcome this. I have every faith in you, Cloon.'

Clooney had mostly remained in his bedroom for the rest of the weekend – he lay on his bed, fully clothed, fully booted – and, at one stage, distinctly heard his mother pour out the bottles of wine she'd leftover from Christmas. She didn't have to, he'd wanted to tell her – he was not going to allow so much as a glass of Rock Shandy pass his lips in the future. That's if he had a future. He'd have been lying if he said that the thought of ending it all hadn't crossed his mind, albeit fleetingly.

Much as he'd chastised himself for what had occurred, there was one puzzling thought that ran through his mind.

How on earth did that happen?

Yes, he'd foolishly decided to take a couple of mouthfuls of wine, but that was all – a couple of mouthfuls. He acknowledged that he'd been extremely nervous and hadn't eaten much earlier on in the day.

Even still!

In addition to being unable to pronounce a single word clearly, HE HAD GOTTEN HIS PENIS OUT LIVE ON TELEVISION!

Clooney's post-mortem was interrupted when Tony announced his arrival with a jolly 'Hello.' The only reason Clooney had agreed to meet his agent was because of the chap's unique ability not to judge others' indiscretions. He treated his clients like his children and seeing as Clooney's own mother had forsaken him, he was in desperate need of a surrogate parent.

'How are you, kiddo? I could murder a sandwich – have you ordered yet?'

How kind of Tony to open with the current state of his hunger pangs rather than launching into a 'what-were-you-fucking-thinking?' castigation. Clooney knew his agent was trying to diffuse the situation and take the sting out of the fact that he'd sabotaged his entire career. It didn't make him any less grateful.

'Let me order a selection of things we can both pick at. You're looking a bit gaunt today – you could do with a bit of nourishment, kiddo.'

As Tony went to the counter to place the order, Clooney wondered what strategy, if any, the agent extraordinaire might have to limit the damage. Perhaps he would suggest laughing it off and releasing a press statement explaining that the moment had gotten a little too much for Clooney but, if given a second chance, it would be Harry falling asleep listening to Clooney's many tales and anecdotes. Or Tony might encourage him to embrace the American way: taking full responsibility, admitting his mistakes, describing how ashamed he was to let down his family and friends, before disappearing to some clinic for a stint in rehabilitation.

Vanishing for a little while might be the only remedy to the situation, but that would certainly annoy his publisher – authors needed to be available for promotional opportunities, although Clooney wagered that the only question any journalist would want to ask him now would be about his overindulgences. And the new series of *Brú na hAbhainn* would start filming in just over a fortnight, so even if he did flee to the hills, it couldn't be for long.

'The clip has been viewed fourteen million times in the past three days,' Tony announced as he returned to his seat.

'What?'

'And Manoscritto is cancelling your book. And …'

'And?'

'*Brú na hAbhainn* is terminating your contract. I'm just off the phone to Úna – she said she tried to call you.'

Úna was the executive producer of the series, and Clooney had always enjoyed a friendly relationship with her, so he was sure she had indeed called directly to give him the head's up first, but, coward that he was, Clooney's phone was off.

'She was lovely about the whole thing,' Tony added, 'but her hands are tied.'

Clooney blamed neither *Brú na hAbhainn* nor Manoscritto; with fourteen million views, and counting, he had brought shame to both. He was supposed to be their ambassador, but instead, he'd disgraced them in front of the entire world. From now on, Clooney knew that the first thing anyone would associate with *Brú na hAbhainn* was a drunk actor who publicly humiliated himself.

'What the fuck am I going to do, Tony?'

'First things first,' Tony replied as a waiter placed a large plate of sandwiches in between them, 'you're going to eat. You can't make any rational decisions on an empty stomach.'

Clooney did as instructed; whether he would manage to keep the ham-and-cheese option down remained to be seen.

'If all else fails,' Tony continued, mayonnaise on his lip and a glint in his eye, 'we could always get you a gig flogging underwear, Mr I'm-a-fucking-Chippendale!'

FORTY-THREE

It was a week since his disastrous appearance on *Friday With …* and things were going from bad to worse for Clooney. He made an ill-judged decision to accompany a concerned Isla shopping in Navan. As they walked the short route from his house to Dunnes Stores, he was the target for a torrent of catcalls, a few jeers and one rotten tomato (at least he hoped the red, gooey substance was a tomato). The cap he wore offered him little anonymity.

'Don't go anywhere near the Newgrange Hotel tonigh', loser!' one threatening motorist shouted at him as he stalled at the traffic lights. 'It's me nan's birthday, and we want there to be at least one drink left for her t'enjoy, ye drunken prick!'

'Look at you, thinking you're all hard,' Isla roared back at him. 'Let's see if you're this cocky when you're thrown into jail next month for not paying child support – I was talking to Orlaith last week, and she told me everything. Don't drop the soap in the showers!'

Isla draped her arm around her best friend before leading him into the supermarket. The onslaught of abuse reminded Clooney of what he'd endured as an effeminate teenager, walking to his Friday evening dance class, or his speech and drama lessons on a Saturday morning. Anyone who grew up in Navan knew well that the town had an extraordinary ability to make or break you; in Clooney's case, it had made him …

Made him get the hell out of the place as quickly as he could!

As he grew older and wiser, he'd eventually realised that the bullying he'd received wasn't personal; it had been that age-old trick of knocking others down to build yourself up. He had yet to hear a truly happy person say bad things about another, and that always gave him much comfort – knowing that those who'd hounded him had, more than likely, been the unhappiest kids in the playground. As such, when he now reflected on his childhood in Navan, it was with fondness. But, today, as he trailed Isla between the Dolmio jars and the penne pasta, those hairy moments came flooding back.

'I don't know why I allowed you to convince me to go fucking grocery shopping with you – I'm going to get lynched!'

'Well, they'll have to get past me first, and I've been working out in the gym,' Isla replied, flexing her muscles. 'Besides, your dad called and begged me to bring you out. Your bedroom is ponging,' he said.'

'At least it doesn't smell as bad as my shitty career.'

They walked towards the back of the store, passing the off-licence section. Clooney gave a little shudder; he almost wanted to pick up the many wine bottles and smash them against the walls – they were to blame for his undoing.

I was also to blame, in fairness. Why couldn't I have shown more restraint?

This was the closest he'd ever gotten to realising his childhood dreams, and he'd sabotaged it. Maybe he feared success and, instead, had retreated to the safety net of the familiar?

Failure.

Clooney's body started to overheat – the frozen foods section they passed offered little relief. His breathing became short and rapid. His chest tightened. He knew exactly what was happening to him.

'I have to get out of here, Isla – I'm having a panic –'

'Oy, *Bastardo*! You owe me one of these!'

Clooney spun around, trying to locate the voice of his latest aggressor. In front of the wine shelves, he saw a young woman holding one of the bottles aloft. Was her accent Italian?

'Who's this bitch?' Isla asked, dropping her basket to the floor and rolling up her sleeves.

'It's okay, Isla – just ignore her.'

'You theft my bottle last Friday!' the woman shouted, ill-prepared to give up without a fight.

Clooney had little interest in indulging this belligerent woman so, rather than break stride, he prompted Isla towards the till.

'*Aspetta*! Along with the bottle of *vino*, you need to make payment for my medication.'

Clooney tried to ignore the unhinged woman, but her colourful accusations had attracted the attention of other shoppers. He could feel his cheeks redden and his forehead moisten. His breathing became even more laboured.

Why did you leave your bloody bedroom?

'I'm sorry, but you must have me confused with –'

'*No*! You are naked drunk man from the television, no?'

'Yes, he is,' an overly helpful cashier interjected. 'The absolute shame he's brought to the town.'

'Shut it, Wendy,' Isla sniped. 'You're hardly one to talk – the fucking state of you with Tommy Gilroy in the Newgrange residents' bar last month. You probably have the warmest ankles in Ireland, what with your knickers always wrapped around them!'

The Italian inched closer to Clooney. 'And it was my *vino* that result in you, how you say, make tit of yourself.'

'Yes, I made a tit of myself, as you quite rightly point out, but I'm afraid it hadn't anything to do with you or your wine,' Clooney said in between pants. 'Why you would want to take credit for such an embarrassing moment is beyond me.'

'I don't want credit, I want cash!' she shouted. 'That psychotic beeeetch is so mean and tight and hairy but robbing my two best treasures was the straw that snap the donkey's back. She won't pay me money she owe me, so I'm sorry, but you pay me now!'

Flummoxed by this vile encounter, Clooney turned to flee. However, after a moment or two of processing these wild allegations, some of the fog started to clear.

'Wait – who might this "psychotic bitch" be?' he asked, back still turned; he was almost afraid to hear the answer.

'Your ex-girlfriend. Vonnie. *Dio mio*! I don't know what you ever seen in her. She crazy!'

Clooney's mind raced back to that blasted evening. He was sure he'd received the bottle as a gift from *Friday With …* That nice runner had given it to him. But why hadn't Debbie received one? And why hadn't the runner said it was from the producers or Harry or whoever? And why would they give a guest a bottle of alcohol just before going live on air?

Because the bottle was from Vonnie.

'What medication were you taking?' Clooney pressed, darting towards her.

'For my depression. And I am so depressed now. First, this pissy Irish weather – and now theeees!'

'This can't be happening …'

'It has happened. You Irish – never take responsibility for you drinking. It's all one big joke. I'm not laughing here.'

Clooney took out a €50 note from his wallet and handed it to her.

'Sorry about the whole situation.'

'So you should be,' she mumbled as she disappeared back into the off-licence.

A shell-shocked Clooney stumbled backwards, tripping over Isla's basket; he heard a jar smash, but he didn't care. He decided that Vonnie would suffer the same fate as the pesto. She'd laced the wine with anti-depressant medication and watched him humiliate himself in front of a million people. It was genius; he gave her that. But it warranted only one outcome.

Death.

FORTY-FOUR

Vonnie's terraced house was a skip and a jump from the River Boyne Railway Bridge, a commanding structure that greeted all those entering Navan from the Dublin direction. The railway line was primarily used to transport zinc and lead concentrates on behalf of Tara Mines – but back in the 1990s, and for decades before that, it had also been where many of the town's youths used to hang out and drink Woody's alcopops or smoke cigarettes robbed from their parents.

These days, there was so much barbed wire surrounding it that the local tearaways had decided to carry out their anti-social behaviour in other, more welcoming, parts of town.

Vonnie liked nothing better than strolling up and down the train tracks, regardless of the weather, standing in the centre of the bridge and looking down on the River Boyne and the ever-expanding town. It made her feel omnipotent: here, she was invincible. Everyone below her was her subject, and all craved to reach her dizzy heights! If the occasion called for it, she'd even throw stones down at walkers or drivers, then duck. Her wonky aim meant she invariably missed her targets, but it gave her a thrill and reinforced her misguided sense of power.

Today, more than usual, she was in the mood for carnage.

Even though her success the previous week had left her feeling untouchable, something was niggling her. Her sleep had been disturbed and her appetite compromised – two aspects of her life that she treasured.

It's just a passing phase, she'd attempted to convince herself.

The troublemaker played with a selection of stones in her hand and wondered which one she should throw first. After opting for the darkest of the pack – it had sharp edges which would create havoc with the window of a truck or a van – she leaned onto the bridge's wall, raised her arm and flung the stone as far as she could. Immediately, she ducked and closed her eyes, hoping to be rewarded with the sound of something smashing. Hearing a pathetic splosh from the river below, Vonnie conceded that she had been a little wayward with her efforts. Her empty stomach and fuzzy mind were not helping matters.

If at first you don't succeed ...

She stood up and was about to lift her arm again when she noticed someone racing up the back entrance to Meadowbrook, the estate where a certain shamed actor lived. Her glasses were currently fogged-up – stone-throwing was a physical undertaking after all – but she was almost positive this was the man himself! He had a distinctive way of moving and walking – his knees did something peculiar, they knocked off each other – and he wore the same peaked cap Clooney favoured when he wasn't in the mood to style his hair.

'I don't ask too many favours, God, but please – let me hit him right in the middle of his ugly head!'

She began her routine of leaning on the wall, raising her arm, then firing. However, this time, she didn't hide or close her eyes – she remained standing, her gaze following the direction of the stone.

'Keep going. Keep going. Keep going,' she encouraged it as it soared across the sky. 'Keep go– Damn!'

She'd missed, although just by a hair's breadth. Her close-but-no-cigar attempts did have an effect; Clooney turned to see who was responsible for the random attack. Vonnie couldn't help herself.

'Yahoo! Hello there, stranger! I hope you're sticking to 7-Up tonight. We don't want a repeat of last week's embarrassing incident!'

She wasn't sure what was to be achieved by taunting him, and before she'd figured it out, he was sprinting towards her.

He'll never be able to jump the fences, Vonnie assured herself.

He did.

He was getting rapidly closer, yet she remained where she was; not as an act of defiance but more because she couldn't live without him.

She needed him to talk to her.

Shout at her.

Interact with her.

Anything!

She now realised that the cause of her upset over the past few days was down to the fact that she'd missed him terribly – even if she still hated his guts. Maybe she'd overstepped the mark on a few occasions, but surely 'friends for life' forgave each other?

Now they were going to have an exchange. Ever the dreamer, this Piscean would pitch the idea of rebooting their relationship and starting over. When she saw his angry, bloodshot eyes directly in front of her, Vonnie fully realised how much she wanted him back in her life. It was confirmed: her love for him was stronger than ever! How cute that they were now reunited. She vowed to throw more stones at him in future if this was the positive outcome.

I only hope he stays off the wine – it doesn't suit him.

FORTY-FIVE

Clooney faced Vonnie. Their noses touched. Her rancid breath assaulted his senses and made him want to vomit. But even if she'd smelled of peony on a rainy summer's morning, he still would have been left reaching for the sick bucket. Clooney had never felt such venom for anyone or anything in his entire life.

That worried him.

He never shied away from a good debate or argument – that was his combative father's influence on him – but he was aware that, sometimes, when passions were roused, he could lose the run of himself, resulting in saying or doing things that he mightn't be proud of later. As a result, the old trick of counting to ten was one he'd implemented time and time again. However, as he continued his wordless showdown with the woman who'd succeeded in destroying his entire life and career, he knew that no matter if he counted for a hundred years, he'd still want to gouge her googly eyes out – and, after everything she'd subjected him to since their ill-fated meeting, every judge in the country would deem his actions justifiable.

Vonnie decided to break the awkward silence. 'Nice to see y–'

'Don't. Just don't, Vonnie,' he whispered, valiantly keeping his rage in check. 'Do you think, after what you've done, that we can exchange pleasantries like normal people?'

'Normal?' Vonnie hissed. 'Don't you ever use that disgusting word in my presence again. I'm unique. *We're* unique.'

'Oh my God! There is no fucking "we" for crying out loud! There never was!'

Blood boiling, Clooney took a significant step back; it was safer that way – for both of them.

'Why are you so determined to ruin my life, Vonnie? The only thing you could accuse me of is being kind to you at Isla's blasted party. I chatted with you for a little while and, if I recall correctly, gave you plenty of support and encouragement. I even gave you the guts of €100 to paint that piece of shite –'

'Excuse me,' Vonnie interrupted, outraged. 'That *masterpiece* will be worth ten times your scabby fee in a few years. Look at Vincent van Gogh – his career only took off after he popped his clogs.' She laughed. 'That's actually funny – you know, van Gogh was Dutch … clogs … for God's sake, Clooney – that deserves a smile at least. You're always clipping my wings!'

If Clooney had had a knife to hand, he'd have clipped more than her wings. Heck, by the time he was done, van Gogh's severed ear would have been a tiny scratch in comparison.

'This is the thanks I get?' he continued, refocusing. 'Because you didn't get to kill me in Connemara, you decided to ruin my career, live on national television? I am a fucking laughing stock! If it hadn't been for your mouthy housemate, I'd have thought it was my fault that I lost everything. My acting career. My journalism work. My book deal.'

'A book about me –'

'Zip it – I'm not done. Not even close! My mother hasn't talked to me in a week, and I can hardly blame her after the humiliation I've caused her and my family. Even my Ozzy Osbourne-type friends told me to "Sort it out, Clooney." Since last Friday night, I've had panic attack after panic attack. I've been waking up in a cold sweat – if I manage to doze off in the first place – and my sheets have been so drenched, you could almost mistake my bed for a fucking paddling pool.'

Vonnie tried, unsuccessfully, to suppress a laugh.

'It's not funny, Vonnie. What you've done to me – and God knows how many other people – is not normal. It's not the done thing; it's just not. Do you see that? Are you aware of that?'

'I'm only aware of one thing.'

'What?'

'I love you!'

'What?' Clooney shouted, horrified. Over the course of writing his book, he'd worked with numerous mental health experts, all of whom had suggested that Vonnie's behaviour in Connemara had sprung from a deep-rooted attachment to him, yet hearing those three words now – earnestly delivered, without a hint of irony – was chilling. Clooney realised more clearly than ever that there was little point in communicating with her the way he would with anyone else. She was damaged, very much so, and what she needed was professional help, not the scorching he'd intended to give her. Yes, they both were in a mess, but, having just gotten off the phone with Tony, he remained hopeful that he could still emerge from this situation with something resembling a career. Vonnie, on the other hand, would need more than a smart agent and carefully worded press release to get herself back on track.

'Look, Vonnie. Why don't the two of us take a little walk up towards the hospit–'

'Stop!' she roared. 'Don't even say it!'

Things became even clearer for Clooney. The mention of 'hospital' was a trigger for Vonnie, so he obviously wasn't the first person to suggest it.

'I would prefer you to hate me, rather than think I'm crazy,' she pleaded, edging towards the wall of the bridge. 'I thought you were different. That's why I loved you.'

'It's okay, Vonnie. I've upset you. Why don't we both go and have a sit down –'

'Stop talking to me like I'm an idiot! It's so patronising. Speaking to me like a fucking child! I'm forty-four years old for crying out loud!'

It was undoubtedly true that she was crying out loud. Unnoticed by either of them, a large group of curious passers-by – including an extremely concerned Isla – had suddenly gathered on the road below, curious about the escalating drama.

'Vonnie, look at me,' Clooney instructed, very much aware that she was creeping closer and closer towards the wall. How foolish he now felt for challenging her about the situation directly – and in such a hazardous location. 'If you meant what you said just now about loving me, then you'll have to trust me.'

'How could you question my love for you?' she replied, finally stopping. 'Didn't I kill that guy in Jamaica for us? For *our* relationship?'

'What?' Clooney's chest tightened; his breath escaped him. Few trains still used the track on which they currently stood, but at that moment, he felt like a locomotive had crashed into him. Maybe Vonnie's words were a figment of his imagination. After such a gruelling week, it was a wonder he was still able to function at all.

'What the fuck did you just say, Vonnie?' he asked through the wheezing. 'How do you know about Renardo's death?'

'Was that his name?'

Clooney's mind raced back to Jamaica, looking up at his new lover taking a photograph of the group. Then, out of nowhere, the bridge collapsing. It couldn't have been Vonnie.

It just couldn't.

'How did you do it?' he probed, anxious to discredit her claim.

'I cut the ropes of the bridge. But that doesn't matter now. What matters –'

'Where was the bridge?'

'Oh, God, this is tiresome – I can't remember. April Fools?

April Falls? May Falls? June Falls or something? Something Falls – or maybe it should be *Someone* Falls! A dangerous spot. A death trap! Anyway, I shouldn't be too boastful of my accomplishments as I failed to drown that slut the day before when you guys were scuba diving. You weren't terribly faithful during that trip, were you, Clooney? And your language was atrocious, shouting out "bollocks" when that pervert's mangled body bloodied the river. We'll need to discuss all of that sometime down the li–'

'Arrrrrrrrrrrrrgh!' Clooney let rip with a mighty, feral roar. 'I'm going to fucking kill you!'

Before he could make good on this threat, Vonnie jumped onto the wall, out of his reach. The drop below was a good seventy-five feet at least. The large group gathered below on the Ring Road released a collective cry, with the loudest scream coming from Isla.

Adrenaline rushing through him, Clooney leapt towards Vonnie, ready to send her someplace she could cause no further harm: the bottom of the River Boyne. Just like she'd done to Renardo.

'You fucking psychotic nut-job! Your time is well and truly up!'

He grabbed her by the ankle, to prevent her from escaping.

'Get off me!'

As she tried to free herself from his grasp, Vonnie lost her balance and tipped backwards. The onlookers screamed in horror as they watched her body dangle over the edge of the bridge.

Clooney still gripped her ankle. All he had to do now was release his hands and it would be curtains; he would finally be free (at least until he got sent to prison). But he wanted answers first.

'What did Renardo ever do to you? How could you do that? How could you kill such a beautiful, innocent person? Do you not have a fucking conscience? How can you sleep at night?'

But the woman currently trying to claw her way back onto the bridge was ill – very ill. He would receive no satisfaction from her answers or irrational logic. He had to get rid of her before she did any further damage to the people he loved. Who would she take out next?

Isla?

His mother?

His father?

Tony?

Prison or hospital would be too good for her. She was a menace and needed to be eliminated. It was the only way.

'I hate your hideous guts, you cruel, fucked-up psycho! And now you're going to pay for what you did to Renardo!'

Eyes closed, Clooney released his grip. Blood pumped through his giddy veins. He'd done it. He'd killed her! His emotions were a mix of fear and exhilaration. He'd never felt more alive! Except that, unbeknownst to him, his earlier vacillating had allowed Vonnie to hoist herself back onto the bridge – all those muscles formed throwing stones had stood her in good stead.

'What the –?' Clooney didn't take any time to dwell on his failure. He lunged at her, but he'd missed his chance.

'Not today, you mealy-mouthed bitch!' Vonnie screamed. Deftly, she picked up one of the stones, her weapon of choice for years, and whacked him across the head. Dazed, Clooney stumbled backwards and caught his foot on one of the wires that lined the tracks.

'Oops!' she mouthed as she watched what happened next.

Clooney staggered before crashing down on top of a concrete pole, whacking the back of his head in the process. He was knocked out cold.

When he woke up four days later, his world – once again – had changed irrevocably.

FORTY-SIX

'Clooney? Kiddo? Are you awake?'

Clooney blinked. He had no idea where he was, but he recognised Tony's voice and could make out the silhouette of his mother to the left of him. He scanned the space and knew that he wasn't in his bedroom, although he couldn't determine where exactly he was.

'Don't rush, Cloon,' his mother advised. 'Take your time; there's no rush.'

What on earth happened?

He tuned in to a soft beeping sound coming from somewhere behind his head. When he turned to identify it, he spotted something resembling a drip. With his eyes, he followed the tube that hung from the bag and realised it was attached to his arm.

'You're lucky to be alive.'

He didn't recognise the voice. Whoever it was, she removed something from the foot of his bed – a clipboard – and began scribbling notes on it.

Hospital.

'And I'm told we're particularly lucky that you're alive – you're a hero! You saved that woman's life.'

He started to remember.

Valerie. On the bridge. No, that isn't her name. Vanessa?

She'd tried to jump off. He'd tried to push her off. Why, though?

Veronica?

But he'd saved her, apparently – and somehow ended up in hospital.

'What ... what day is it?'

'It's Tuesday.' His father. 'You've been here, sleeping, for the past four days. And you promised you'd help with mowing the garden!'

'Norman!' his mother scolded.

'I promise I'll help when I get out.'

'You won't be doing much physical activity for some time, I'm afraid,' the doctor cautioned. 'And that means no work either – is that clear, Tony?'

Clooney's agent laughed.

'Oh yes,' Clooney remembered, his chest tightening, a familiar feeling. 'I don't have any work to do. Thanks for reminding me, mate.'

'I'm not laughing at you,' Tony reassured him, 'I'm laughing at the irony that you've never been in more demand than this week, and here you are, stuck in hospital!'

'What? I don't understand.' Clooney tried to sit up; it wasn't an easy task.

'Kiddo, you're an international superstar. A pin-up! Everyone, the world over, adores you. You are a hero!'

'Stop messing; I'm not able at the moment.'

'It's not a joke,' his mother added. 'What do you call that thing-a-ma-jig, Tweeter?'

'Twitter.'

'Exactly – you've been top of the pops since Friday evening.'

'Top trending,' Tony corrected. 'It's true!'

'Because I stopped Vonnie from jumping?'

Vonnie, that's it.

'Because, even though she tried to kill you last year, and then sabotage your life and career on *Friday With ...*, you found the humility not only to forgive her but even help her in her hour of need. You've brought the topic of suicide into the mainstream – it has been such a taboo for centuries. And all those things together combine to make the perfect hero.'

Something wasn't quite adding up. Clooney knew there was an aspect to the incident on the bridge he was forgetting – but what?

'How do you know how things played out on the bridge? It's all a bit fuzzy.'

'No matter what we all think of her,' his mother said, 'Vonnie has played a blinder since the whole horrid ordeal. She's been interviewed by RTÉ, BBC, CNN – everyone! Hasn't she, Norman?'

'She has. And she's been quite eloquent as well, in fairness to her.'

'She told us exactly what happened,' his mother continued. 'That she called you, begging for forgiveness, which you gave her without a moment's hesitancy – but still she was so guilt-ridden that she couldn't live with herself any longer, and decided it was best for the world that she disappear for good.'

'Witnesses saw you running from the back of Meadowbrook to the bridge and pulling her down from the wall,' his father took over. 'It was even filmed with lots of telephones. I have to say, Cloon, your mother and I are extremely proud of you.'

'I always knew that you had a big heart, Cloon. Didn't I always say that, Norman?'

'You did.'

'As soon as you're back on your feet, kiddo, we're going to make you into a millionaire,' Tony promised, almost salivating at the prospect of overflowing coffers. 'The phone hasn't stopped ringing. Our email account crashed twice. Girls and gays are writing to say how gorgeous-looking you are!'

'Really?' Clooney's sluggish blood flow suddenly sprang to life. 'Gorgeous, you say?'

'Yes, kiddo. This is your time. The world loves you and wants you both.'

'Both?'

'Well, yes. You're a double-act now. Manoscritto wants to re-edit the book to include this new, happier ending. Lucy is talking about a global release. The producers of *Friday With …* want the two of you on the show as soon as you're fit and ready –'

'Which won't be today or tomorrow,' the doctor piped up from the corner of the room.

'I've had offers from America for reality TV shows following you and Vonnie around. Magazine covers. Interviews – *The New York Times* has already done a profile on you. I mean, kiddo, the world is your oyster! This is it – everything you've ever dreamed of. You and Vonnie are the new Sonny and Cher. Liz and Richard. Heck, you're the new Adam and Eve!'

'And the world wants a bite of the apple,' his father joked.

'But …' Clooney half-remembered something. Something connected to Jamaica.

'Okay,' the doctor interrupted in an authoritative voice, 'the man of the hour needs to rest. You can call back again later this evening. Oh, Tony, please see if you can send those photographers away – they're blocking the entrance. And I've also no time to be putting make-up on or fixing my hair every time I pop out for a cigarette.'

Clooney's parents and agent each took their turn to kiss the patient.

'Wait,' he called out as his visitors reached the door. 'I can't work with her.'

'Why not, kiddo?'

Clooney felt a knot form in the pit of his stomach. He wasn't the hero Tony and his parents described – far from it. Memories of the incident flashed through his mind. He couldn't quite piece together the entire puzzle, but one thing he was now sure of: Vonnie's version of events was far from truthful – in fact, it was an out-and-out lie. He hadn't tried to save Vonnie.

I tried to fucking kill her.

'Well, Mr Irish Brad Pitt? Isn't that what they're referring to him as, Tony?' Clooney's mother said.

'That's right, the Irish Brad Pitt.'

Clooney caught his reflection in the mirror that hung on the wall beside him. The bandage wrapped around his head gave him an air of rugged authority. In fact, he felt he had never looked more desirable in his entire life. 'The Irish Brad Pitt? Really?'

'Well? Why can't you work with her?' his mother repeated.

The Irish Brad Pitt? Damn!

'Nothing. Doesn't matter.'

FORTY-SEVEN

According to his CV, Clooney had many strings to his bow, but the only skill he'd full confidence in was his ability to fake it. At the drop of a hat, he could force a smile and pretend he was having a good time – even if, deep down, his emotions were humming along to Beethoven's Fifth. As he stood in a spacious warehouse recently reinvented as one of Dublin's leading photography studios, Clooney was forced to call upon that particular qualification – and he was excelling with gusto.

He'd been discharged from hospital the previous day. Now that the medication had worn off, his mind was slowly becoming his own again and what he saw before him was … complicated.

The Daily Mail had flown over that morning to interview him and Vonnie, and while Vonnie didn't have to pretend she'd taken up residence on Cloud Nine, Clooney wasn't so lucky. He was inches away from the woman he'd tried to kill for sabotaging his life (and, if instinct served him correctly, for another, more sinister, reason he couldn't quite remember). Shamefully, he was now going along with the false narrative that he, the hero, had saved her from hurling herself off a bridge. It made him sick to the stomach – not that anyone present would have guessed.

The theme of the photoshoot was the magnetism between him and Vonnie: no matter how they tried to get away from each other, they were always drawn back together. Vonnie, who'd recently been the recipient of successful laser eye surgery and some laser hair removal above her lip, sat proudly on top of a giant fake magnet, yapping away to the journalist about her favourite flavours of ice-cream, her battles with bronchitis and her blossoming success as an adult artist. For this shoot, she'd decided to take a breather from her outrageous costumes and, instead, channelled Audrey Hepburn from *Funny Face* by donning a simple black turtleneck with matching pants. She'd earlier told the stylist that she 'wanted to be the sole focus and not share the limelight with my amazing, revolutionary outfits!'

Clooney, below her, was equally low-key in his appearance – Jimmy Dean, circa *Rebel Without a Cause*. While he delighted in what he'd seen staring back at him from the mirror a little earlier, now, striking a series of silly poses, all he could visualise was the outcome of the inevitable confession. He was confident the general public would understand the situation and not judge him too harshly for wanting to kill the person who had created carnage in his life for the past year. Yes, it was apparent to all that her mental health was compromised and, in hindsight, he should have run to the nearest garda station and sought assistance rather than confronting her in the first place. But surely the public would understand his plight.

Wouldn't they?

Of course, he would probably lose his now-thriving career.

The offers would stop.

The interest would wane.

He'd be living in his parents' home forever and a day.

In fact, more than likely, he'd be a laughing stock once again, despised the world over. Not only for attempting to kill a mentally ill woman, but for then going along with her fantastical version of events. What he'd endured following the original *Friday With* … would be nothing in comparison. But it was a better fate than getting into bed with someone who made the devil seem like Mahatma Gandhi. If he was to have success, professionally and personally, it had to be for the right reasons – and he wanted to enjoy it without that demon at his side.

Yes, as adept as he was at putting on a mask, Clooney knew deep down that he must tell the world the truth.

And it really was the world.

Tony hadn't been exaggerating when he said they were global stars. There were six-figure endorsements with some of the biggest brands in the world on the table; his revised autobiography was number one on Amazon US and UK and the video of him 'saving' Vonnie had been watched almost forty million times.

It must be a slow news week, Clooney had thought at first when he began to see how their relationship had caught the imagination of the world. But the fuss hadn't died down. What was happening to Clooney was just what he'd dreamed about as a teenager, but he'd never imagined it would come with such a considerable caveat.

Fuck. That was the word he was repeating over and over. *Fuuuuuck!*

'Now, Clooney, could you try to walk away from Vonnie, but imagine that you're being pulled back by her captivating force? And show those lovely, muscly arms of yours to our hundreds of thousands of readers.'

Lovely, muscly arms... Hundreds of thousands of readers...

Ever the professional, Clooney complied with the photographer's orders. As he stretched his 'lovely, muscly' arms out, he realised this might be the last time he would be in a studio getting his photograph taken. In the future, the sound of cameras clicking would be those employed by the tabloids as he entered courtrooms, say, or stumbled out of an off-licence at eleven in the morning, laden down with bottles of vodka in brown paper bags. Like those dark days in Connemara. Still, it was better than living a lie.

Wasn't it?

He recalled his mother's repeated advice over the years: always tell the truth, regardless of the consequences. She of all people would be proud of him, and that pride would surely trump the whispers and piteous looks she'd be subjected to at every Sunday mass from now on.

Wouldn't it?

'Now, Clooney,' the photographer instructed, 'if you have the energy, I'd like Vonnie to pretend to pull you up to her so if you could lean against the magnet again and give her your hand?'

Tony would advise him how best to word the admission. There might be an attempted-murder charge to contend with, but Clooney's father had numerous contacts in the legal world, and surely they could get those dismissed.

Couldn't they?

Whatever the outcome, he'd embrace it with dignity and courage. He'd made his decision: he was going to leave this ridiculous photoshoot, jump in a taxi, head over to his agent and kick off proceedings.

Just one last moment to savour being a hero.

'Clooney, that's wonderful news!' the reporter screamed.

Being a legend.

'And thank you, Vonnie, for giving me the exclusive!'

Being a superstar. A pin-up. 'The Irish Brad Pitt.'

'I've just tweeted the announcement on our official Twitter account. Now the entire world knows your secret. Have you anything to add, Clooney? Clooney?'

'Yes?'

'What are your thoughts on the amazing news?'

'Sorry, what amazing news?'

'That you and Vonnie are expecting.'

FORTY-EIGHT

'Hold on a second, kiddo; I know you want to say something to me, but if I don't get this contract in the post by lunch, I worry they will change their minds.'

'Tony, this is impor—'

'Ninety thousand euro for half a day's work – can you believe it! All those years you grafted for tuppence, kiddo, are long in the past! Ah, here it is!'

Clooney felt Tony's office was the physical manifestation of his own mind: chaotic. Located in Ranelagh, his agent owned the four offices collectively known as Tony Bannon Management, along with the rest of the building. His husband, an interior designer, had renovated the other spaces, now occupied by a variety of tenants, including a pole-dancing school and a television production company. It was a hub of activity, but even so, Clooney's overnight meteoric rise to worldwide fame had left Tony and his team in a tizzy, and the order that formerly existed had been unceremoniously flung out the window. Clooney wondered whether the unexpected success had gone to Tony's head somewhat. The phone hadn't stopped ringing since he'd arrived ten minutes earlier, while Tony's two assistants were starting to drip with sweat, going in and out of the various offices, passing on messages – all related to the man of the hour.

'Wouldn't it be magic if we could get some of your film and television scripts across the line now, kiddo? All those years you spent doubled over a computer, living off clean air, are paying off at long last. I'm sure I could get a fortune for them!'

'I'm not interested in the mon–'

'I'm going to set up a meeting between you and my accountant, by the way,' Tony announced as he handed him the contract and pen. 'I know you're sensible enough not to squander your newfound wealth, but it would be no harm to discuss how best to save or invest. Hopefully, you'll have longer than fifteen minutes, but, you know, just in case.'

Robotically, Clooney scribbled his autograph on the bottom of the contract and wished fate had never afforded him his moment of fame. He'd come to Tony's office not to augment their chests of gold but to empty them. Pleasant compliments aside, every aspect of the situation with Vonnie was reprehensible, but the fabrication of the pregnancy was one lie too many. He hadn't been intimate with a member of the fairer sex since his college days, for God's sake! Although using a word like 'fair' to describe Vonnie was nothing short of a liberty. Even though he stood a chance of landing a custodial sentence and risked being an international laughing stock until the day he relinquished life, Clooney had no option other than to reveal the truth.

'Tony, Vonnie isn't pregnant.'

'Of course she isn't.'

'You knew?'

'When I first heard it, I wondered had she done something untoward while you were in the hospital, but then I slapped my wrist for even thinking she'd stoop to such levels.'

Clooney laughed.

'Then I concluded the poor thing just got a little carried away by the situation. She always seems to have trouble distinguishing between what's real and what's make-believe.'

'And were you not going to bring it up?' Clooney quizzed, surprised at how calm his agent was over this untruth. 'You know I had nothing to do with the lie?'

'Bring it up? It's fucking genius! There are two things magazines absolutely scream for – a celebrity gaining or losing weight, and a pregnancy. Listen to the phones ringing. We've been receiving five times the volume of calls since she made the announcement and, let me assure you, kiddo, the phones were already hopping like frogs beforehand.'

'Yes but she's not fucking pregnant, Tony. It's all just a load of bullshit. The whole bloody thing!'

'Okay, calm down. This is obviously all very overwhelming for you – as it would be for anyone. Fame is tough –'

'It's nothing to do with fame; it's because it's all a big charade and Vonnie is much more dangerous than any of us realised.'

'Kiddo, I can talk to her today. We can say it was a false alarm – the excitement of the past few weeks has led to her body doing all sorts of crazy thin–'

'Tony, it's not just the pregnancy …' Clooney took a deep breath; he was going to come clean. Tony didn't have a judgemental bone in his body, so Clooney knew he wouldn't be outraged by the fact that he wasn't actually the all-forgiving hero the world had assumed, but a hot-tempered, poor man's Jack the Ripper – and whatever repercussions followed, Tony would embrace with dignity. Clooney had made his decision: he was going to tell the truth.

'I didn't save her, Tony. I can't quite remember every minute detail, it's still a bit of a haze, but one thing that I am sure of is that there was no brave rescue. She wasn't trying to jump off the bridge; I was trying to throw her off it.'

'Oh my God!'

It was Tony's assistant, Gemma, standing in the doorway. And her tone indicated, not shock at what Clooney had begun to confess, but excitement.

'Sorry for cutting across you, Clooney, but you are never going to believe what that last phone call was about.'

'Not now, Gemma,' Tony scolded. 'We're in the middle of something.'

'I know but, Clooney, you're going to want to hear this.'

'What?' Clooney didn't want to hear it – particularly if, as her demeanour suggested, it was good news. No matter what offer or revelation Gemma had to report, he was adamant he'd refuse, before continuing to discuss a damage-limitation plan with Tony.

'The organisers of the Met Gala in New York have just called to say they were so impressed by the grace and humility you showed to the woman who tried to kill you – not only saving her from suicide but also by starting a family with her – that they want you to attend the next event!'

'You are kidd– ... The Met Gala?'

Each year, Clooney whiled away hours poring over images of the A-list event. He had never allowed himself to imagine being in attendance – it was exclusively for the crème de la crème, and even though the actor was a dreamer, he was worldly enough to know that securing an invite was next to impossible. Even still ...

'That's very nice of them, but I'm afraid I'll have to decline.'

'But,' Gemma protested, 'it's fashion's biggest night out. The world's most famous stars will be there!'

Clooney shook his head; he'd made his decision: it was over. He was determined not to allow the glitz and glamour he'd been obsessed with all his life to seduce him any longer. 'No, I'm sorry.'

'That's not all,' the assistant continued, unperturbed by Clooney's rejections. 'There's talk that Jean-Paul Gaultier wants to dress you.'

'Jean-Paul? I don't believe you ...'

'It's a no, Gemma,' Tony interrupted, a note of reluctance in his voice.

'The theme is "From the Periphery to Centre Stage", which

is obviously why organisers are so keen to have you and Vonnie present because, you know –'

'Gemma, that's enough now.' While Tony was certainly impressed by this glorious, exclusive invitation, he wasn't by his assistant's insistence. But she couldn't help herself, and who could blame her?

Gemma sat on the edge of the desk – the best news was yet to come. 'Some of the guests already confirmed include Nicole Kidman, Leonardo DiCaprio, Oprah, Julia Roberts, Lady Gaga, Ariana Grande, Taylor Swift and Lizzo to name but a few! But, this year, guess who's also rumoured to be attending, performing some new music?'

'My love,' Clooney interjected, 'I'm going to have to stop you there. Unless it's Madonna, my answer remains the same. No.'

'It's Madonna.'

FORTY-NINE

Clooney stood in a tent, naked save for a disposable thong. He'd just received a spray-on tan – his first in many years. In his early twenties, he'd been addicted to them, indulging almost every other week. Thankfully, he'd eventually found sense and stepped away from the spray gun. The stained bedsheets he could tolerate; the unpleasant waft had been endured, the impact on his bank account had been considered inconsequential. No, what finally put him off for good was the tan he'd received the night before a friend's wedding, where the beautician had been a smidge over-zealous and left him looking like a lump of coal. No amount of scrubbing had improved the situation so, the next day, when he and Isla gathered to cheer on their pal, he was forced to blame his strange, darkened state on a television role. Somewhat ironically, if it weren't for the tan, everyone would have seen his bright red, embarrassed cheeks.

But now, on the verge of being at the same event as Madonna – saviour of all those awkward teenage years when he'd battled his sexuality – he decided his pasty skin would be an insult to her influence on him, and booked himself in for a dollop of much-needed grooming the night before departing for New York. If things went awry, as they had before, that gave him twenty-four hours to scrub, scrub and scrub some more!

As he waited the seemingly interminable twenty minutes for the tan to dry – legs and arms stuck out like a starfish – Clooney noticed how quiet the voices in his head now seemed. The whirlwind of tormented self-loathing mutterings had been replaced by calm tranquillity – of a kind that had evaded him since he'd first laid eyes on Vonnie. Dubious and immoral as most of it had been, everything he'd been through with her now seemed to have been worthwhile.

Almost.

Yes, they'd played fast and loose with the truth, but if the consequences of telling a few white lies meant being in the same room as the Material Girl herself, well, he wished he'd indulged his inner Pinocchio earlier!

However, even though his celebrity status was as a result of his relationship with Vonnie, Clooney knew that moving forward, he was going to have to find a way of breaking away. Tony had promised to handle the pregnancy situation, but Clooney knew that freeing himself from Vonnie would be a much more complicated affair.

Maybe Madonna will have a similar mishap to that time at the Brits and come flying off the stage to land slap bang on top of the Wicked Witch of the West! he thought mischievously. *If that tree didn't kill her, maybe the Queen of Pop will!*

These naughty fantasies were interrupted by his phone ringing. Even though he was under strict instructions by the beautician to remain rooted to the spot, Clooney's giddy mood encouraged him to waddle over to his jacket, and with delicate precision, prise his mobile from his coat pocket.

It was Vonnie.

'Hi there, what's up?'

'Clooney!' She sounded hysterical. 'Clooney! We lost the baby!'

'Did we? I'm so sad to hear that.'

'Well, it's not so much that we lost it; it turns out that I wasn't pregnant in the first place! My body has been doing strange things since you saved my life on the bridge. It has been overwhelming, hasn't it?'

Tony had remained true to his word.

'It most certainly has, Vonnie. I hope you're okay?'

Her tears and heavy breathing quietened.

'I was going to call him Ren if he was a boy.'

'I beg your pardon?'

'Ren. Exotic, don't you think?'

Clooney froze. Was it a coincidence that her choice of name was short for Renardo? He hadn't talked about Renardo to anyone following his trip to Jamaica. There had been no mention of the accident in his autobiography or in any subsequent interviews. Was it just a coincidence?

'Why "Ren"?'

'R.E.N. Remember Every Nanosecond,' she replied coquettishly. 'I want us to remember every nanosecond. Clever, don't you think?'

Clooney breathed a sigh of relief.

'If we have more success the next time,' she continued, 'maybe we can call him ...'

'How are you getting on, hun?'

A broad-shouldered, immaculately maintained beautician entered, smile fading when she saw Clooney where he ought not to have been.

'Who's that?' Vonnie spat out without even attempting to hide her jealousy.

'Is that Vonnie on the phone?' the beautician asked without even attempting to hide her excitement.

Clooney nodded.

'Vonnie, it's Michelle here – I've just given your fella a spray-on, and he looks only gorgo.'

'Does he now?'

'But don't you worry, he has eyes only for you. He has been shiteing on about ye for the past hour, haven't ye, hun?'

It seemed it wasn't just Clooney and Vonnie who were partial to telling porkies.

'I sure have!'

'An' come here to me, Vonnie – how ye getting on with the morning sickness. I remember when I had Hunter, I was in absolute –'

'I lost the baby!' Vonnie screamed, with impressive commitment.

'Ah, stop the lights. I am so sorry, hun! There'll be more chances, don't ye worry!'

As the two women chattered away about pregnancies, Clooney made his way back to the tent. Only minutes earlier, he'd delighted in embracing the crazy situation in which he had found himself. Now, that wretched niggling inner voice was starting a racket within.

Remember Every Nanosecond.

If only he could …

FIFTY

Vonnie had never been too enamoured with Madonna. She'd hummed along to 'Like a Prayer' or 'Vogue' when they came on the radio but had never gone down to the Record Sleeve to buy any of her albums. Now, as she watched her darling man – dressed like a futuristic Che Guevara – scan the Metropolitan Museum of Art's Great Hall for a possible glimpse of her, she liked the woman even less. She couldn't understand what all the fuss was about, although judging by the high-pitched pandemonium surrounding the singer's possible arrival that night, she was clearly in the minority.

Since the incident on the bridge, the media had positioned Vonnie front and centre; her image graced every magazine and newspaper – and the editorial that accompanied these photos was usually positive and supportive. Vonnie was tickled pink to discover that she'd become a 'modern-day role model' as the *Huffington Post* had described her, as well as an inspiration to Bohemian types forced out to the edges of society. She was lionised for her quirkiness and reluctance to adhere to the status quo. Vonnie had always known she was a leading lady; the only surprise about her rise to superstardom was that it had taken so ruddy long! Yes, this was her moment.

Until fucking Madonna, that brazen hussy, swooped in and unashamedly stole it! Has she not had enough attention over the years? Vonnie thought, leaning against one of the many free-standing pillars that lined the limestone hall. Despite her grumpy form, she couldn't help but admire the three impressive saucepan-shaped domes above her and the delicate marble mosaic floor beneath. The recent laser surgery carried out on her eyes had been a great success – ever since, she'd found herself noticing things that generally would have eluded her.

If only I could now drown out the nonsense people are talking around me, she wished, tired of being forced to listen to some celebrity dressed as the Ugly Duckling complain that she hadn't eaten in a week to fit into her anodine costume.

'And you call yourself a role model? You need your nourishment!' Vonnie hissed at her fellow guest through an enormous vase of lilies. But her words fell on deaf ears as the duck, on the advice of her publicist, waddled over to the sweeping Grand Staircase, keen for a photo-op with Madonna should she arrive.

Playing second fiddle to the Material Girl didn't sit well with Vonnie – she'd just lost a make-believe baby for heaven's sake! And even though she stood among the world's brightest stars, all dressed by fashion's biggest names, not one of them came close to competing with Vonnie's own ensemble, which she'd put together herself using pink and orange cushions scattered with pieces of popcorn and crisps. An hour beforehand, the photographers had snapped frantically on the red carpet, and Vonnie knew, in that moment, she'd made the right decision to turn down the many designers falling over themselves to dress her for the event. Nobody could make her shine brighter than she could herself.

'The world is full of couch potatoes, doing sweet fuck all,' she'd earlier informed a reporter from *Elle* magazine, 'and the only way to make a change is to get off your fat arse and do something. And make sure that something is big!'

And then, abruptly, the attention had been snatched away from her with everyone's talk about bloody Madonna – especially her darling man, currently yapping away to someone – Rihanna? – beside a giant statue of a pharaoh.

'These past few weeks have been surreal,' she could overhear Clooney tell this celebrity, who was dressed as a wall. 'But never in my wildest dreams did I think that I'd be standing in the same space as the greatest living musician! Present company excluded, my love!'

Yawn.

Vonnie was hungry. There had been a few *hors d'oeuvres* floating about on arrival, but they were of no use – rather than fortifying her, she exerted more energy chewing the I-don't-know-what-you-call-thems.

All around her, fake bitches were gushing, 'You look stunning, sweetie!' 'Who dressed you?' 'We're holidaying in the Riviera this summer; you should join us!'

Yawn, yawn.

Vonnie had had enough. Sick and tired of being an afterthought, she decided to leave this sorry excuse for a fashion show and go on the hunt for something more substantial than those vile bits of rabbit food. Instead of politely slipping out, Vonnie made her mood known to those around her, but the guests were too mesmerised by themselves to care.

There was a handful of buff security men standing on either side of a door leading out to a makeshift garden that doubled as a smoking area. She squeezed past some woman dressed in a kimono – Jennifer Lopez? – but didn't receive so much as an acknowledgement.

How the mighty had fallen!

Out in the near-deserted garden, there didn't appear to be much by way of food, but she was, at least, free from the hoity-toity silliness running amok within. As she walked towards the fake fountain, a couple of giddy middle-aged men approached her for an autograph.

About bloody time.

Beatifically, the couch potato obliged, delighted she hadn't been completely sidelined.

'We've been waiting all night to see you,' they gushed. 'You are such an inspiration to us – we hope you know that, Vonnie.'

'I do, and it means the world to me,' she robotically replied as she scribbled her name on a tatty notebook. One of them looked like Ricky Martin, but she wasn't certain.

Look how professional I am – giving these fans my time! Would that wagon who may or may not be arriving tonight be as accommodating to her minions as me?

Before the ink had dried, the autograph-hunters had fled, anxious to see who else they might approach.

Charming.

It was still bright and warm, although Vonnie wondered if it was her fabulous costume that was keeping her so well insulated. She sat down at the edge of the fountain. It was nice to have a moment to herself, following the mayhem of the previous few weeks.

'Excuse me; may I have a word with you?'

Vonnie looked around to see who the owner of the thick American accent was.

'My name is Len Blumberg; I'm a television producer. One of the biggest producers in the industry if I may say so.'

Cocky, isn't he?

Sitting down beside her was a tall, handsome man with short curly hair, stubble and sallow skin. He commanded great authority, and his suave demeanour instantly struck Vonnie.

'You're one of the biggest producers in the industry, you say. I'm Vonnie, but you probably already know that,' she said, matching his confidence.

'I most certainly do. You don't seem to be enjoying the gala – I thought it would be exactly your type of event, given your interest in fashion.'

'I might have to launch my own gala next year. There are too many clones in there for my liking.'

'Is Clooney a clone?'

'I didn't think he was, Larry –'

'Len.'

'Until tonight. I thought he was unique. But he's in there, waiting for "Madame" to arrive.'

'Madonna?'

'He's obsessed with her.'

'How obsessed?'

Vonnie gave him a quizzical look. There was something about this encounter that intrigued her – and not only because it was the most attention she'd received since entering the museum.

'What did you say your name was? Lance?'

'Len. And I'm producing a new reality TV show I was hoping you and Clooney might take part in. But there's a little twist … Are you good at keeping secrets?'

'The best.'

'Nice outfit, by the way – very avant-garde.'

'If you think that's avant-garde, Leyton, you should see what's underneath.'

FIFTY-ONE

'Would you like relish on this sandwich, my love?'

'That would be wonderful. You know how to treat me like a queen, don't you? My prince knows just how to treat me like a queen!'

Rebecca, the director of the reality show pilot, sat to the side of the camera and nodded enthusiastically at Vonnie's comment, clearly delighted by how well this unlikely couple was interacting. 'Keep going,' she encouraged – her husky, cigarette-damaged voice contrasting with her sunny LA disposition.

'I'll leave the tea here for you,' Clooney said, placing a large steel pot in front of his supposed true love, whose current outfit could easily have been mistaken for a miniature – and mutilated – version of the Statue of Liberty. 'Give it a few minutes to brew. You like it nice and strong, don't you?'

'Yes, the same way I like my men.'

'You messer!'

Back at the counter, Clooney, dressed in a more sober outfit – a tailored, petrol-grey three-piece suit – garnished the top of the sandwiches with a sprinkle of chives before returning to the table with them. He'd been devastated a few weeks earlier when Madonna had failed to appear at the Met Gala, apparently too busy filming a music video, but the news that had arrived later that night back in the hotel had cheered him considerably.

Len had invited the formidable Irish duo to take part in a new reality series called *Crazy For You*, which documented not only the love between celebrity couples like Clooney and Vonnie, but also between these celebrities and their own idols. Produced by one of America's most successful TV companies, the selling point of the project was the opportunity celebrities would receive to watch a cut of the episode in the presence of these idols – footage that would subsequently be included in the overall series.

In Clooney's case, his idol was, of course, Madonna.

The pilot episode was being filmed in a beautiful, modern apartment in South Dublin, which viewers would believe was Vonnie and Clooney's new home. In truth, it was nothing of the sort.

When it came to reality shows, it seemed there was very little reality.

'I hope you didn't put cheese in these,' Vonnie chided, 'I'm trying to keep the weight down.'

'I can't make any promises, my love – but, as an aside, you know I'd love you no matter what size you are!'

'They all say that, don't they?' Vonnie quipped off-camera to the crew. 'And then you balloon, and they're out the door quicker than you can say "calories"! Am I right?'

Rebecca nodded once again. Clooney couldn't help but be impressed by how effortlessly Vonnie took to the role of leading lady, although it hardly came as a surprise given her narcissistic nature. If there were Olympic medals handed out for the kind of game she was currently playing, she would be top of the podium. This was her moment, and she was grabbing it with both hands.

Speaking of grabbing with both hands, Vonnie swiped the sandwich from the plate and, without waiting for permission from the chef, started wolfing it down. Not that Clooney minded; they'd been filming all morning and were both in dire need of nourishment.

'And cut!'

The floor manager quickly handed Vonnie a bin to spit out the half-chewed sandwich, but she swatted him away.

'Are you kidding?' she scolded between frantic bites. 'Wasting good food? Those poor people starving in Somalia couldn't compete with the hunger I have.'

Clooney took half of his sandwich and headed over to the make-up stand, grabbing a protein shake from his bag. He wanted to ensure that his hair remained in position and that the bags under his eyes remained concealed. What would Madonna say if her greatest fan looked like a cast member from *Whatever Happened to Baby Jane?*

'My love, you wouldn't mind taking off the slap from under my eyes and reapplying it,' he asked one of the make-up artists. 'It's looking a bit cracked, don't you think?'

'Of course, just sit down in the chair.'

Clooney took a bite of the sandwich as he allowed the make-up artist to work her magic on him. He stole a glance at his phone – numerous missed calls from his parents, his siblings, Isla and other friends. He knew what they wanted. They'd been calling constantly since Vonnie had announced that she was, then wasn't, pregnant, trying to find out if he'd completely lost his mind – pretending he was all of a sudden straight and in the middle of a love affair with his one-time stalker? Worst of all, now allowing it to play out in front of the world in *Crazy For You*!

And all because of his fascination with a particular pop icon.

They were, understandably, anxious; probably wondering if the blow to the head on the bridge had been worse than the doctors initially thought.

Clooney returned the phone to his pocket. He'd call them back. Eventually.

Yes, the condition of his mind might have been up for debate, but the angular face that hid it was slightly more pleasing. Ever since Len Blumberg had offered him and Vonnie the opportunity to be participants in the coveted pilot episode, Clooney had locked himself in the gym and followed the strict regime of a monk – if monks ate five chicken fillets and ten egg whites per day, that is. His extreme efforts had resulted in a glow he hadn't seen since his youth, and muscles he'd thought were reserved for bodybuilders alone.

'Clooney, I want to go over the next section with you.' Rebecca pulled up a chair beside him. 'It's going to be about the pregnancy. If the tears don't come naturally, stare into one of the lights – that should activate a bit of moisture.'

'Fear not, forcing out tears is one of my few talents.'

'That's what I like to hear. So Vonnie is going to talk about how the doctors told her the baby wasn't forming properly in the womb, and how they advised her to terminate.'

'Wait? What? There never was a … Who told you that?'

'Vonnie – she was very distressed, informing me of the ins and outs on the phone last night. I told her to save some of the emotion for the camera. Madonna, a mother of six, will be gripped by this particular plot point.'

'I see,' Clooney said, suddenly less anxious to dismiss Vonnie's version of events. He spotted Isla entering the room. *Shit.* He gave her a little wave.

Not wanting to interrupt the discussion, Isla loitered a few metres away and sipped on a cappuccino. Clooney could tell she was worried and wanted to talk to him. Apart from Tony, she was the only other person who knew the entire truth about the ridiculous, you-couldn't-write-it situation.

'You must both have such strong faith,' Rebecca continued, scribbling some notes along the side of a script.

'Faith?'

'Insisting that God alone should decide the fate of your baby.'

'You've used that word twice: "baby". There wasn't one; you know tha–'

'Do you know what? Let's save all of this for the interview – that way, your answers will sound fresh and spontaneous. I have to say, though,' the director added, 'I was extremely taken by how you both dealt with the situation around the pregnancy.'

'Which was?'

'As if you don't know.'

'As if I don't know.'

'Those orphanages in Africa must have been very grateful for the generous donations you made.'

'Sorry, what?'

'Madonna will love to hear that – you know four of her children were adopted from orphanages in Malawi.'

Clooney nodded – of course he knew that. He also knew that he was an even bigger charlatan than Donald Trump.

'Oh, before I go,' Rebecca added as she rose to her feet, 'I also want to address your sexuality. I know you were openly gay until Vonnie entered your life, so I'd love to explore that abrupt change to heterosexuality as it were.'

'Right.'

Clooney gave his director a little smile, relieved at the chance to mull over the best way to reflect on Vonnie's many creative de-pictions of their relationship. No sooner had Rebecca disappeared than Isla was sitting in her seat.

'I can imagine what you're going to say.'

'M'dear, I hope you know what you're doing,' she whispered.

'I don't.'

'I didn't think so. You're in too deep here.'

'It's Madonna, Isla. This reality show is giving me the chance to work with her! Not shake her hand at some event – actually collaborate with her. How could I say no?'

'I understand, sort of, though I'm more of a David Beckham gal myself. But the further you continue into this make-believe world, the more difficult it's going to be to escape. You tried to kill Vonnie that day on the bridge for crying out loud – not save her!'

'Sssh!'

'And now you're pretending she's your girlfriend. I blame myself – I should have never introduced you two in the first place. God, why didn't you listen to me when I told you she was a rotten egg?'

She squeezed the muscles on his arm, impressed.

'And I see you're also preparing to play Hulk Hogan in a biopic of his life. You look … great, in fairness.'

'Do I?' Clooney beamed.

Isla scanned the room, crew members setting up lights and cameras. She laughed. 'I'll say this about you, m'dear – you've some neck.'

Clooney turned to the mirror to inspect, horrified. 'Do I? Does it look too bulky?'

'I meant … Oh, it doesn't matter.'

'Clooney,' a floor manager called out, 'we're going to need you in a minute.'

Before he was whisked away, Isla took her best friend's hand. 'All I'm going to say is this … Remember that story we learned in primary school – that fella, Icarus? Well, I feel you're flying way too close to the sun, Clooney.'

Her words began to sink in – helped by the fact that Vonnie was now pretending to be a horse, jumping over furniture and getting crew members to feed her from their hands.

What had Clooney signed up for?

'You could say the knock to your head was the reason you went along with all these inventions. Even still, the fallout is going to be enormous.'

'I know.'

'I'm not saying this to alarm you, but you need to know what might be in store. Will that agent of yours know how to put the pieces back together again when it all goes tits up?'

'Vonnie keeps making up things, Isla. There's no stopping her. She knows she has me by the short and curlies and is having a field day. Not only is she saying she was, in fact, pregnant earlier on, but she's also now claiming we like to spend our Saturday nights having tea parties with fucking porcelain dolls. So tomorrow, we have to re-enact that.'

'That sounds like a bit of craic.'

'Isla! How did I go from trying to fling her off a bridge to sitting on a rug forcing Earl Grey into fucking porcelain figurines?'

'Two words: fame and Madonna.'

They sat in silence for a moment, reflecting on the crazy trajectory Clooney's life had taken. Then they laughed.

'Dolls!'

Roared, doubled-over.

'On a rug!'

Tears streamed down their faces. They had to fight to catch their breath.

'Earl fucking Grey!'

Their hysterical laughter was a brief reminder of the innocent fun they used to enjoy before the madness took over. What Clooney would give to go back to those simpler times, even for a moment.

'Hey!' Vonnie cried from the kitchen area, clearly jealous. 'Don't leave me all alone, Clooney-wooney. And tell that snotty bitch she's not welcome on our set, the way I wasn't welcome in that kippy staffroom.'

Isla, not wanting to cause a scene, rose to her feet.

'Clooney-fucking-wooney?' Clooney muttered, fixing his make-up. 'I'm doing this for Madonna.'

'I don't know why you gays are so obsessed with her –'

'Shh! I'm batting for the other team now, don't forget.'

'I forgot. Would ye give me cousin Lottie a go now? She always had a soft spot for ye.'

'If I'd a few bottles of whiskey in me, I'd do me best.'

'It's whiskey I'll be needing when all of this goes to pot. Which it will. I am the worst best friend in the world.'

'I've always said it.'

'You divil!'

Clooney kissed Isla on the cheek.

'I'm only messing. You're the best.'

'Stop. Now go on – don't keep Herself waiting.'

He swiped Isla's cappuccino. He needed it more than she did, he thought as he returned to the side of his partner-in-crime.

Crime being the operative word.

FIFTY-TWO

Before carving out a career as a travel journalist, flying had petrified Clooney. Once, as he made the simple forty-minute journey from Belfast to Edinburgh, he'd become so panicked that he had disappeared into the toilet and removed his clothes. Every single stitch. It was only when he saw his hairy body in the mirror that it dawned on him: if the plane did crash into the North Channel, how would his poor mother deal with the news that not only was her son goosed, but his body had been found in the toilet, in the same state of undress as when he'd first entered the world?

'I hope he wasn't involved in any seedy Mile-High Club business!' he had imagined her worrying.

Although perhaps she'd have been the first to understand. She too struggled with nerves while airborne. The only time in her life she'd been drunk was on a shaky flight to Tallinn when the turbulence was so horrific she'd guzzled six glasses of Sauvignon Blanc – twice her maximum capacity.

But once Clooney's anxiety had finally been identified (he'd discovered that Irish doctors weren't forthcoming in making diagnoses of the mental health variety, feeling more at home with tonsillitis or a sprained ankle), he'd worked extremely hard at diffusing its impact. One of the upshots was that he no longer had an issue with flying. In fact, he'd almost say he enjoyed it.

And never more than now when travelling to the fairy-tale skiing resort of Sölden in Austria's dramatic Tyrol Valley. There, the most exciting element of *Crazy For You* was set to occur: Clooney and Vonnie would watch footage from the pilot episode with none other than Madonna!

Ignoring his wired state, Clooney sipped on his seventh coffee of the morning and wondered what it would be like to finally be in the legend's presence. He was confident they'd get on famously.

This cappuccino's pretty strong, he thought as he felt himself getting jittery. He vowed it would be the last. His daily intake was usually limited to one, and he knew he'd be completely strung out if he didn't rein it in.

Madonna loved skiing and brought her family to resorts whenever she got a chance. But she hadn't become the biggest-selling pop star in the world by sitting back during such holidays, so the special screening was set to take place somewhere in between her visits to the slopes and saunas.

'Do you mind if I sit here?' Rebecca asked. Clooney made a gesture for her to sit down. 'I just wanted to thank you for all your hard work over the past couple of weeks. You were very professional at all times, even when I detected there were other places you wanted to be.'

'Really? God, I'm sorry. I truly relished –'

'The prospect of meeting Madonna? You're not the first gay guy to –'

'Gay?' Clooney said with a sarcastic smile. 'I thought the series was presenting me as a fully converted heterosexual?'

'I think there are a lot of things in this pilot that could be characterised as fictional, don't you?'

'I have no idea what you mean,' he mocked. 'I hope you're not suggesting we were dishonest. Because you'd be correct!'

The director smiled.

'You love her, don't you?'

'Vonnie?'

'Madonna.'

'I do.' He paused. 'When I was a teenager growing up in

Navan, admitting you were a fan would have left you with your head flushed down the toilet. Now, I wear my obsession proudly on my sleeve.'

'I've worked in the industry for many years, and I've huge respect for her. But you – I'm interested in knowing why you love her so much.'

'I've never really thought about it. I've just been always drawn to her.'

'Try thinking about it now.'

'Okay.' He rested his head on the headrest and shut his eyes for a minute. 'This is probably going to sound corny ...'

'I'm American. The cornier, the better!'

'Since time immemorial,' he began, adopting the kind of voice used in museum narrations, 'the main suppressor of the gay community has been the heterosexual alpha male.'

'Good opening. Strong. Go on.'

'He maintained his absolute authority by suppressing every section of society that wasn't an exact mirror of himself. Women were weak and hysterical. People of colour were criminals. Muslims were terrorists, and so on.'

'I should be filming this.'

'Don't you dare, I'm talking absolute shite here.'

'You most certainly are not. Go on – I'm genuinely interested.'

'He invented a clever narrative about us gay men – convincing the world we were insatiable perverts who should be feared and despised. It's a narrative that was hugely successful for centuries, particularly amongst the God-fearing contingent. How most of us wish we were as fucking promiscuous as we were made out to be!'

Rebecca gave an encouraging laugh, and Clooney could tell she appreciated being told something truthful at last.

'Of course, the more you're called a pervert, the more you start believing it. The number of people within the gay community who battle self-loathing is astronomical, even now.'

'I can only imagine.'

'Statistics show – Jesus, I sound like a newsreader now –'

'Once a journalist ...'

'Absolutely! Statistics show that alcoholism, drug addiction and mental illnesses in our community are all way higher than among our heterosexual counterparts. How could it be otherwise?'

'You don't need to tell me – I'm from Kansas.'

'Ironically, home to one of the gayest films of all time.'

'Oi, the straight community adores *The Wizard of Oz* as well.'

'What community doesn't, in fairness? Anyway, the best allies of our particular community have always been those who've courageously stood up to the patriarchy and challenged its domination. People who have said, "No, mate, shove your toxic masculinity up your arse." And no one, I mean, no one has done that more often and more successfully than Madonna.'

'I'll give her that.'

'And she's made some fabulous records along the way, don't ye think?'

'What's your favourite?'

'God, you're full of questions today. Em, I know most people would say "Like a Prayer", but I've always had a soft spot for "Secret".'

'Well, Clooney, your secret is safe with me,' Rebecca assured him, tapping her nose before getting to her feet.

'I've never articulated any of that before. There must be something about you that I ... trust.'

These words stopped Rebecca in her tracks. She suddenly looked pale. Was the flight taking its toll, Clooney wondered.

'I don't know if I can do this anymore,' she mumbled to herself.

'Are you feeling alright?' He was concerned now.

'Clooney.'

'Yes?'

'There's something you should know –'

'Rebecca?'

It was Len. His tone was odd.

'It doesn't matter,' Rebecca said to Clooney before disappearing back to her seat.

Alone, the soap-star turned reality-star closed his eyes once more, taking comfort from having articulated his feelings to the director. Now he could get excited about meeting the Material Girl!

But what was it Rebecca had wanted to say to him before being interrupted?

He put it out of his mind and focused instead on the big day ahead.

He was right to savour the moment while he could. In twenty-four hours, his life would, once again, be turned upside down.

This time, permanently.

FIFTY-THREE

'I can't ski! I want to go back to the hotel!'

Vonnie wasn't impressed by the afternoon's itinerary. She and Clooney were due to meet Madonna the following morning, and meantime had been invited to take their chances on the slopes.

Vonnie had scowled at the idea – not only because her leg hadn't fully recovered from Treegate – but because she detested being told what to do. Throughout her early years, people had bossed her about, patronising her at every turn – and, to this day, being ordered to do something triggered an unpleasant feeling within.

That morning, as the bus drove through the Tyrol Valley from Munich airport, Vonnie, immersed in the majestic Alpine landscape, had felt like a snow queen. It was gratifying that society had finally seen fit to elevate her to the lofty position she'd always known was hers by right. Her royal status felt confirmed when the production team had checked into the Das Hotel Central – a luxurious, five-star getaway complete with picture-book turrets, timber balconies and even clothes-free spas for those wanting to relax the way nature intended. Quite rightly, the manager had allocated her the presidential suite.

Leaving her suitcases unpacked – and swimwear untouched – she'd joined fellow nudists in the spa and, after sweating much of the jet-lag out of her system, allowed a couple of hunky masseurs to pummel her muscles and pedicure her feet. She'd felt invincible; there was nothing she couldn't do!

Except for ski.

'My boots keep slipping out of the skis,' she moaned as she cartoonishly returned to a vertical position, dusting snow from her goggles. 'I want to return to the hotel. I'm hungry. And cold. And wet. And my leg hurts. And my bronchitis is playing up again.'

She could tell Clooney and Hans, their jolly, bearded instructor, were getting fed up with her. Clooney had shown promise as a skier – he too was tackling the slopes for the first time – and Hans had said he'd be able for a more challenging course. But so long as Vonnie kept face-planting in the snow, Clooney wasn't going anywhere.

Hans had met many unconventional couples during his six seasons as an instructor, but none as odd as Vonnie and Clooney. There was something about this pair that didn't add up. The loathsome female hadn't been able to keep her hands off her poor boyfriend in the chair lift earlier, but Clooney's body language had screamed he would rather be anywhere than in her clutches. Hans had reminded himself that his job was to help them master the basics of skiing, not act as relationship counsellor. And so he'd focused on the task in hand. But it was proving more difficult by the minute.

'Vonnie, remember, ja – tits to ze valley, ass to ze peak!'

In an attempt to help the duo learn the basics, Hans was sharing some tricks (he'd even suggested smoking a joint to 'loosen ze body, ja') – but his unorthodox suggestions weren't working on Vonnie. His efforts, just like this strange Irish woman, were falling flat.

'I tried that, Herr-whatever-you're-called but, just like the last two times, my boots fell out of my skis!'

'Are you sure you're clipping them back properly in place?' Clooney asked. He was becoming increasingly frustrated and anxious to resume the lesson. Vonnie didn't care for his tone. In fact, she didn't much care for his attitude in general over the past few days. He'd jumped at the chance to sit alone on the plane, and had the audacity to request his own bedroom in the hotel. She didn't buy the 'I'm a terrible snorer' excuse, but felt it would have been inelegant to make a scene in such beautiful surroundings; unbecoming of a lady.

Had he forgotten it was she and she alone who'd elevated them to this lofty position? If it hadn't been for her impressive quick thinking – and magnanimous humility, forgiving his two murder attempts – they'd be scrubbing mildew from the cobwebs back in Navan. Instead, they were making a pilot for a ground-breaking reality show and were currently holidaying right where a significant portion of James Bond's *Spectre* had been filmed a few years previously – something every single resident of the town repeated over and over again. ('He gets around,' she'd tartly gibed to one of the waiters earlier, remembering some previous connection between 007, Jamaica and, of course, Navan).

'Vud you like to stop, Vonnie?' Hans enquired. 'You don't look too happy.'

'I'm not a quitter! How dare you!'

'Why don't you get yourself some hot chocolate or *gluhwein* in the bar, and relax and enjoy the stunning views?' Clooney cut in. 'We have a big day tomorrow. You don't want to be stressed or anxious beforehand.'

Is he trying to get rid of me? Again?

He took her for a fool, thinking she'd believed all his grovelling and bootlicking while filming the pilot. Vonnie knew fine well his performance had been for the benefit of the old tart they were due to meet the next morning. And now that he was in striking distance of his idol, poor Vonnie, who'd stood by him through thick and fucking thin, was being asked to exit stage right. She thought that, by now, she'd have been used to Clooney's repeated, cruel abandonment of her, but it hurt every single time. He really was no different to the rest of the bullies who had goaded her all her life. The only real difference between now and the time he'd tried to kill her on the bridge were his unsightly muscles.

If only the cad knew what I've planned! Nobody takes Vonnie for granted! Nobody.

'Do you know what, Clooney, that's a splendid idea,' she said as she shuffled off towards the bar. 'Skiing is for babies anyway.'

No sooner had these words escaped her mouth, than a boy, no more than three or four years of age, crashed into her as he throttled down the piste at full speed. Not for the first time that day, Vonnie tumbled to the ground. Clooney giggled like the girl he was behind her. She somehow resisted the urge to turn around and lacerate him for his rudeness.

After all, this snow queen would soon be having the last laugh.

FIFTY-FOUR

'Where's Rebecca?' Clooney asked.

No answer.

Just as he was about to ask again, Clooney got distracted signalling to the waiter that he didn't want any bread. He wanted to be as lean as possible for the following morning. Non-carbs, on the other hand, he was accepting with open arms – a day on the slopes had left him with quite the appetite! And if the chandeliers and exquisite tableware were anything to go by, the restaurant's food was not something to be ignored.

'Should we give her bedroom a shout?' he continued as he sipped his Evian. He knew what directors were like – working around the clock – so if Rebecca was locked in her room doing last-minute edits, maybe something nourishing could be sent up?

'She had to return home to LA, unfortunately,' Len answered without looking up from his menu. 'A family emergency, I believe.'

'Oh, I see.' Clooney was disappointed, and surprised, to learn this news. Not only because Rebecca was the pilot's director but, more importantly, because he felt she'd become a close friend and confidante. And an invaluable point of stability amidst the giddy madness of the past month. 'I hope it isn't anything serious?'

'Sorry, what?' Len asked robotically, clearly uninterested in pursuing the conversation. 'Waiter? I think we're ready to order. You're ready, Clooney, aren't you?'

Clooney nodded and smiled politely; something wasn't adding up. He looked around the rest of the long table and counted those in attendance; apart from Vonnie and himself, there were ten others present: the twelve disciples – all looking forward to the hotel's celebrated food.

But all of a sudden, Clooney found he'd lost his appetite.

'Has anyone been to the bar yet?' Len asked, indulging a hiccup. 'The cocktails are delightful – if a little on the strong side. We should pop in after the meal for a nightcap. Who's in?'

As the others debated the wisdom of joining him or not, Clooney looked over at Vonnie. Unusually, she sat at the edge of the table rather than the middle where she could be the centre of attention. She appeared detached from what was going on – yet wore a slight smile, almost as if she harboured a secret.

Yet again, something wasn't adding up.

Clooney placed his order absent-mindedly – a schnitzel or strudel; something beginning with 's' – and tried to quieten his worries.

This is what happens when you neck a gallon of coffee. You stop thinking straight!

Was that all it was? He was over-caffeinated?

You're hungry. Your energy levels are low.

Yes, but …

You're tired. Up early and on the slopes all day.

Again, yes, but …

The past few weeks have been a whirlwind of emotions and tomorrow is the climax. Of course you're going to be a bit rattled!

That was it. Exactly. He was a little on edge. It was completely understandable.

How many millions of people around the world would give their proverbial right arm for this opportunity! Now, put a smile on that sullen face of yours and enjoy yourself!

And so he did. Until …

'Rescue me,' Vonnie began warbling, one of Madonna's lesser-known songs from her 1990 greatest hits album, *The Immaculate*

Collection (to this day the bestselling compilation by a solo artist). 'I'm drowning; baby throw out the rope.' She turned to Clooney and winked. He shivered.

FIFTY-FIVE

Clooney hadn't slept a wink. He had never claimed the best relationship with shut-eye, but the night before meeting his childhood idol, even Rip Van Winkle would have turned into an insomniac. All night he'd played out various scenarios for the following morning's brunch and screening with Madonna.

Would he be seated beside her or across from her?

What would she eat? What would he eat?

What if a *käsekrainer* sausage fell out of his mouth and onto her hand! He decided he'd just sip on a coffee. Or, better yet, green tea with a slice of lemon floating on top – that would surely impress the notoriously health-conscious Queen of Pop. Would he ruin things by talking too much or making inappropriate comments? What kind of feedback – if any – would she have on the footage from the pilot? What if it didn't meet her expectations? What if he didn't come across well on camera? She hadn't risen to the top of her game by suffering fools.

But, even in the middle of all this speculation, two questions kept recurring ...

Why did Rebecca leave?

And what was Vonnie up to?

Over the night, he had repeatedly looked at the clock: *If I doze off now, I'll get five hours' sleep.*

Now I'll get four hours'.

Three.

Two.

Realising he'd just one measly hour left, he flung the duvet off and got up. As he rubbed his eyes, he decided to neck back a few coffees in his room, out of sight. That should keep him going until after the screening.

He stepped out onto the balcony for some fresh air – few places provided such a revitalising and rejuvenating atmosphere as the Alps, he was quickly discovering. It was in the minus-degrees zone, but he took pleasure in the way the crisp air hurt his face and skin. It wasn't the same as an uninterrupted eight-hour sleep, mind, but it would have to do for now. He looked down towards the entrance; there was a small battalion of fans held back behind newly erected railings. Word must have gotten out that Madonna was in town, and her Austrian devotees had wasted no time in descending on the hotel. Clooney admired the various posters and banners held aloft in tribute to their queen, even though he couldn't quite make out what was written on them. He was delighted his days of being one in a crowd of thousands, all vying for a look, an acknowledgement, had come to an end.

The last thing he wanted in Madonna's presence was a sniffling nose, so he moved to return indoors. He had also to begin the long process of beautifying himself. But as he turned around, he heard a shout from below.

'Aussehen! Es ist Clooney!'

He returned to the edge of the balcony and looked down. Was his sleep-deprivation playing tricks with him or had the hundreds of fans below gathered to cheer him on rather than Madonna? Surely not…

'Clooney! *Wir lieben dich!'*

Oh my days, they had!

'And I love you, too!' he shouted back, effortlessly falling into the role of superstar. Now that the posters and banners were held in his direction, he could make out various images of himself and Vonnie, some with flourishes of love-hearts around them;

others with images so graphic they'd have brought a blush even to the cheeks of the raunchy superstar he was about to meet. He turned a blind eye to some of the less flattering pictures of himself, particularly the side-angled ones. He'd investigated getting a little surgery a couple of months earlier, but the clinic had advised him he'd need ample time to recover in private, which just wasn't an option given the hectic filming schedule of *Crazy For You*. Instead, he made peace with his imperfections – the aesthetic ones, at least.

'*Wir lieben dich!*' the crowd shouted again, louder this time. Feeling like Eva Perón, Clooney waved to his admirers.

These guys seem to love me, flaws and all, he thought. *And who needs sleep when you've adoring fans like these guys energising you!* He blew several kisses. *Thank God I never listened to my conscience telling me to come clean. If I had, I'd be still in my parents' house, hiding under a duvet, trawling through online forums full of pricks jeering me. I'll take this lifestyle any day of the week! Yessiree Bob!*

Swept away by the moment, he grabbed a box of chocolates from the table in his bedroom and began throwing them down at the crowd.

'Sweets for my sweets!'

They couldn't get enough of him. He could have hurled the contents of his giddy bowels onto them, and they'd still have been in their element (not that he'd dream of doing such a thing).

'Life is good! Thank you, Universe, for making this happen! Please, never let it stop!' he called out.

No sooner had the words left his mouth, than a knock sounded on the door – heralding an end to his giddiness.

FIFTY-SIX

'Vonnie, why are your bags packed? Where are you going?'

Vonnie, dressed in oversized white winter gear, stood in front of Clooney, laden down with three suitcases. She'd arrived in Austria with just two; the third, newly acquired, was bursting with items stolen from her bedroom and various rooms across the hotel.

'I'm going home!'

'Sorry, what?'

'You heard me.'

'I couldn't have because I know you didn't just say you were going home.'

Vonnie had suspected it would be fun watching Clooney's pathetic little heart break in front of her – but she hadn't realised quite how much.

The attempts to kill her she could forgive.

Writing a tell-all book, she could overlook.

Loving another woman more than her, however – well, that would not do.

'I am.'

'But ... Why? We're due to meet Madonna in the ice Q in an hour. Why on earth would you want to leave?'

'I'm not interested in Madonna. Apart from you, I don't think anyone is these days.'

'There's no need to be rude.'

'And I miss my cats. I can't believe that wretched airline wouldn't allow me to bring my twelve furry friends on-board. Have they not heard of emotional support animals, for crying out loud? Sometimes, it seems like the world is against me.'

'Are you kidding?' Clooney shot back. 'They adore you!'

'Why can't you listen to me properly for once – listen to what I'm actually saying. I'm not interested in this charade anymore.'

'What charade?'

'You and me.'

She brushed past him, flung herself on the couch and looked around for the complimentary box of chocolates. She was livid to find they were gone.

'Fat, greedy bastard,' she muttered to herself. 'I'll have a coffee, thanks. And make it strong – I have a long day of travel in front of me, so I need a little pep to my step.'

Clooney, unable to hide his devastation, obeyed. He dashed over to the coffee machine and set to work making her an espresso.

'The truth is, as an adult, I'm an artist, and I must return to my true calling. This isn't the life for me.'

'Why are you talking this way, Vonnie? I thought you enjoyed making the pilot –'

'You prefer her to me.'

'What?'

'You prefer Madonna to me. Admit it.'

'So that's what's going on – you're jealous.'

'I most certainly am not.'

'My love –'

'Oh give that grotesque silver tongue of yours a rest, will you?'

'Vonnie. You're being unreasonable. Look at what you'd be throwing away. I'm not just thinking of myself here, but you as well. This is your moment – they only come around once in a lifetime. Haven't you enjoyed being pampered and adored over the past few months? You – *we* – are superstars.'

'Are we?' she asked innocently, knowing precisely the current value of her stock.

'Vonnie, listen to the crowds outside. They love us! They love you, in particular. You've become an icon, breaking the mould.'

'I've always tried to do that over the years. I've never conformed.'

'And now is the time for your dedication to be celebrated throughout the world. If you think you're popular now, wait until the pilot goes to series and the world gets a first-hand look at how intelligent, witty and inspiring you are.'

'Do you really think I'm intelligent, witty and inspiring?'

'Of course I do. So does everyone! You'll be offered exhibitions in every museum in the world – the Louvre. The Prado. The Guggenheim. I'll call my brother now in the Musée d'Orsay and organise something.'

Vonnie looked blatantly towards the coffee machine. Her espresso was ready, and it wasn't going to reach her hands unaided. Clooney took the hint.

'Would you like sugar?'

'You see – you don't know me at all. If you were really and truly my soulmate, you'd know exactly how much sugar and milk I take. I bet you know whether Madonna takes sugar, don't you?'

Oh, she was enjoying watching him squirm.

'I do actually,' he nodded, his cheeks turning a rosy shade of pink.

'Do you know what, Clooney, you can forget about the coffee. I'd better be making tracks.'

Vonnie returned to her suitcases, pocketing a large handful of coffee capsules on the way, then headed towards the door with her ever-expanding belongings.

'Vonnie! Wait. You're too impulsive. There's no way they're going to commission a series without you. Every contract we've been offered has been for the two of us. Every interview. Every photoshoot. We only work as a duo. We can't split now; it's far too early in our career!'

'But it's all built on a lie.'

'Yeah, your lie,' he muttered under his breath.

'Sorry?'

'Nothing. Look, what is going on here, Vonnie? Are you discovering you have a conscience at long last –'

'Excuse me? How dare you! I've always had a finely tuned conscience.'

'Or is it because I've been dividing my attention between you and Madonna? If it's the latter, I'm sorry. I got a little bit carried away. After today, everything will return to normal, I promise. It will be just you and me. The way you like it.'

'Just you and me? Friends for life?'

'Friends for –'

'It's no good, Clooney. I've seen how you swoon over her. You crumble at the mention of her name. You never acquired big, bulging muscles for me, did you? And look at how you're behaving now – don't you think I can't see what you're doing? Trying to manipulate me, all so that you can meet that bitch. You don't give a shiny shite about me, admit it. You're using me to get to her.'

Clooney held his head in shame; what Vonnie was accusing him of had merit – plenty of it. But surely after everything she'd subjected him to – chasing him with knives in Connemara, poisoning him live on national television, faking a pregnancy – he deserved a little treat or two?

'You've never felt that way about me, the way you feel about her,' Vonnie continued. 'Sometimes, I even think you detest me. For instance, the original version of that book you were about to release; I doubt you spoke too highly of me in it.'

Clooney couldn't argue.

'I feel you've just been using me for your own personal gain.'

'My love –'

'Don't!'

'Sorry. But Vonnie, if you leave now, that's it – the whole thing is over. We both return to our humdrum lives. We'll never be able to recapture this splendour. You've only got one shot at life.'

'Okay.'

'Okay?'

'You're right. You only have one shot.'

She reached into the smallest of her three suitcases and pulled out a gun.

'Here,' she said, placing it in Clooney's trembling hand. 'One shot. To kill that trollop.'

She returned to the couch.

'And for future reference: I take one sugar and no milk.'

FIFTY-SEVEN

'If you don't kill her, I'll tell the world everything – and I mean *everything*.'

Clooney stared at the gun now cradled in his sweaty hand, too afraid to stir in case he accidentally activated it. If the owner had been anybody but Vonnie, he would have laughed and assumed it was a toy. But the owner was Vonnie, who had possibly killed her mother and had undoubtedly attempted to kill him. Over the past few months, Isla and his mother had tried to warn him time and time again, but Clooney hadn't been able to resist the lure of becoming besties with the world's most famous woman – Madonna. Now, in punishment for his vainglorious, starry-eyed folly, he either had to kill a living legend or kill his career and reputation.

Even if he escaped a jail sentence for what had occurred on the bridge, he'd be forced into a self-imposed prison. Clooney knew the consequences of revealing their chicanery at this stage of the game would be disastrous. He wouldn't be able to leave his house again – that's if the family home remained standing, and wasn't razed to the ground by lynch mobs.

'Vonnie, you're upset and emotional,' he said, his calm voice belying his inner turmoil. 'Of course I'm not going to kill Madonna. Or anyone for that matter.'

They stared at one other without a single blink between them.

'Alright then,' Vonnie conceded, lowering her hand.

Clooney breathed a sigh of relief.

'If you don't kill her, I will.'

'What?'

'You heard me, you wimp!' She jumped to her feet and snatched the gun from Clooney's hands. 'I'm going to blow those trampy brains out of her wizened face – and there's nothing you can do to stop me!'

She marched towards the door, a woman on a mission.

'Wait!' Clooney pleaded. The day-dreamer in him had always imagined he was equipped to negotiate high-risk situations, but he suddenly realised that, as with so much of his life, he was more gifted in his head than in reality. Vonnie had a gun and, knowing what she was capable of, Clooney was cautious. He didn't want to provoke her.

'There's no need to do this,' he pressed. 'Why don't we both make our apologies and return home? We can call it a day and park all these ridiculous showbiz escapades. It doesn't suit us. The pressure has gotten the better of us, and there's no shame in that. Look at Britney. Look at Amy. Whitney. Michael Jackson. This fame game kicks the shit out of most people. Not everyone is built like …'

Vonnie turned around slowly.

'Like who?'

'No one.'

She raised her hand and pointed the gun square at him.

'I'm going to ask you one more time. Like whom?'

'M … Ma … Madonna.'

'You can't help yourself, can you? Even in your darkest hour, you can't help but sing her praises.'

'She is pretty formidable, in fairness,' he feebly replied.

'Yeah? Well, let's see how formidable she'll be when her cerebrum is dripping from the chandeliers! She's already shown the world every jingly-jangly bit of her body – the insides of her brain are the obvious next step.'

She opened the door and marched out into the hallway, a girl possessed.

'Vonnie! Please!' The door slammed behind her.

Oh, Lord! What had he been thinking all these weeks? Look what he'd created. If only he could journey back to his meeting with Tony and follow through with his plan to put an end to the entire farce. Instead, he had let Gemma seduce him with an invitation to the Met Gala. He'd allowed his desire to meet his childhood idol overrule his good sense.

Clooney didn't know whether to stay in his bedroom and hide under the sheets or follow her and try to rugby tackle her to the ground. Sweat began to seep from every pore on his body. He could feel his breathing become laboured, his mind dizzy. He'd never fainted before, but the heavy feeling currently enveloping him suggested he was about to. He could hardly breathe. His downward spiral was interrupted when his phone vibrated on the table beside him. His parents – again – calling to give out to him for the lack of contact.

'"Papa Don't Preach"!' he cried, suddenly remembering that if he didn't act swiftly, he'd be responsible for the murder of the world's bestselling female artist. 'Move your ass, Clooney! Quick!'

Dressed in just a white singlet and Calvin Klein boxer shorts – and armed with nothing more dangerous than his phone – he ran with the kind of speed shown by skinflints (like Vonnie) when it's their turn to buy a round of drinks.

He had work to do.

As long as the freezing Alpine air didn't kill him first.

FIFTY-EIGHT

Clooney knew – because the hotel manager had told him – that the ski lift that brought visitors to the futuristic ice Q restaurant atop Gaislachkogl Mountain, some 3,000 metres above sea level, was the world's fastest. But as he sat in the enclosed gondola, making his way skywards, he felt an ageing snail would have shown more speed. He could see Vonnie standing in another gondola a short distance above him, but knowing that his pleas for calm had been in vain, he tried to preserve his energy for the showdown that was set to come.

The ice Q restaurant, slowly revealing itself above him, was a stunning and innovative glass building that appeared to link the top of the snowy Alps with the heavens above. It was the definition of exclusivity, with waiting lists and high prices for anyone outside the select few who were lucky – and wealthy – enough to have bagged a seat. It's fame was partially thanks to James Bond.

Yes, that name again.

A few years earlier, Daniel Craig and 500 of his colleagues from the *Spectre* production had transformed the ice Q into a futuristic clinic. As Clooney and Vonnie inched closer to the property, Clooney prayed there would be no need for doctors or medical assistance on this particular morning. He also longed to call upon a sliver of James Bond's prowess so that he could take down the villainous Vonnie. Unlike the spy's favourite tipple, Clooney was both shaken and stirred. But before his mind drifted off to Renardo and the Jamaica Inn – so closely linked to 007 – his phone vibrated in his hand.

Rebecca.

'Hello? Rebecca? Can you hear me? Len told me –'

'Clooney, don't talk – listen to me carefully. There's something you need to know. All isn't what it seems. There is no –'

The gondola suddenly lurched in the wind, causing the phone to slip out of Clooney's hand. Luckily, he managed to catch it before it fell to the floor.

'Rebecca?'

'Cloon?'

'Mam?'

Bloody call-waiting.

'Mam, I can't talk –'

'How are you, Cloon? I've been so worried about you!'

He could hear the truth of that in her voice.

Clooney remembered once asking his mother if she'd slept well the night before. She'd replied that she hadn't enjoyed a good night's sleep in over forty years, not since his eldest brother was born. It was the curse of being a mother, he'd often thought.

Much as Clooney wanted to protect her, he suddenly wondered whether he should give her the head's up that her youngest son was a cad, and that any pride she and his father might feel in him was the result of lies and deceit. Should he tell her he was minutes away from something so explosive and shocking it might even surpass the assassinations of John Lennon and John F. Kennedy? How would she react to the possibility that her baby boy's supposed girlfriend was set to feature in the hall of infamy along with Mark David Chapman and Lee Harvey Oswald?

Maybe I'll get her to pass me onto Dad, he decided, certain that his father would be better equipped to receive the cataclysmic news. As the gondola continued its ascent towards the ice Q, Clooney vowed to come clean. Already, he felt a weight lift off his tense shoulders.

'Mam,' he said, voice cracking with emotion. 'I need to speak to Dad for a second.'

'Cloon? Cloon?'

'Yes, Mam? Can you hear me?'

'Cloon, it's Mammy.'

'Yes, Mammy, I know. Look, I haven't much ti–'

'How are you getting on in Austria? I hope you're keeping warm; it's freezing on the Alps.'

'I'm as snug as a bug,' he lied. Apart from his underwear, all he had to protect him from the ice-cold temperature was a blanket he'd swiped off a chair in the hotel foyer. 'And before you ask, I am eating plenty!'

'Good boy. We haven't heard from you in so long. I've been worried sick.'

'I know, Mammy, it's just been a little hectic. But fear not, I'm not dead or anything.'

Not yet anyway.

'Speaking of, do you know who died, Cloon?'

My happiness?

My integrity?

My career?

My life?

So long as the answer wasn't Madonna, he couldn't bring himself to care.

'Who?' he politely probed, on the off-chance it was someone close to her. It rarely was – usually a former neighbour or the sister-in-law of one of the ladies she did aqua aerobics with at the local leisure centre.

'You probably don't remember him …' As soon as his mother uttered those words, whatever little empathy Clooney had left, disappeared. His mother continued to describe – in real-time detail – the final two months of poor Mr Garraway's life. The couple of attempts Clooney made to get her to incorporate brevity into her reporting were in vain.

'The removal mass is tomorrow evening at seven. I have lunch with Tilly and Nora in Dublin on Tuesday, so your father and I will go to that and pay our re–'

'Dad – yes! – can you put Dad on the phone?'

'He's doing the lawn at the moment, and without a hat on his head! Who does the lawn without a hat in November! Who does the lawn in November! He's idle this week – looking for things to do.'

Clooney heard his mother rap her knuckles on the window with the force of an MMA fighter.

'Norman! Norman! Where's your hat? Come in this minute and put on your hat. What? I don't care if you're moving and active; you'll catch your death in this weather. One funeral is enough this week. Sorry, Cloon,' she continued, returning her attention to the phone call. 'So go on, tell me – have you met Madonna yet? What's she like? I hope Vonnie has been well behaved. I have to say; I'm not too convinced by your romantic relationship –'

'Look, Mam, there's something I've got to tell you.'

'Yes?' she sounded worried again. 'Is everything okay? Do you have enough money? Do want me to lodge a few bob into your –'

'Mam! Please, listen, this is important, and I haven't much time.'

'Cloon, you're scaring me.'

Clooney sighed. She was already up to high doh, and he hadn't even begun to reveal his misdemeanours. 'You're not to freak out, okay?'

'Let me decide on that! What is it? Vonnie? What has she done? I've never trusted her – not for a second. And you, letting on you were her boyfriend, and you gay! The lies! I always knew you were gay – the way you used to dance at all the birthday parties when you were a child. The way you moved – so beautiful. Oh, you would have made a gorgeous dancer. You should be on one of those dancing contests. You'd win hands down. Could Tony sort something out –'

'Mammy!' he cut in sharply before pulling back. 'Thank you. That's all very nice to hear, but, well, your instincts were correct.' He looked up towards the self-proclaimed artist a few gondolas above him. 'Everything has been a lie.'

'What has? You two? I knew that. Haven't I been saying that all along to your dad? We both knew. We thought in this day and age, you wouldn't have to lie anymore.'

'It's not just our romantic relationship that was untrue. That's only a small part of it. I didn't save Vonnie that time on the bridge. I wasn't the magnanimous hero that everyone made me out to be. The opposite, I was actually –'

His confession was interrupted by the sound of more knocking on the window of his parents' house.

'Mud, look, I've put my hat on me!' he heard his father proudly declare.

'Good! And keep it on this time, do you hear? Good boy. And by the way, Cloon just said he is still gay.'

'He's going grey? Like me?'

'No, gay!'

'Very good. I hope he knows we've no problem with that –'

'I know you don't!' Clooney shouted down the phone, trying desperately to get the conversation back on track.

'I'm just going to pop in next door with yesterday's newspapers,' his father continued. 'I'll be back in about ten minutes.'

'Okay, make sure you keep –'

'Mam!' Clooney yelled. 'Can you listen to me? This is important!'

'Sorry, Cloon. Go on.'

'Keep what, Mud?' his father interjected again.

'Your hat. Doesn't matter – I'm on the phone to Clooney. He's got something important to say.'

'He hasn't cancer, has he?'

'Jesus, I hope not. Cloon, you haven't cancer, have you?'

'No, Mammy!'

Since his father had cancer a few years earlier, the pair had become obsessed with the Big C. Every wrinkle was a cancerous mole; every cough was lung cancer.

'No, he doesn't,' she informed him.

'Tell him I look forward to opening my presents,' his father joked before pottering off to visit Clooney's godfather, who lived next door.

'Don't mind him, Cloon, we don't want anything. No sweets anyway – your father's belly is almost the size of the one of those Alps you're skiing on.'

'Mam, please!' Clooney was desperate. Vonnie's gondola was moments from arriving in front of the ice Q, so the disclosure about his transgressions had to be made post-haste.

'Sorry, Cloon.'

'Stop saying sorry, just focus.'

'You're scaring me, Cloon.'

'The bridge, Mammy. What the various videos captured wasn't the truth – I didn't intend on saving Vonnie, I was trying to kill her.'

'Oh my God, why?'

'I don't quite know, but it was something other than her spiking my drink before *Friday With* ... I shouldn't have gone along with her version of events, but I became so seduced by all the fame and fortune – especially because it offered me the chance to meet Madonna.'

'You've always idolised her, haven't you?'

'Yes and now Vonnie has become so jealous of her she wants to kill her!'

'What do you mean? Actually kill her?'

'What other kind is there?'

Vonnie's gondola had disappeared out of sight, which meant she was now directly in front of the ice Q – and metres away from Madonna.

'Mammy, I have to go. I love you, okay?'

Silence.

'Mam?'

His heart thumped – had his mother forsaken him? He looked at his phone and realised he was out of coverage, hardly unexpected considering he was north of 3,000 metres above sea level. Whether she'd abandoned him or not would have to be revealed at another time because he was about to arrive at his destination.

Suddenly, the ski lift abruptly stopped.

'What the …?'

He looked towards the lift station. Brazen as you like, Vonnie stood beside the rotating chain, which now had several skis wedged into it, preventing it from moving.

'*Was machst du?*' one of the security men roared, running towards her. But Vonnie didn't wait around to explain her actions. She set off towards the ice Q. Clooney watched as the security men tried to free the skis from the large chain, but it was more complicated than anticipated. Clooney didn't understand German, but he presumed the instructions shouted by one security man to his colleague in the office were to turn off the lift because the loud vroom of the engine stopped dead. Instead of going into battle with Vonnie, Clooney was left dangling over a scary, if beautiful, 3,000-metre drop with no phone coverage.

'Well played, Vonnie. Well fucking played.'

FIFTY-NINE

Vonnie sauntered into the ice Q restaurant. Instead of being impressed by the magnificent innovative design, her sensitive eyes were pained by the amount of light hijacking the space. It made no difference to her that the glass walls afforded second-to-none views of three countries, or that the building's architecture gave the impression that she was floating on air; if she had her way, she'd have opted for good, old-fashioned brick walls and curtains any day of the week.

She spotted familiar faces – Len and a couple of the other members of the team, all fussing over a woman who sat hidden in a corner. The expression on their faces put her in mind of a bunch of adoring puppies. Vonnie felt revolted.

Why is everyone obsessed with this bloody woman? What does she have that I don't? Well, one thing that Madonna will never have is my man, Vonnie reminded herself. That much was certain. She placed her hand over her bulging pocket, comforted and emboldened by the weight of her gun.

'Would you like something to eat, Ms Gallagher?' a waiter enquired, holding out a tray of appetisers. 'There will be brunch served shortly, but maybe you'd like something small beforehand?'

Vonnie was impressed that this soft-spoken man was familiar with her name and also her appetite. She was famished. She'd worked herself into such a tizzy that nourishing herself had been the last thing on her mind.

'*Danke,*' she replied, aware of the importance of manners in such lofty environments. 'I'll take three. After all, they're only small.'

The waiter gave her a knowing smile; they were barely mouthfuls. Despite the minuscule size of the appetisers, Vonnie thoroughly enjoyed the symphony of unusual flavours. What they were, she couldn't confidently say, but she detected something resembling a sausage and rebuked herself for stopping at three. But the waiter had vanished so she would have to make peace with her oversight. She turned towards the entrance: no sign of Clooney. Even though she'd deliberately delayed his arrival, she wanted him to witness what she was about to do – otherwise, where would be the fun?

From where she stood, Vonnie couldn't quite make out her target, still hidden behind fawning devotees. She hadn't intended on there being much collateral damage, but if a stray bullet lodged in someone else's skull, so be it.

She returned her attention towards the action – or lack of – outside. Surely the ski lift should be working again? After the horn-tooting the hotel had indulged in about it being the fastest and most high-tech of its kind, it should have been child's play to remove a few harmless skis. But obviously not.

'Vonnie!' Len shouted as he clocked her. 'What are you doing, standing over there on your own? Come over. There's someone who wants to meet you.'

Vonnie regretted positioning herself so visibly, but now they'd summoned her, she decided she might as well get the bloody show on the road.

'There's a seat here for you in front of the monitor,' Len continued.

Vonnie looked out the window. Still nothing, apart from end-less, sun-kissed snow. She wished she had her sunglasses to hand but, somewhere amidst the chaos of the morning, she'd misplaced them. No one could fault her if she decided to pursue a legal claim against the restaurant for exposing her delicate peepers to such danger.

Eyes are the windows to the soul. People need to be more careful about how they treat them, she thought as she sauntered towards the group. Her target's hair came into view. Even though Vonnie's eyes had been through the mill, she could tell those wavy curls had been blow-dried once too often. In fact, Vonnie reckoned, a single match would send them up in flames. Just like Clooney's career.

That would save me a bullet, she thought.

'Vonnie, we're just waiting for your side-kick to arrive. Any minute now. I hope you're not too lonely without him.'

'Actually, there's something I wanted to say before Clooney arrived, Larry –'

'Len.'

'I know it's not in the script, but I've organised a little surprise for you.'

'Maybe you can save it until later,' Len suggested, his firm tone indicated that he didn't want the morning's itinerary to veer off-piste.

'I love surprises,' came a voice from the other side of the table. A voice Vonnie was familiar with. 'Tell us what it is?'

Vonnie reached into her pocket, yanked out the gun and pointed it at Madonna.

'Your death. Ye man-stealing wench!'

SIXTY

Clooney thought the world could have ushered in a new millennium in the time he'd been left dangling in the gondola. In reality, it had been just moments, but his fear of heights, colliding with his desire to prevent his childhood idol meeting a grisly end, made it seem an eternity.

The two security guards seemed to suffer from a case of Tweedledum and Tweedledee. One talked animatedly into his phone while the other feebly attempted to remove the half-broken skis from the chain. When they both disappeared into the office, Clooney realised the only way to complete his mission was to take matters into his own purple, frozen hands.

Please don't tell me I'm going to have to channel my inner Pierce Brosnan and venture out of this gondola and climb up the lift myself?

No sooner had the thought crossed his mind than he remembered that his instincts for successful plans had been questionable in the last few months.

Don't be stupid, Clooney! You're wearing nothing more than fucking underwear. It's minus six degrees outside, and you haven't been to the gym in days. Do you think you could hoist yourself up that wire and pull yourself to the summit? Granted, it's only about twelve metres but look at the drop below, ye gobshite! God only knows what lies beneath the snow. And even if you don't crack your skull on a jagged rock, you'll freeze to death within minutes – particularly if you're waiting for those two imbeciles to rescue you.

The most sensible thing for Clooney to do was remain seated with his warm blanket to stop him morphing into an icicle.

However, as he'd just recognised, he hadn't been a great decision-maker in recent times, so rather than listening to his own advice, he jumped to his feet and began the short – impossible – journey up the ski lift. He pushed open the door, no easy feat on account of exemplary health and safety precautions.

'Don't look down. Don't look down,' Clooney repeated out loud while attempting to scramble to the roof of the gondola, which rocked back and forth perilously. The slippery surface wasn't helping matters either. Frustratingly, his recent absence from the gym was apparent and, as he struggled to hoist himself onto the top of the gondola, his arms started shaking. This awkward and inelegant rescue mission certainly wasn't the swift process usually depicted on the silver screen – *Carry On* films aside.

What was I thinking?

The initial burst of adrenaline now gave way to what seemed to be symptoms of hypothermia. His giddy arms were completely useless – they may as well have been yanked from his torso and thrown into a dustbin.

Keep going. You've no choice!

Ignoring the top part of his body for a moment, he sought the assistance of the lower half. With his left foot remaining on the seat within, he tried to swing his right leg up onto the roof – but a combination of fear and wintery conditions had stiffened his limbs. Instead, his foot only managed to hit the top of the door frame – the jolt leading him to lose his balance completely. Lacking control, his entire body swivelled around, his chest whacking the outside corner of the lift with a bang – the sticky frost that offered a temporary grip proving an ally at last. Clooney attempted to roar, but his voice was as unforthcoming as the rest of his body.

Keeping his focus in front of him rather than below him, he slowly scaled the gondola, inch by inch, second by second.

Almost there – you're almost there!

With all the energy he could rally, he thrust himself onto the top of the gondola – *hurray!* – but balanced in a haphazard, unsafe position. He struggled to catch his breath. His body, having taken on a bluey-purple hue, could now barely move. If he hadn't been battling a brain freeze, he'd have reprimanded himself for being so fucking stupid.

Clooney could just about make out cries from somewhere – the two useless security men – and correctly assumed these were directed towards him. He didn't need his full faculties to conclude his actions were being called out for their recklessness. Reaching out towards the wire, he realised his movements were even slower and clumsier than moments earlier – not at all what they needed to be like to haul himself up towards the station.

Don't be so negative, Clooney! Come on, you've come this far – there's no turning back. You've got this!

But just as he attempted to place his hand on the wire, another, louder roar came from the security guards. Clooney couldn't make out what they were saying to him – 'el-trick, el-trick!' – but his racing heart told him he hadn't time to ask. By now, Vonnie was surely just short of pulling the trigger – if she hadn't done so already – and he needed his mind and body to be allies and assist him in his ambitious rescue mission.

'El-trick! Don't touch! It's El-trick!'

What on earth were they talking about, Clooney thought as, with tortoise-like slowness, he moved to place his hand on the wire.

'El-trick! El-trick!'

He noticed that the closer he got to it, the warmer his hands felt.

If I wrap my entire body around the wire, I'll warm up nicely, he decided as he called on all his inner strength for another push.

'El-trick! Hands off! El-trick!'

Were they shouting out 'hat-trick' in their broken English? Were they encouraging him to count to three before diving onto the wire? How thoughtful.

Okay, so. One! Two! Th–

Before the word passed his chattering teeth, the ski lift sprang to life and started to ascend towards the station. The sudden bolt was such that it almost threw Clooney off the gondola and onto the snow-covered rocks below. Fortunately, thanks to the numbing conditions, most of his near-naked body was stuck to the roof.

Seconds later, security guards and a multitude of rescuers surrounded him. One of them sprayed something from a large can that helped free Clooney from the embarrassing position he'd foolishly put himself in.

'That vire vas electric. You vould haf been killed instantly!'

At last, Clooney understood what the security guards had been trying to say to him – but he was still in no position to reply; it appeared he had left his voice, along with his dignity, somewhere above the Alps.

They lifted him down from the gondola and wrapped a funky-coloured blanket around him. Things became foggy, and he couldn't quite grasp where he was or who these people fussing over him were.

Was he in Ireland? Was he on a school tour? Where was Isla? They always sat together at the back of the bus. Where did all the snow come from?

Is that a woman pointing a gun at someone in the building opposite me?

'Madonna!'

The heart and mind are extraordinary things, as Clooney now discovered. Finding strength and focus from somewhere, he freed himself from the group and raced towards the ice Q, his bare feet so numb it was a miracle they allowed him to move. But move he did. Paying little heed to a surprisingly unconcerned security man, he pulled open the door and raced inside, knocking over a waiter carrying some sweet-looking appetisers, before crashing over a couple of chairs and tumbling to the floor. He raised his head and saw Vonnie's outstretched arm with the gun, pointing in the direction of a small group sitting around the table. He attempted to shout, but his voice, as unresponsive as the rest of his body, remained mute. He pushed the upturned chair towards the table, but even though it made something resembling a fuss, neither Vonnie nor those around the table turned. Surely, someone else could finish his valiant rescue mission? That security man, for instance? Had Madonna, the most famous woman in the world, no bodyguards? Maybe they were already trying to appease Vonnie, and he couldn't hear?

But he wasn't going to take that chance. He forced himself back onto his feet and stumbled towards Vonnie, mouthing the word 'stop' repeatedly as he went. He tripped over but managed to catch hold of the side of the table, and although the cutlery and crystal glasses went flying, he kept himself vertical. Clooney pressed forward – why was nobody looking at him? Why was everyone frozen to the spot? If anyone had the right to freeze, it was surely him, after what he'd just experienced on the ski lift.

'Stop! Vonnie, please!' he mouthed in vain. 'STOP!'

He stood about a metre away from the aspiring assassin and, with all his might, bounced off the floor and lunged at her. He didn't quite reach his target however, landing at Vonnie's feet instead, but that set him up perfectly to drag her down to the floor.

Which he did.

Bizarrely, when she landed on top of him, a series of balloons and streamers fell from the ceiling while silly music began to play.

'What the fuck?' Clooney said.

This time, his words were heard by everyone around him.

SIXTY-ONE

In the past few days, the excitement Vonnie had initially felt about the fake series had begun to wear thin.

When Len had first pitched the cutting-edge concept for a 'reality show within a reality show' at the Met Gala, Vonnie had thought it sounded genius. *Crazy For You* would feature celebrities, like Clooney, under the impression that they were filming a run-of-the-mill series documenting their lives. Once completed, so the story went, they would watch the footage in the company of their idol – in Clooney's case, Madonna. But what Clooney didn't know, although everyone else did, was that this straightforward premise was a smokescreen for the show's real concept:

How far would you go to save your idol from death?

Len and the show's creators aimed to observe and analyse the deep obsession that people harboured for the famous, and examine the lengths they were prepared to go to protect them.

That's where the set-up had piqued Vonnie's interest.

Just before the screening, Vonnie was required to announce to Clooney that she was going to kill Madonna, which she'd convincingly done earlier that morning. Clooney was then expected to prevent this murder, while also contending with the fact that he needed to protect Vonnie – his 'loved one' – from a lifetime behind bars.

Crazy For You.

At first, Vonnie had thrived on the fact that Clooney was oblivious to the real purpose of the reality show. Aware of how smitten he was with Madonna, she'd known there was nothing the chap would refuse to do for the sake of meeting her. Tea with porcelain dolls, a day impersonating farmyard animals or – Vonnie's personal favourite – getting him to wax her hairy legs. She'd revelled in the power she wielded over him.

Eventually though, the charade had begun to grate on her. Seeing the guy she'd been in love with reduced to a whimpering idiot … How she regretted agreeing to the whole saga. Until she stumbled on an alternative ending to the reality show within a reality show, that was.

Forget fake: really and truly, Vonnie was going to kill that up-her-own-arse superstar.

Now that would be an exciting season finale!

The world was rightly obsessed with Vonnie already but, by God, wait until they got a hold of this. She'd be a gun-toting icon – immortalised; worshipped. A modern-day Calamity Jane!

Except that when she'd arrived at the ice Q, it turned out that her target hadn't even had the decency to show up to her own execution! Len or Larry or Lennox – whatever that unbearable executive producer was called – had pulled the wool over Vonnie's eyes as well as Clooney's.

There was no Madonna. There had never been a Madonna. Just some bloody lookalike who deserved a bullet for being so tiresome.

So Vonnie's gun would remain unused.

For the time being.

SIXTY-TWO

'A reality show within a reality show? I don't get it.'

A team of medics had just visited Clooney, currently slumped on a red velvet couch beside a warm fire and, while he wasn't quite in rude good health, he was feeling infinitely more alive than an hour earlier. The hot whiskeys certainly helped. But these fresh revelations – that Vonnie's threats to murder (a fake) Madonna were all a part of an alternative reality show that he hadn't even known existed – made him wonder if he'd been too hasty dismissing the doctors.

'Yes, Clooney,' said a woman dressed to look strikingly like the "Hung Up" hit-maker. 'It's called *Crazy For You*, and it explores how far fans will go to protect their icon. Neat, huh?'

Not really.

He recalled the warning Rebecca had tried to give him, which must have been why she and her loose lips had been given their marching orders.

'I heard you being interviewed earlier this year,' Len announced from behind him. 'You mentioned that you were Madonna's biggest fan, so we thought you'd be the perfect candidate for the show.'

'Do you remember the Met Gala?' Vonnie continued. 'When you were blubbering like a big fat baby because Madonna never turned up? Leroy approached me –'

'Len.'

'Len approached me and pitched the idea: a reality show made under the pretence that it was a simple warts-and-all glimpse into the lives of two lovebirds ...'

Despite his sorry state, Clooney couldn't resist a snigger at the mention of their romantic status.

'But the show was really about these past few days, and whether you'd take the side of the love of your life –'

'Or your side, Vonnie,' Clooney interjected.

'No, or Madonna's side.'

'Of course,' he laughed. The joke went over Vonnie's head.

'You certainly proved yourself a worthy contender,' Len added with a grin. 'We were watching everything on the monitors in here! I must admit – those stunts on the ski lift were off the chain!'

'Literally off the fucking chain! I could have died! You think this is an honourable way of conducting business?'

Pleased as Clooney felt that he wasn't going to be thrown into the slammer – at least not for the moment – he struggled to reconcile what Len and the others were telling him.

'So the idea all along was that Vonnie would convince me that she was going to kill Madonna –'

'Which you did extremely well, Vonnie,' Len complimented.

'Thank you.'

'And then I'd have to prevent the murder somehow?'

'We didn't expect you to climb out of the gondola,' Len interrupted, 'but believe me, that is going to make good television. Great television!'

'And if I'd fallen? Or died from fucking hypothermia?'

Everyone looked awkwardly away from Clooney.

'And she's not even here to meet me or say congratulations? Surely that's the least she could have done, no?'

'My thoughts exactly,' Vonnie critiqued, squeezing her concealed gun.

Len raised an eyebrow. 'Madonna has no involvement in the show. Why would she?' he snapped.

'All the stuff we filmed,' Clooney continued, still trying to puzzle out the pieces, 'Vonnie and I living together, the miscarriage –'

'Was it a miscarriage, though?' Len questioned. 'For that to happen, you'd need an actual pregnancy.'

'So the reality show I thought I was taking part in was all fake?'

'And that wasn't the only thing that was fake, am I right?'

Clooney couldn't decide if this was an innocent comment or a thinly veiled threat.

'Look,' Len continued, voice full of authority, 'just like all groundbreaking television, things got a little out of hand.'

'Out of hand? Is that how you describe it?'

'Who hasn't dreamed of being an action hero? A saviour? Don't tell me it didn't give you an erection thinking it was you and you alone – in the entire friggin' world – responsible for Madonna's life? Of course, it only succeeded because Vonnie turned out to be such a convincing would-be murderer!'

The group laughed, including Vonnie. Clooney remained stony-faced.

'Oh cheer up, Clooney!' Vonnie added. 'You didn't think I was actually going to kill Madonna, did you?'

Well, you did try to kill me in Connemara. And you probably killed your own mother, so I wouldn't put anything past you, he thought, trying unsuccessfully to join in with the merriment.

'Listen, misery guts,' Vonnie jeered, 'you need to return to Jamaica and jump back into that waterfall in Mayfield Park or Junefield Park or whatever it's called! You were so much more relaxed then – well, at least until …'

Clooney froze. At this stage, he'd frozen so often he was ready to qualify for the Winter Olympics.

'Until?'

How does Vonnie know about the waterfall and what happened there? I never told her.

'Relaxation. That's exactly what we all need now,' Len interrupted. 'It's been an action-packed few days.'

'How did you know about that, Vonnie?'

She didn't even bother to blush, but Clooney knew she was hiding something, and his stomach turned.

'Come on, James Bond, why don't we make our way back to the hotel and hit the spa?' Len suggested, ushering everyone towards the restaurant exit, anxious to bring an end to this post-game analysis before anybody's lawyers were called. 'I think I might join you for a couple of hot whiskeys, Clooney – they smell heavenly. Make sure we keep the cameras rolling, boys.'

Clooney followed the crew out of the ice Q, certain now that beyond the smokescreen of this reality series, Vonnie was, in fact, a murderer! That was the missing piece of the jigsaw. Now it all made sense.

The bridge in Navan. That's why I tried to kill her. She'd confessed. Mayfield Falls.

That was what she'd admitted all those months ago that he hadn't been able to remember: she'd been to Jamaica. And while there, she'd attempted to drown Pippa.

And she'd successfully killed his sweet lover, Renardo.

SIXTY-THREE

Vonnie was the true artist, not Madonna.

A visionary, some might say.

But nobody had ever given her what she felt she was her due. Now she had the world's undivided attention, at long last. And she had no intention of relinquishing it.

If I succeed in this simple task of killing Clooney and then myself, my name will live on forever!

Buoyed by what she'd committed to, Vonnie followed the other members of the team into a hot steam-room and placed her towel on the bench. It didn't bother her in the slightest that she was alone in being fully naked – although she would have thought those working on a series about Madonna, never knowingly over-dressed, would have been a little more comfortable in their skins.

The chatter that had been going on since the big reveal in the ice Q was now at an end and the room was quiet. The heat was a stark contrast to the conditions outside. Not that she minded the cold. Over the years, various housemates had rudely likened her cottage to an igloo, and her body was well accustomed to a bit of chill. But she had to admit, she was enjoying the feeling of blood in her cheeks and sweat down the sides of her thighs.

'Aaaaaagh,' she roared, oblivious to the atmosphere of peace and calm. She noticed how quiet Clooney was – and, how hairy! There was a grooming facility in the hotel; maybe she should book him in for a little priming?

Why is it me who does everything in this relationship? she wondered, exasperated.

She noticed too that he looked a bit distant. Granted, he'd endured a dollop of drama on the ski lift and would probably be nursing a sniffling nose for the next few weeks but, all the same, there was something about his demeanour that she didn't like; a look on his face she recognised. It was an expression she'd seen once before: on the bridge in Navan when he'd launched at her. He was angry with her. For what?

He'd better not be acting like a baby just because I concealed the true nature of the reality show from him. Jesus, get over yourself!

But instinct told her it wasn't that. It was something else. She smiled at him and tried to brighten his mood.

'I know what you did,' he suddenly mouthed, eyes cutting through her like newly sharpened knives. 'Renardo. And Pippa. And your mother.'

Vonnie had to think for a moment who he was talking about, Mammy aside. Then it dawned on her.

Those lecherous perverts from Jamaica?

Even so, Vonnie wasn't sure what all this attitude was for. Had she not already told Clooney about her hand in the chap's death on the bridge? Why was he suddenly acting like this was new information? Vonnie was taken aback by this trivial banality suddenly reappearing in her life.

This is draining, she thought to herself.

'Too hot for me,' Len announced, rising to his feet. 'I'm going to take a dip in the pool.'

The rest of the team followed him, leaving Vonnie and Clooney together. They sat in silence for a few moments. Uninterested in playing further games, Vonnie rose to her feet. Clooney's foul form was toxic, and that self-help book she'd read on the flight over had advised her to steer clear of such energies. She placed a hand on the door, but before she could push it open, Clooney grabbed her wrist.

'It's over. You're over, you murderous bitch!'

'What's gotten into you? You need to lose the aggression and attitude, do you hear?'

No sooner had the words escaped her mouth than she realised she was fighting a losing battle; his face was even more threatening than on the bridge.

He must really have liked that guy.

'Enjoy your last few minutes of freedom, Vonnie, because this is where everything catches up with you, once and for all.'

'What about you – you're no angel either! You tried to throw me off the bridge, remember?'

'And I'll face the consequences. My biggest crime is going along with this farce for as long as I did. Not anymore. You're going to rot!'

He then stormed out, leaving Vonnie alone. She sat back on her towel and allowed the new developments to sink in.

Oh dear.

There was only one choice left. She needed something more significant.

As charming as it is, I'll have to wipe out the entire hotel.

SIXTY-FOUR

Clooney waited by the reception desk. A sense of calm washed over him for the first time in ages. He had just called the local *Bundespolizei* and the Garda Síochána back in Ireland and explained everything. He'd rambled and mixed up his story, but felt sure his message was clear: Vonnie was a murderer and she needed to be arrested immediately.

He had also left a long-winded message for his parents, explaining everything. There was going to be an enormous fallout, and he'd probably spend his life having stones thrown at him or, if he were lucky, being asked to take part in endless humiliating, Z-list-filled reality shows, ridiculed at every turn. But whatever the future held, it would be one free of guilt. He just needed the police to arrive, arrest Vonnie for dear Renardo's murder and Pippa's attempted murder, and wait to see what happened next.

I'm so sorry, Renardo, he said, looking towards the heavens. *You were such a kind, beautiful soul, and because of me and my stupidity, your life was cut short.*

Clooney accepted there would be plenty of work to do to get his life back on track and understand why he had encouraged this whirlwind of chaos and tragedy. Maybe a good counsellor could help him understand his vanity and insatiable desire to be liked by others? He certainly wasn't guiltless in any of this – far from it – but he wanted to make amends.

'I'm sorry. I'm sorry. I'm sorry.' As he repeated those words out loud, Clooney felt his eyes well up.

What have I done?

The ecstasy and excitement of beginning the process of redemption were superseded by extraordinary guilt. How had he ended up in the foyer of a five-star Austrian hotel, begging his deceased lover for forgiveness while his lover's murderer sat in the spa beneath him, with a fake Madonna strutting her stuff somewhere nearby?

What have I done?

The anxiety he'd battled so often reared its hideous head. His mouth dried, his cheeks flushed and his skin moistened.

What have I done?

He looked around the foyer – it was nearly abandoned save for a couple of receptionists dressed as milk-maids.

What have I done?

His self-torture was briefly interrupted by the sound of a police siren outside. Clooney moved towards the glass doors and saw two squad cars pull up in front of the hotel. This was it. No turning back now.

But before he could introduce himself, a deafening noise sounded from the alarms around the building. The quiet atmosphere of the foyer fled and in its place came pandemonium. Screaming guests emerged from the restaurants and bars, from lifts and stairwells.

'Gas! Gas! Gas!'

A single whiff informed Clooney how potent this was, and he knew it would result in one thing.

An explosion!

Staff valiantly attempted to bring order to the mass exodus, helping the elderly and children, trying to quieten the deafening roars. People tripped over each other, pushing anybody who got in the way of their survival. A cacophony of languages and accents, soaring in volume, polluted the air, but there was no need for a translation; it was evident no one was passing the time of day or complimenting the morning's breakfast. They were fighting for their lives. Clooney stood in the middle of the commotion, unable to move.

It couldn't be, could it?

He immediately knew that this was, yet again, Vonnie's work.

What have I don–

Before he could finish his thoughts, he saw her. The artist-as-an-adult slowly walked out from the basement area, face and hands black with dirt. She carried a lighter in front of her, her finger menacingly placed on the spark wheel. She came over to him and grabbed his hand.

'This is how it should end, Clooney.'

Her eyes were lit with fantastic excitement. She'd never looked happier.

'Now that all those scaredy-cats have fled, it's just you and me. And possibly a few rich guests in their bedrooms, too drugged on Valium to get the hell out of Dodge. Oh, and Liam, trapped inside the sauna.'

'Who's Liam?'

'Whatever that backstabbing Judas producer is called.'

'Len.'

'Who cares? It's over, sweetcheeks! This hotel might boast five stars, but not a single one of them is a lucky star because, in a few short moments, this overrated kip will just be a mound of rubble.'

This was not how Clooney wanted it to end, however.

'Not on my watch!' he hissed, shoving her to the floor. 'And before you say I shouldn't hit women, you're not a woman – you're a fucking monster!'

He raced towards the exit. Fortuitously, the doors immediately opened wide, and the blast of fresh air invigorated him. He'd made it! The police, who'd arrived following Clooney's complaint about Vonnie, were leading guests across the snow-covered entrance to safety. Additional sirens could be heard in the distance. More police cars. Fire brigades. Ambulances. Assistance.

'Help!'

It was Vonnie, behind him, sprawled on the floor. It seemed she had banged her head against the tiles and was struggling to move.

'Help!'

How Clooney wanted to leave her there, in the middle of her own sorry mess.

There would be no court case.

No media scrutiny.

No fallout – well, limited at least.

Tony, along with a good lawyer, could handle the damage control and maybe, just maybe, Clooney would have a life again. All he had to do was keep moving and leave her there to go up in her own flames. But …

He couldn't.

She didn't deserve an easy way out. She owed Renardo his day in court. Besides, it just wasn't in his nature to leave her, regardless of what she'd done. He could never live with himself. He took a long, deep breath and ran back in. Bending down, he placed his arm around Vonnie.

'Come on, Vonnie, give me your weight.'

But before he could pick her up, her limp body sprang to life, and she wrapped her arms around his legs and dragged him to the floor.

'Didn't you hear what I said, Clooney – just you and me. *Friends. For. Life.* Jesus, Scorpios can be so devious at times.'

'Come on, Vonnie, get up,' Clooney shouted, struggling to free himself from her grip. 'We need to get out of here.'

'Exactly! Out of here – out of this horrible, cruel world! That's why I'm going to blow the place up with the two of us in it! (And Leo in the sauna). *Friends. For. Life*! That's what you said!'

Vonnie could see the police and security guards racing across the grounds outside, making for the hotel's entrance.

'Don't bother!' she roared, revealing the lighter in her hand. 'It's too late! Although, could you do me a favour and send my friend, Cheesy Teasy, a box of Easy Singles. Just make sure her mother doesn't get to them first or she'll confiscate them, the bitch.'

'No, Vonnie!' Clooney pleaded. 'Don't do this.'

'Stop being so dramatic! The little girl only has IBS – sure who doesn't? Let her eat cheese! Let her eat cake! Let them all eat cake! Oh, that's catchy. I should copyright that – *Let them eat cake*. Catchy.'

'Marie Antoinette, yes! Remember? When we first met? You loved dressing up – there'll be so many more chances to wear fabulous costumes. Please, don't do anything foolish now. Just take a breath. Actually, maybe not in here – let's go outside into the fresh air, and we'll both take deep breaths. Please, Vonnie. For me!'

'You think a lot of yourself, don't you? I've gone off you now – you and your hairy arse! I've gone off you all! And by the way – you were shit in bed!'

'What are you talking about? We never slept together!'

'Oh, yeah. Anyway, back to more pressing matters …'

Vonnie held the lighter aloft.

'See you on the other side, bitch!'

THE END

ACKNOWLEDGEMENTS

Even though there's just one name on the cover of this book; in reality, so many people have been instrumental in its release.

The amazing dream team at Mercier Press: Deirdre Roberts, Wendy Logue, Sarah O'Flaherty and Alice Coleman. Maybe there's truth in the claims that Cork is the greatest county in Ireland!

My editor, Emily Hourican. I'd probably need her assistance to properly articulate how magnificent she has been over the course of this project!

Máire and Seán O'Donoghue – I knew what I was doing when I chose them to be my parents!

My boyfriend, Gabriele Bianchi, and our cat, Prince, for keeping me company during the writing process.

My friend and agent of fourteen years, Lorraine Brennan. Being a Libran, you often change your mind, but I'm glad you never changed your mind about me.

My mentor and dear pal, Alexander Fitzgerald.

All my friends and family who offered support throughout the writing of this book, as well as my two earlier efforts, including Vanessa Keogh, Eamonn Norris, Déaglán Ó Donnchú, Stephen Wall, Gayle Norman, Gillian McCarthy, Ruth McGill, Gary Murphy, Bairbre Ní Chaoímh, Christina Edge, Angela Steen, Esther McCarthy, Jennifer Zamparelli, Máire Ní Mháille, John Donohoe and Louise Ferriter.

All the lovely new friends that I've made since becoming a writer: Sinéad O'Donnell, Eimear McKeever, Don Jimmy Tormey and Thea O'Brien.

The incomparable Áine Toner and Aisling O'Toole for sending me to Jamaica and Sölden to write travel features on behalf of *Irish Tatler Man* – two of the backdrops in this book. Thank you to the Jamaica Inn, Das Central, Ann Scott PR, Burson Cohn & Wolfe, the Jamaica Tourist Board, Ikenna Lewis-Miller, Lisa Adelle-Jondeau and Sarah Fitzgerald who organised those life-changing trips.

The gang in *Ros na Rún* and all my friends in Connemara – #clannrosnarun.

The Irish media and bookstores who have been so supportive of my work over the past number of years.

And last, but by no means least, Madonna – when you read the book, you'll know why!

Crazy For You is dedicated to my best friend, Ruth Keane (Betty). We've been a two-person army since playschool.